PETER

Printed in the United States of America

Editing by Ariel Ryan
Copy Editing by Anthony Bolkema
Book design by Myriad Creative

First Printing, 2015

ISBN 978-0-692-46517-2

Jonathan M. Wenzel
www.PeterPanCanFly.com
www.JonWritesBooks.com
hi@JonWritesBooks.com

Peter
A Tale from Neverland

Jonathan M. Wenzel

For Heidi.
My best friend and greatest adventure.

I hold no reservation in believing that this tale, if ever discovered, will be regarded as anything more than a story.

I do not write this for my sake, but for yours. I write so you may see that what once was still lives in one corner of the world.

I write so truth may be divided from fiction, darkness from light.

But disbelief has blinded you.
May this tale carry you back home.

PROLOGUE

A full moon watched waves lap at the rocks and boulders that lined the small island's shore. The island was just large enough to hold a single structure – an ancient stone fortress. The abandoned, crumbling tower must have served as a lookout post or a lighthouse ages earlier. But now it served as a meeting place for a gathering that could only take place at night.

Dark shadows stretched out from the rocks, reaching out towards the looming tower. The hiss and crash of seawater against the ancient stones whispered sinisterly as it trailed back to the sea.

"He'sss late," a wet voice hissed.

"Patience, Kall" a second voice chided.

Kall peered out though one of the building's narrow, barred windows, his dark eyes searching for the boat, searching for the man.

Other voices began to speak in the dark.

"Krie! This is a mistake, they lost their voice here long ago."

"Perhapss they have changed."

"Changed!? Never!"

A small, elegant voice cut though the din. "The time for debating has passed, my friends."

The room fell silent, all eyes turning to the speaker.

"We have all agreed that we do not trust him," he continued. "We have chosen this location, far from our respective domains. And when he comes, we will hear what he has to say and tell him our decision."

The regal speaker smiled at his companions. "There can be no harm in listening, can there?"

Before anyone could answer, Kall straightened. "Tam," he said. "He comess."

They could hear the faint sound of oars creaking in their oar-locks and splashing against the waves. A deep, gruff blend of singing and humming caught on the wind and sailed up to the small group waiting inside the stone fortress.

The man nosed his boat towards the rocky island's lone dock and jumped nimbly to the berth, mooring line in hand. He looped the rope through one of the several docking rings that lined the dock. Satisfied with his work, he shuffled towards the tower. His scabbard chains jingled and his red scarf snapped in the wind as he walked up the stone steps. He hummed and whistled to himself as he approached the large, wooden doors. He put his hand on the oversized iron door rings, smiled, then pulled them open.

Pale moonlight rushed greedily through open door, spilling down the stone hall and painting the old walls in dim, grey light. The sound of the man's footfalls clicked and clacked on the hard stone tiles. He crossed the twenty paces to a smaller door opposite the first, pushed it open, and stepped inside. The room was dark, save for a few small, golden lights that seemed to hover around the room. He smiled broadly and stroked his long, black beard. He removed his hat and bowed deeply.

"Good evening," he smiled. "I thank you for agreeing to meet me." He returned his hat to his head and looked up and around the large room. "A bit out of the way, but I take no offence."

"Your offence does not concern uss," a wet voice hissed.

"Now, now," he replied, pausing to search for the speaker's name. "Shiiklah," he said, finding it. "I come as an ally."

"An ally!?" another voice hissed from the other side of the room. "We have no reason to trust your kind!"

The man folded his hands together – a sign of pleading. "I ask only that you judge me by my actions, not by the actions of others."

"But the actions of countless others have all been the same, Edward. It is only because of your persistence that we've agreed to this meeting," Tam said from the center of the ring.

"We're not all liars and cheats, Tam," Edward said, the corners of his mouth tugging down in a frown. "I only ask for the chance to show you, to show all of you," he said, looking at each face as he spoke.

"The Council is afraid your motives are that of conquest, like the others," Tam replied.

"Ha-ha!" Edward laughed. "I have all I desire." He balled his hand into a fist and held it against his chest. "Damnation seize my soul if I give you quarters or take any from you; I wish only to be a part of your Grand Council," he swore.

"Why you?" Tam asked.

"Why indeed, my shiny little man. There has not been one of my kind in this place for a long time. Our reputation has been stained by carnal men, but I am not a carnal man."

"Edward," Tam said, approaching the man. "We have discussed your request to join our Council, and we feel that the voice of man does not yet have a place in the Grand Council. That pla-"

The crack of Edward's pistol cut him off as he erupted in a flash of light. A fine golden dust drifted to the ground where he had been a moment before.

"I thought you might say that," Edward muttered, slinging the discharged pistol over his shoulder.

The length of silk that was tied to the end of the gun kept it from hitting the floor behind him and pulled the other end – an identical gun, only this one was loaded – from under his arm and into his outstretched hand.

"Betrayer!" a menacing voice hissed. Edward shot the speaker between the eyes and spun on his heels. Slamming the door shut behind him, he sprinted down the hall. He stuck his index finger and thumb into his mouth and whistled, the sharp report echoing through the cavernous hall. Reaching the large doors, he pulled them shut just as the hall doors exploded off their hinges. He slammed home a large shiny bolt that was obviously not a part of the original door and sprinted towards his boat, taking the steps two at a time.

This time the boat was not empty; it was filled with six men. They were dressed in various garb, some in loose-fitting shirts and vests, others shirtless – all of them pirates. They pushed the boat away from the dock and began to row as Edward reached the landing. He ran faster now, stumbling forward more than running, towards the end of the pier. He reached the end and jumped, sailing through the air and landing in a heap in the middle of the boat.

His men helped him up then watched the tower in silence. The doors shook as the tower's trapped occupants hammered on it.

Pressing their hands to their ears, the pirates waited. Without warning, the tower exploded, fire and flying stone replacing the old fortress. Debris pelted the men as they cheered and laughed, patting each other on the back.

The explosion subsided into a simmering mess of smoke and flames.

"I guess things didn't go so well in there, eh Capt'n?" one of the men asked.

"Not at all," Edward smiled, brushing stone and dust off of his hat. "Things couldn't have gone any more according to plan."

"Do we get the treasure now that the Council is out of the way?" another man asked.

"Almost," Edward replied. "The head may be severed, but the body is still dangerous. We'll need more than our humble crew if we wish to take the island."

"A fleet, then?" one of them asked.

"Aye," Edward replied.

"And then the treasure?" the same man pressed.

Edward nodded.

"Is it gold, Captain?" another man asked.

"In a matter of speaking," he replied, putting his hat back on and turning to face the speaker. "But gold like you've never imagined."

ONE

Waves crashed against the ship's bow sending sprays of seawater sparkling into the evening air. The forty-gun warship, *Dawnriser,* sliced through the waves, the might of the ship turning each powerful wave into a harmless eddy. Each wave conformed to the will of the ship's rudder, each wave submitted to the power of the ship and her captain's will.

A tall man with chocolate-brown hair stood at the foredeck, his bright eyes scanning the horizon. His beardless face, bronzed from months at sea, was oddly both optimistic and haggard, as if the man had lived two different lives. The foremast creaked behind him as a renewed breeze filled the topsail, surging the frigate forward.

His name was Captain Benjamin Hornigold.

And he was the Pirate Hunter.

Another man, this one Hornigold's first mate, William Till, stood beside him. William's own eyes scanned the horizon ahead of them. William was a head shorter than his captain, but well-muscled in a way that suggested he had spent more time taking orders than giving them.

"Is that him, Cap?" William asked, pointing towards a dark speck in the distance.

"Aye," he confirmed, peering through his spyglass at what could only be a ship.

"I wonder what surprise he'll have for us tonight," William thought aloud, stroking his beard with his free hand.

"It makes no difference," Hornigold replied, his jaw tightening. "He's just another pirate."

"They say he's killed a thousand men!" a reedy voice behind them squeaked. "And that he's faster than lightning." The speaker, Crewman Riley, was a scrawny man, a child really, no older than seventeen. He squinted towards the black dot on the horizon, fear as much a part of his face as skin.

"Well it's obvious that they have never met William Till," Hornigold smiled, turning to address the young sailor.

"Second to you, sir," William smirked.

Hornigold chuckled, rolling his eyes. He, along with everyone on the ship, knew that William Till was second to no man when it came to combat. The man moved like lightning. Hornigold did not. But he was smarter than most and a proven tactician. And he was wise enough to know where his deficiencies lay. He knew that with the sword, there was no match to William. Although the man would never admit it, it was said that William could have your own blade out of your scabbard and pressed to your throat before you could even finish challenging him.

William had spent his younger years working his way through the naval ranks. Electing to gain experience from apprenticing himself to officers over attending the Royal Naval Academy, he gleaned wisdom and skills from the men around him rather than from books. Throughout the years he begin climbing ranks, learning from superior officers—who quickly became fellow officers before becoming his own subordinates. His conduct and leadership style eventually gave him something he could have never demanded: respect. William Till was an officer of the people. When William spoke, people followed, not just because they had to but because they wanted to.

Normally a man like that would make Hornigold uneasy; he had been betrayed by his own lieutenant in the past – another man loved by the crew. But William was as honest and true as he was fast and deadly. And he had no regrets about placing his old friend at his side.

The stairs creaked and a gruff voice, thick with accent of the Irish, spoke.

"Storms' rising up from the west, it's bound to be rough."

"They say that storms follow him, Mr. Langdon, and that he's pure evil, that he has fire in his eyes," Riley wailed.

"Now that I'd like to see," the Irishman said, cresting the steps and watching the clouds darken on the horizon. "With stories like that, I almost hate to bring him down. How'll we frighten children into going to bed when he's gone?"

Benjamin smiled, imagining horizons without dark blemishes, seas without chaos.

"When do ya expect we'll catch up to them, Captain?" the Irishman, Langdon, asked.

"Morning," William answered for his captain. He drew a long dagger from his scabbard and tested the edge with his thumb.

"Well then, I guess we've got work to do, don't we?" Langdon said, glowering at Riley.

"Huh? Oh, aye sir, yessir," Riley replied, scurrying down the stairs.

"That kid is something else," Hornigold said, watching the awkward sailor make his escape.

"He's your nephew," Langdon said. "I like him, he reminds me of you."

Hornigold glared at his friend and officer. "To the plank!" he said jokingly.

"You first, limey," Langdon quipped.

The three friends laughed. It was good to laugh, it reminded him that they were still human, that they were different than the men they hunted.

"The great Edward Teach," Langdon said. "Finally in our sights."

"He's calling himself 'Blackbeard' now," William said, still inspecting his dagger.

"Blackbeard?" Langdon exclaimed." "Why? What kind of a name is that?"

"His beard, I suppose," William replied. Then smirking, he looked up and said, "It's black."

"Well, it's stupid," Langdon insisted. "And anyone with a fool-name like that deserves to get blown out of the water."

"Ready the ship, old man," William said, chuckling over the

man's ranting.

"Old man?!" he retorted, saluting smartly. "Oi, you're older than I am! Maybe I should make up your bed for ya? I could bring ya some tea."

"Irishmen," William snorted, shaking his head and returning his blade to its sheath. "Back to work, or I'll throw your potatoes overboard."

"Not my beloved!" Langdon mocked, clutching his hand to his chest. Then he saluted, and descended the steps.

"So what are you really thinking?" William asked Hornigold, after Langdon had left earshot.

"As your captain or as your friend?" Hornigold replied, his eyes fixed on the ship and the setting sun.

"I'm concerned that you have to ask," William responded.

"I don't know, Will. I've got a different feeling about this one. Something doesn't feel quite right," he said solemnly. He looked away from the horizon, his eyes meeting his lieutenant's. "It feels like our course has been set, and we're just along for the ride."

William smiled reassuringly. "At the end of the day, he's just a man. Just another pirate," he said, looking from his captain to the ship on the horizon and then up to the sky. "That crazy old fool is right though, a storm is coming." He turned and walked away, disappearing down the stairs, leaving Hornigold alone with his misgivings.

"So it seems," the Hornigold said to himself, watching the dark clouds gather strength around them. "So it seems."

He let the sounds of his ship against the waves drown his doubts. He opened his eyes, staring out once more at the tiny ship in the distance. It seemed to be sailing right into the setting sun.

Tonight would be no different than a hundred other nights. He would run down his quarry, then capture or kill him.

He would bring order to chaos.

He was, after all, the Pirate Hunter.

It was a name he neither chose nor savored. He was just a man – a former pirate himself – doing his duty, trying to make right a few of the many wrongs he had done in his life. He was known all throughout England and across most of the Pacific as the man who was reducing the Great Pirate War to a bad memory. In less than seven years, he had captured or killed over twenty-five pirates.

When face to face with an unconventional enemy, unconventional tactics were called for. The men Hornigold hunted didn't use the same code of conduct gentlemen used. So he adapted to better fit the men he stalked. When hunting pirates, one had to think like a pirate, and having once been a pirate himself, this was an easy task for Hornigold.

After accepting the General Pardon offered to all pirates by the King, he had been hand-picked to help end the pirate insurrection.

Working side-by-side with shipwrights, he had helped produce one of the deadliest ships ever built. He choose his crew by hand, trained them, and armed them to the teeth. In the last seven years, Hornigold had become one of the most respected and feared captains. His tactics were brilliant. He had managed to out-think every pirate he hunted, every pirate but one.

But tonight felt different. Maybe it was the fact that the man he hunted was one of the most renowned pirates in the Caribbean. Or maybe it was the fact that this man had once been Hornigold's own first mate.

Years earlier, during his own life of piracy, he had become acquainted with the ruthless and brilliant Edward Teach. The two men had become fast friends and Edward eventually signed on with Hornigold as his lieutenant. But after sailing together for a few years Teach's ruthlessness began to drive the two men apart. Eventually, they parted ways. Hornigold left his life of piracy, accepting the pardon, while Edward resolved himself to unleash chaos and destruction wherever he could. It was oddly fitting that Hornigold was tasked with bringing Edward to heel.

"*It's nothing*," he thought to himself, beginning to walk toward his cabin. He paused and looked back towards the horizon and the setting sun and the ship he pursued. "Rest up, Edward," he spoke to the ship in the distance. "Tomorrow you sleep in chains."

TWO

awn was beginning to break as the *Dawnriser* came within a hundred yards of the pirate vessel. The *Hellmaiden*, as she read, was a good third smaller than the *Dawnriser* but still seemed menacing in her own right. Painted in grays and blacks with random streaks of red, she gave the impression that she was a ship of death. Hornigold lowered his spyglass and turned to his lieutenant, who had joined him again on the forecastle.

"There doesn't seem to be any sign of movement," William said, placing the glass to his own eye and scanning the ship ahead. "It could just be the dark, but the jeering has usually started by now, and I don't see a soul. What are you orders?" he asked.

"Are the men prepared?" Hornigold asked without looking.

"Your men are ready. They await your order," was William's reply.

Every man was armed with two pistols, both of which were fastened to a length of silk as to not lose them in the heat of battle. It was an old pirate trick; two pistols were better than one. Pirates may have been outlaws, but they weren't stupid. In addition to the pistols, each sailor was given a sword and a dagger. This degree of armament was unheard of for other servants of the empire. To lavishly equip every sailor in the navy to this extent would doubtless bankrupt it. But Hornigold had insisted on making every member of his crew as armed and deadly as the men they hunted.

When they were less than a ship's length away, William gave Langdon the order to issue the General Pardon.

"The King's most excellent Majesty, taking into his gracious and serious consideration the long and great troubles…" he read.

The pardon was a fresh start. It wiped a man's ledger clean so long as the pirate cast off his life of treason.

"No one ever surrenders," William said wryly.

"I did," Hornigold said quickly, smirking.

Langdon finished reading the pardon and waited for a response, but the only response came from the creaking of the mast and the waves slapping at the hull. In fact, there hadn't been any movement since they had fallen within hailing distance of the *Hellmaiden*.

"Lieutenant," Hornigold began, "prepare for boarding."

"Aye, sir," he replied.

Langdon turned towards the sailors, all traces of his normally lighthearted mood gone.

"Boarding crew, to arms!" he roared. "Gunner, ready cannons. Pikes, to arms! Ready weapons, men!"

The ship came alive with sailors brandishing grappling hooks and boarding axes. Below deck, Langdon oversaw the loading of the *Dawnriser's* forty guns. In a matter of minutes, stations began to report in.

"Boarding ready, sir."

"Gunner ready."

"Ship prepared for battle," Langdon reported.

"Very good," William replied.

He turned toward Hornigold. "The ship is prepared, sir."

The captain stared for a long moment, watching the *Hellmaiden* bob in the water, silently mocking him.

"Lieutenant," he said slowly. "Bring me Teach."

"With pleasure, sir," William replied, dipping his head in acknowledgment.

The lieutenant walked to the deck railing and began barking orders. "Douse those lights, men! We've given them their chance! Grapples, on my ready! Pikes and axes, to bear!"

Time slowed to a lull as the *Dawnriser* glided slowly next to the *Hellmaiden*.

"Now!" he bellowed.

Lights were extinguished and grappling hooks sailed through the early morning sky as the *Dawnriser* winked out, blending in with the dark waters.

"Heave, men! Break yer backs!" Langdon cried.

The *Hellmaiden* groaned under the strain of being pulled. She drew closer and closer to the *Dawnriser*, anchor lines creaking with her weight.

"Charge!" William yelled and then unsheathed his daggers and leapt, clearing the distance between the two ships. The deck swarmed with His Majesty's finest, swords drawn and ready for battle.

But the ship was empty.

"Search below deck." Hornigold ordered quickly, coming aboard to stand beside William. "Look everywhere, there has to be a crew on this ship," he snapped.

Hornigold exchanged glances with his lieutenant, his jaw clenched tight.

"Sir?" William asked, eyeing his captain.

"Just find him," was Hornigold's sharp reply.

The crew dispersed, tearing the ship apart, searching for the crew that had seemingly vanished. Langdon led the search, sending men throughout every section of the ship. Finally he made his way up from below deck, sweat beading on his forehead.

"There's no sign of 'em, sir," Langdon reported, wiping the sweat away with his sleeve. "I just don't understand how–" his report was cut short as gunfire ripped through him, hurtling him into Hornigold. The two men crashed to the deck in a heap. The port and stern came alive with firelight, creating a deadly crossfire, with Hornigold's men in the center. Bullets poured into the ranks of sailors still on deck.

William instinctively dropped to the deck, angry bullets hissing above him.

"Hit the deck!" Hornigold bellowed, heaving his dead shipmate off of him.

He swore, spitting blood out of his mouth, and looked up at William. "They must have been hiding on the outside of the ship," he shouted.

"Aye!" William shouted back, quickly counting off the number of pirates in the ambush.

"Charge, men!" Captain Hornigold ordered, scrambling to his feet and diving into the battle. William followed his captain as he climbed to his feat and charged. He fell upon the pirate horde, his dual blades singing into their ranks. The deck was alive with the sound of death and battle as British sword clashed with pirate cutlass.

"This isn't right," the lieutenant yelled to his captain, driving a shoulder into a pirate, sending the man screaming into the dark water that spanned the two ships.

There was a roar from the ship's starboard as more pirates, who had been hiding on the seaside railing, charged into the sailors' unsuspecting flank.

"Not good," William muttered to himself, watching the pirates moving to flank them.

He tripped an unfortunate pirate, killing the man before he hit the deck boards. He parried a downward strike aimed at his head, then lashed out with his other dagger, the blade biting into the man's wrist. The pirate howled in pain and his sword tumbled from his hand. William spun, plunging both daggers deep into the man's side and released them. In the same breath, he caught the pirate's falling sword and hurled it, burying it in the chest of another advancing pirate. Both pirates fell to the deck dead. William rolled, ducking under a third pirate's swinging blade, and retrieved his daggers from the dead pirate's side. He spun on his new assailant, quickly dispatching him as well.

The skirmish continued to rage with the close range of combat drawing massive casualties from both sides. Hornigold's men, however, were bearing the worst. William knew they would lose if the battle continued on like this. Something had to shift. It was beginning to turn into a free for all, void of any order.

"Full force, starboard side!" William ordered. "Charge, men! Give 'em hell! Ben, we've got to break that flank," he yelled, pointing with one dagger toward the group of pirates hacking at his men. Ignited by William's rousing call, the *Dawnriser's* men surged forward, channeling their attack into the main force.

The charge pushed the pirates back. Some fell to the sailor's hungry blades, others fell off the ship. Hornigold and William fought with their backs to each other, spinning and circling their way through the hordes of pirates, desperately trying to break their momentum.

And then it happened. It was so subtle that at first, only William sensed it. The battle's teetering balance dipped, ever so slightly, in their favor. William looked behind him and saw his captain staring back at him. Hornigold was feeling it now too. The two men fought harder. And like an eddy moving against a stronger current, growing in strength, the sailors started to feel the turn. So did the pirates. The sailors fought with renewed intensity, almost physically strengthened by their foe's growing doubt.

"Looks like this may not end half bad, eh Cap?" William called over his shoulder, cutting down another pirate with his blades.

"So it seems," Hornigold yelled back, "but we still need to find Te–"

He was cut off as the deck thundered violently, knocking everyone off their feet.

"*Cannon fire,*" William immediately thought.

"Cease fire!" Hornigold bellowed, turning toward his ship. "You fools, cease fire!"

"It's not us," William yelled, pulling his captain back. "It's him!"

Sure enough, the deck of the *Dawnriser* was swarming with pirates. They poured below deck like rushing water and crashed into flanks of sailors still on board.

"*Why would they fire on their own ship?*" William thought, his mind speeding through the possible explanations.

"Regroup!" he heard Hornigold command.

William raced to the railing and through the *Dawnriser's* gun ports saw pirates below deck, massacring his men and reloading the *Dawnriser's* cannons.

And preparing to re-fire them.

"*They're stealing our ship.*" The realization hit William like cannon blast.

"Ben!" he cried, turning toward his captain, but his cries were swallowed by cannon fire. Decking erupted under his feet as the cannons tore through the *Hellmaiden*. He dived, a reaction he prayed would take him out of the direct line of fire. Horror washed over him as he saw sailors and pirates alike fly through the air in slow motion, propelled by the point-blank cannon fire. Another blast from the cannons thundered behind him – the blast sounded slow and muffled in his overloaded ears. He stared, puzzled as the deck slowly began to come apart around him. Small splinters broke free from the boards and seemed to float away into the air.

Then there was nothing.

Dread ignited deep in Hornigold's stomach, a thick, burning fog that replaced the ember of hope that had been present a moment earlier. He watched, dumbfounded, as the deck erupted under William. That entire section of ship instantly turned into razor-sharp kindling that flew in every direction. The smoke cleared, but William was gone. Anger seared through his veins as he hacked madly at pirates struggling to recover from the blast.

"Fight, men!" he shrieked, continuing his frenzied attack, but even he could hear the hope failing in his voice.

"We can't win this. We've got to get back to the ship," he thought.

"Retreat!" he bellowed, spinning back toward his ship.

But it was too late. Somewhere deep inside the *Dawnriser*, a sharp whistle pierced through the din, and every pirate still onboard the *Hellmaiden* rose to his feet and charged through Hornigold's men, trampling them to the ground.

The battle was lost.

The ferocity of the charge slammed Hornigold into the mainmast. Light exploded behind his eyes as he fumbled to get to his feet. He gasped, feeling what seemed like fire burning in his chest. Instinctively he grabbed his side and winced as something wet and sharp bit into his hand. He looked down, his vision clearing, to see a huge splinter from the mast protruding out of his side. With an anguished cry, he slid himself off the splintered mast and fell to the ground. He pressed hard at the wound with one hand but felt blood flow down from the wound in his back. The sounds of boarding planks clanking off the side of the ships and splashing into the sea registered distantly. He shook his head, a futile attempt to clear it, and stumbled to the forecastle in time to see his ship, the *Dawnriser*, sailing away.

"No!" he croaked, tripping through wreckage to get to the bow.

"My ship!" he moaned, hurling a lose chunk of decking towards it with his free hand. It splashed harmlessly into the water.

He leaned heavily on the railing, his stomach filling with hot blood and anger as absolute defeat washed over him.

He glared at the *Dawnriser* and saw a lone figure with a thick black beard fluttering in the wind. He was doubtless smiling as the Pirate Hunter pathetically howled over the loss of his ship.

"Teeaaaaccchh!" Hornigold screamed, mustering one last breath. Then his legs gave out, folding under him. As darkness closed in, he watched as the man removed his hat and bowed. Then the *Dawnriser* adjusted its course and disappeared in the rising sun.

THREE

Williams's eyes fluttered open. How much time had passed? The cannons' blasts still rang in his head as if they'd just been fired. He rose to his feet before a wave of nausea brought him back down to the ground. Covering his face with his hands and taking deep breaths, William waited for the nausea to pass. Then, more slowly this time, he stood. Painstakingly he made his way over and through the *Hellmaiden*, checking for survivors, but the splintered deck made for slow, dangerous going.

Edward Teach had brilliantly countered their attack and even managed to steal the *Dawnriser*. He shook his head in disbelief. *How did this happen?*

All around, sailors started to come to, some brushing off debris, others crying out in pain, while so many others remained still, never to move again. A sailor approached him and began speaking. He waved the man to stop, then pointed to his own ear, indicating that he couldn't hear.

"Find the bilge," William yelled, unaware of his own volume. "We need to keep this wreck afloat. Make sure the pump is manned constantly!"

The man saluted and made his way down into the ship in search of the bilge pump. If they had any hope of getting home, keeping water out of the ship was the main priority. William picked his way through the ship, issuing orders to those who were well enough to work. He found his daggers a few feet from where he had awoken and returned them to their scabbards. Eventually he found a group of men huddled together, bandaging Hornigold.

"How bad is he?" he called to one of the men, finding that he was beginning to hear himself again.

"Not great," the sailor replied. "He lost a lot of blood, but we managed to stop the bleeding. I think he'll pull through though. Capt'n is tough." The man managed a smile.

"Indeed, he is," William replied.

Hornigold had now managed to pull himself up and was leaning on the railing, watching the *Dawnriser* shrinking in the distance.

"Sir," William called, approaching him. He didn't answer.

"What are your orders, sir?" he asked again.

Again, no answer. Hornigold's glazed eyes stared blankly towards the ship in the distance, now just a small dot.

"Make ready the sails," the captain said finally.

"You can't be thinking about following him," William said carefully. "The ship..." he stammered, looking around, "it's a miracle we're still afloat."

"Make ready the sails!" Hornigold shouted. He paused, sighed heavily, then closed his eyes. "We're not following him, Will. We're going home."

"Ben, I," William started, but Hornigold cut him off.

"Oversee repairs, Lieutenant. I'll be in my–" he began to say 'cabin,' but caught himself, a bitter laugh escaping his clenched teeth.

"Dismissed," he finished instead.

William knew better than to press any further. He turned, leaving his friend and captain to cope with his failure. He carefully made his way back to the main deck, thankful that Hornigold was not planning to pursue the *Dawnriser* just yet. The ship was in no shape to sail, and the men were in no condition to fight. He made his way back to the main deck and began to further assess their damages.

A hand reached out from under a heap of debris and grabbed at his leg.

"Sir," a voice croaked.

William quickly bent down and began removing debris from the buried sailor.

"Riley," William half smiled, pulling the young man to his feet.

"I'm afraid you're stuck with me, sir. It'll take more than exploding ships to end me," he replied.

"Glad to hear it," William replied. "Why don't you head down below deck to see what kind of shape this wreck is in. We've got to get home in this boat so let's make sure she doesn't break apart under us before we make port."

"Yessir," Riley replied, saluting as he disappeared below deck.

William spent the next hour tending to the men, treating wounds, issuing orders, and generally trying to make the best of their hopeless situation.

As it turned out, out of the hundred men who had boarded the *Hellmaiden*, less than thirty were able to sail. The others were put in the captain's quarters, the main hold, and anywhere else they could find room.

William's heart ached at the thought of losing so many men, but he quickly chased thoughts of grief and failure out of his mind; there would be time later for mourning. If he were going to get these men home, he had to stay focused.

It was nearly noon when Riley made his final report.

"It seems we've a spot of luck, sir," he said.

"Is that a fact?" William replied wryly.

"Yea! I mean yes, sir," he replied. "While cannon fire did do extensive damage to the ship – the main deck basically being nonexistent now– most of the damage is above waver level. The chain bilge pump—you know, the pump that gets rid of seawater—is in good order." William gave him an I-know-what-a-chain-bilge-pump-is look and motioned him to continue.

"So if we keep it manned at all times, we should be able to stay on top of the leaking. All in all," Riley shrugged, it could be worse."

"Good work, Riley, I'm assigning you to the pump. Make sure it's double-manned at all times," William ordered, clasping the young man on the shoulder.

Riley saluted and picked his way to the pumps.

Hours passed and the repairs slowly continued. The *Hellmaiden* was technically seaworthy, though barely. The mizzenmast and mainmasts had been completely destroyed, but the foremast could be repaired. With a little imagination and a good deal of prayer, it would hold sail.

By the end of the day, the *Hellmaiden* was ready to sail and, with help from the *Dawnriser's* surviving crew, began to limp home.

FOUR

The noon sun hung high as footprints followed a small girl, racing after a small boy towards the docks.

"Hurry, Mara! It's the Bell!" the boy yelled over his shoulder.

The Bell, as it was simply called, was a clear, bright-sounding bell that only tolled when ships were spotted on the horizon. The Bell gave workers on the docks time to ready themselves and it gave merchants expecting goods time to prepare, but to those anxiously waiting for returning loved ones, it was either the sound of heaven or of impending doom, as many sea-bound men never made it home.

The girl, Mara, desperately tried to catch the boy, but he moved like a sparrow, darting around people in the street, climbing and leaping off crates. His blond hair lay plastered to his head by the wind as he ran.

"Peter!" she yelled. "Wait up!"

Peter halted and turned towards his sister, his blue eyes ablaze in the sunlight.

"Come on!" he called, his face cracking into a grin. "He's back!"

And with that, he turned and raced headlong towards the docks, oblivious to the wake of damage behind him.

"Silly boy," Mara muttered, leaning heavily against a wall and gasping for breath. She wiped her brown hair out of her eyes, picked up her dress, and raced after her brother.

The pair made their way through the docks, squeezing between crates and sneaking past workers too busy with their tasks to notice the two. Others loitered the docks too, fidgeting and fighting against hope as they waited to see if the Bell tolled for them.

Peter found a stick and immediately transformed it into a sword. He thwacked and hacked at make-believe assailants.

"Mara, behind you! Duck and I'll run 'em through!" he shouted, still deep in make-believe.

Mara dropped to the ground as Peter swung over her, dispatching his sister's imaginary attackers.

"To Hell's gates with you!" he cried.

"Hell's gates?! Watch your mouth, or I'll tell Aunt Ellie, and you know what that means," Mara scolded.

"Ha-ha!" he laughed, throwing his head back in defiance. "You're not my mother, you're hardly eleven!" he taunted, expecting a slew of reprimands about respecting one's eldest sister. But none came. "Mara?" he asked. "Didn't you hear me?"

But she hadn't. She stood stock-still, staring past him. Peter turned, following her gaze to see a ship, moving very slowly and riding very low in the water. It was a frigate, smaller than most, painted black and gray with streaks of red in random places. The craft pitched lazily to port. Its splintered mizzenmast, broken where it met the deck, teetered over the side of the ship.

"What happened?" Mara whispered, watching the ship crawl towards the dock.

The ship was a mess of blackened, splintered wood held together with rope and tar. The mainmast was splintered a few meters off the deck, as if God had reached down and snapped it off. The foremast, the only remaining mast, was barely up to the task of moving the ship. Shreds of patched, tattered sails tore and fell away as the ship neared the dock. Pieces of the ship fell off and splashed into the harbor as it inched towards the dock. The crew seemed to be in worse shape than the ship, gaunt from lack of food with hollow, vacant eyes that stared as if unseeing.

Peter had spent enough time on the docks to know that this homecoming was not a happy one; happy homecomings were never silent. He had spent many years hearing the songs of sailors returning home wafting up to his home like a sweet perfume. But there were no songs to hear today, just the bitter silence of beaten men.

This was a ship of death.

The ship creaked to a halt as it nestled against the dock. Rigging and timber showered down from the ship, slapping nosily on the dock. The ship seemed to crumble apart as it came to a full stop.

A man, more solid than the rest, climbed up on the gunwale. With one hand he grasped the rigging above him while his free hand pointed around, issuing orders to everyone within earshot.

"Someone fetch the barber!" he roared. "We've got wounded. Riley, don't bother rolling the sail, cut it loose, but keep it clear of the deck. Ease her in, boys!"

The shock that had captivated the dockworkers a moment earlier evaporated as their hands and feet moved to action by the man's words.

A joyous shock ripped through Peter as he and his sister exclaimed in unison, "Father!"

The man looked down at the two children – his children – and a smile cracked across his dry, peeling lips. "Mara! Peter!"

He leaped off the gunwale and landed expertly on the dock but lost his balance as his children plowed into him.

"Omph," he grunted, falling to the deck.

"Father!" Mara cried, her eyes filling with tears.

"I knew it was you! I just knew it!" Peter yelled, clutching his father fiercely.

The man laughed, smiling through his own tears. "My boy! And how are you, Miss Mara?" he asked, winking at her.

"I missed you so much" she cried, burying her face in his chest.

"I missed you, too," he smiled, messing Peter's hair playfully.

"What happened, father? What happened to the *Dawnriser*?" Peter asked, still gawking at the ship struggling to remain afloat.

"That," William replied, "is a long story."

Peter began to ask more questions when a pompous, nasally voice cut him short.

"Where is my ship, Lieutenant Till?"

William rose and turned to see a short, fat man in his late fifties glaring at him and then at the dilapidated ship.

Peter had seen the man several times, and on each occasion the man seemed nastier than the last. His upturned nose, angry red cheeks, and large stomach reminded Peter of a pig.

"Sir," William saluted, "I think it would be best if Captain Horn—"

"I didn't ask Captain Hornigold, Lieutenant," the pig snorted. "I asked you!" he said, stabbing a fat finger into William's chest.

"We ran into some trouble, sir," William replied, unruffled by the man.

"Trouble?" he snorted, the sneer he had been born with somehow deepening.

"Sir, we were–," William continued.

"I don't want to hear it," he snapped, cutting him off again. "Where is Benjamin?"

"The Captain is below deck," he replied. "Planning our next move, plotting Teach's possible destinations."

"Your next move?" the man squealed. "And how does he plan on getting to him? Because I'm certainly not going to give him another ship," he spat.

"Commodore Sus, with all due–" William started, but the man wouldn't have it.

"Dismissed, Lieutenant," he said, without looking at him.

"Thank you, sir," William replied, saluting the man. Turning, he took his children's hands, and left the docks.

As they climbed the hill to their home, William noticed Peter lagging behind. He kissed Mara on the head and winked to her.

"I'll meet you at home," he said. "Go tell your aunt the news."

She beamed, always enjoying a chance to be the one to bear good news, and sprinted home.

William turned to Peter. "What's bothering you, son?' he asked, dropping to one knee.

Peter shifted uncomfortably and shrugged one shoulder. "Why do you let that Commodore talk to you like that?"

"He's my commanding officer, Peter. I've been placed under his charge," he replied. "I have to submit to him."

"But everyone hates him!" Peter cried. "How can you just let him walk over you?" He exhaled loudly. "Doesn't he know who you are?"

William smiled at his son. "Who am I?" he asked.

"What?" Peter asked, confusion wrinkling his face.

"You asked if he knew who I was. Who am I?"

"You're William Till!" he cried. "The fastest, deadliest, most dangerous man in all of England!"

"No, I'm not," William said softly.

"What? Yes, you are," Peter countered. "You're a warrior."

"But that's not who I am," William corrected. "A sailor, an officer, a..." he smiled. "A warrior. Those are things I do, but it's not who I am." He put his hands on Peter's shoulders. "I'm your father, and that's all that matters to me. Commodore Sus can say whatever he wants to me. Anyone can say anything they want to me. They can take any of those other things away from me and it doesn't matter, because no one can change the one thing that matters. The only title I care about is *father*. Do you understand?"

"I think so," Peter said. "But doesn't it still bother you, the way he talks to you? He only gets away with saying those things because he outranks you."

"Who has more strength?" William asked, drawing one of his daggers. "The man who can fight, or the man who knows when to fight?"

"I don't understand," Peter replied, frowning. "The strongest fighter always wins."

"Not always. Strength lies in knowing how to act in the moment," William continued. He let his dagger roll off his finger, then caught it deftly just before it hit the ground. "Just because you're the strongest doesn't mean running over everyone is the answer or even the best way." He paused for a moment, then continued. "Sometimes it takes more strength to hold your tongue than it does to strike a man down."

"Still," Peter said, kicking at the stone path. "I still wish you would throw him into the bay."

William laughed. "You know, Peter," he said, wiping tears of mirth from his eyes, "I'll tell you a secret."

Peter leaned forward, his eyes wide with excitement.

"Sometimes I do, too." He winked. "I am human, after all."

The two of them laughed and father and son continued to walk home.

"Father?" Peter asked, looking up.

"Yes?"

"Can I ask you something?"

"Anything."

"How many men have you killed?"

His father's smile faded as looked away, considering. After a moment he looked back to Peter.

"What kind of man do you want to become?" William asked, staring straight into Peter's eyes. "Remember the good you've done, not the bad. The first time I killed someone was the worst day of my life. As soon as it becomes about killing, you become no better than a pirate," he said. "No one should have to watch the life fade from another."

Peter shifted, embarrassed over his questions.

"But the day I saved someone," William said, his mouth lifting into a smile as he spoke. "Was the first day I really felt alive, felt that I had a purpose."

"What happened?" Peter asked, his eyes wide, his embarrassment forgotten.

"I was walking home from the docks and a group of men were robbing a woman," he began. "People were avoiding her, crossing on the other side of the street. They'd rather pretend it wasn't happening than put themselves in harm to help her. It made me furious. So I sprinted across the street, wrestled a dagger from one of the men and fought them off. When the fight was over, all that was left was me, her, and a number: one. And that's when my counting began."

Peter stood slack-jawed, then asked, "What ever happened to the woman?"

"I married her," William said. He winked, then sheathed his dagger.

"She was your mother, " he said rising to his feet.

Peter beamed at the mention of his mother. William would often speak of her. He never mentioned how she died, just how she lived. Peter had asked about how she died a few times, years ago, but William wouldn't discuss it. His father focused on life, not death – lives saved, not taken.

It was a lifestyle that seemed very heroic to Peter, and he liked that.

"So how many people have you saved?" Peter asked.

"Not enough," came his father's reply. Then smiling, he added, "Come on, let's go home."

The gate was still swinging on its hinges as William and Peter approached the house. As they drew near, they could hear Mara inside, talking faster than anyone could possibly take in.

"Slow down, child," a female voice was saying. 'There's a wrecked ship in the bay? And what about your father?"

"Aunt Ellie, he's here!" she nearly shrieked.

As if on cue, William opened the door. The startled woman looked from Mara to William.

"Will!" she cried, wiping her hands clean on her apron.

She dashed across the room and embraced her younger brother, a puff of flour surrounding them as they collided.

"Ellie!" William smiled, embracing her.

"You're back so soon," she said, holding him tightly. "You weren't due back for another four months at least, is everything all right? What happened? Is Ben okay?"

"We had an... unfortunate run in with Teach," William replied. "And I hope so. Teach's blow struck true, truer than I would have thought. Ben needs some time alone. There'll be time enough for the full tale later."

Ellie released her brother. Her brown hair, mixed with flecks of flour and hints of silver, fell from the loosely knit bun behind her head.

"Well, anyway, look at you. You're thin as anything!" she said, coaxing stray hairs back into the bun while looking him over.

"I'm fine," he said, waving her off. "And I'm home now. That's all that matters."

"Home safe, yes, but dead sick of pickled cabbage and hardtack I'd bet. A proper feast is in order!" Ellie said, brushing more flour off her apron.

"Oh!" William exclaimed. "You have no idea what it's like to hear those words after weeks of bone soup. I'm half tempted to eat my own children," he joked, winking at his kids.

She started listing off menu items on her fingers: "I'm starting a loaf of bread now. Peter, I'll need you to head to the butcher and get us a turkey—make sure it's fresh; I don't want any more of those rotten old birds that Hackett tries to pass off. And Mara, why don't you run down to the market. I'll get you a list."

Mara opened her mouth to object, but her aunt cut her off. "No, I don't want to hear any of that plague nonsense," she chided. "Vegetables are perfectly safe!"

Mara looked from her aunt to her father and back.

"Okay," she replied, hesitation quivering in her voice. "I can get them. What did you want?"

William smiled with understanding at his daughter as Ellie listed off items for the meal.

"I'll tell you what," he said to Mara. "I'll go with you."

"What about me?" Peter protested.

"I'll bet we can get our vegetables on the table before you can get back with that turkey," William challenged.

A heartbeat later, Peter was gone, the front door slamming on its hinges as the boy flew from the house.

FIVE

ara was in heaven. Her family was complete again, sitting around the table, talking and laughing. It was amazing how one person, her father, could bring so much life to a home. Her father, strong and alive, sat in his oak chair at the table's head. Peter sat next to her, wearing a smile so big it threatened to knock him out of his chair. And of course there was her Aunt Ellie: sweet, but with an excitement about her that was almost electric.

Mara was still amazed how, in the time it took her to blink, her aunt had filled the table with food.

The turkey had been cooked – and perhaps stolen as well. Peter had left the house in such a hurry that he had forgotten to bring money, yet somehow still managed to return home with the bird.

And he, as he kept reminding everyone, had returned home first.

The four of them meandered through dinner. There was no reason to rush. As far as anyone was concerned, there were no chores, no lessons, nothing but William Till.

Their father was home, and nothing else mattered.

They talked about anything and everything that had happened in the months since William had been gone. He told them as much about his journey as he would allow the two children to coax out of him.

They were midway through dessert – an apple and raisin bread pudding – when there was a knock at the door.

"I'll get it," Ellie said, pushing back her chair from the table . "You keep eating."

A few moments later a black-haired man who looked to be in his mid twenties with a neatly trimmed mustache and ensign marks on his shoulder entered the kitchen.

"Sir," he began, "I'm terribly sorry to intrude on your family."

Peter shot the man an angry glare, but William waved him in.

"Not at all, Ensign," he smiled, rising from his seat and walking toward the man. "What can I do for you?"

"Sir," the man began again, clearly uneasy. "Your immediate presence is...requested by Commodore Sus," he said, handing William a letter.

"Thank you, Ensign. Dismissed," William said, taking the envelope and turning back toward his family.

"Yes, sir, thank you, sir. And, if I may add," the man hesitated "it is an honor to finally meet you, sir."

William turned back toward the young man and extended his

hand.

The young sailor gawked at William's outstretched hand and then slowly, tentatively, reached out and grasped it. After releasing William's hand, the young man straightened visibly and saluted.

Mara chewed thoughtfully. It was moments like this that reminded her of the awesome respect her father commanded.

William walked the man out then returned to the dining room. He read the letter. His expression became unreadable as he folded the letter and returned it to its envelope.

"What is it?" Ellie asked.

"My orders," William replied. "I've been given a captain's commission and ordered to bring back the *Dawnriser*."

"What?!" several voices cried in unison. Mara wondered how a full stomach could suddenly feel hollow and empty.

"When do they want you to leave?" Ellie asked.

"We sail at the end of the week."

"That's four days!" Peter screamed, slamming his fist down on the table.

"You've just returned!" Mara yelled, hot tears pooling in her eyes. "You've been gone for months and months and now you're just going to leave again?"

"I know," William whispered, placing his hand on top of her own. "I know. It's awful, you two have every right to be upset."

"It's that pig, Sus!" Peter raged. "Who does he think he is? He hates us, he wants us to be miserable!"

"Enough!" William barked. Every back at the table straightened. "I did not raise my children to be animals!" he shouted. "I'm going to go down to the barracks and see what this is all about," he said.

"I'll look into pushing our departure date back. The men are in no condition to set sail yet anyway."

Mara began to cry.

"It's not fair!" Peter snarled. "You just got back, and now you're leaving again!" Peter shoved off from the table and ran out of the room.

"It's okay, Mara," William whispered, wrapping his arms around her. "This trip will take no time at all. I'll be back before you know it." He tipped her head back so her eyes looked into his. He wiped her eyes dry and smiled at her.

"Now, let me find that brother of yours and see if I can't calm him down a bit," he smiled.

"Good luck," Mara replied, coughing a laugh through her tears.

William found Peter sitting on the steps leading up to the house. He closed the door behind him and sat down next him. Peter's eyes were puffy from crying, and he knuckled at one eye as his father sat next to him.

"It's not fair," Peter protested. "Sus hates you because he's jealous." William listened.

"And the only way he can be sure you won't take his job is if you're out there," he pointed to the dark waters.

"Perhaps. It's more than that though," William explained. "Teach is a very dangerous man and now that he has the *Dawnriser*," he sighed heavily, "it's going to be a lot harder to bring him down. People could get hurt, could die."

"She was quite the ship," Peter mused, his attention shifting at the mention of the stolen ship.

"Yes, she was," William agreed.

"Father?" Peter asked.

"Yes?"

"Don't go," Peter said, his red eyes pleading. "Just stay. Haven't you done enough?"

William stared at his son for a long moment. "I have to go to make things better for you two," he explained.

"Make things better here," Peter said quietly. "There are other men who can fight and you're gone all the time. Please. Don't leave us again."

The noises of summer filled the silence that followed Peter's plea. William had been away at sea for a long time, most of his children's lives in fact. Peter was right about that. He was also right that there were others who could take his place. Maybe it was time to take a step back and focus on what truly mattered. He opened his mouth to respond but something held his tongue.

Duty.

The word was almost audible. More than anything, he wanted to tell Peter that he'd go down to Sus' office and resign his commission. He wanted to hold his son and tell him that he'd never set foot on another ship, that he would stay right here with him.

But he couldn't.

"I'm sorry," he whispered. He closed his eyes, grateful that the night hid his tears from his son. Then he rose to his feet and began walking toward the docks, away from his son, toward his duty.

"I'm growing up," Peter called from behind him. "And you're missing it."

William didn't turn, he didn't even slow. He wished he could stay. More than anything he wished Peter understood why he had to leave. He wished he wasn't a sailor, wasn't a warrior and he wished a hundred other things – things that could never come true. But more than anything, he wished he could stop time and keep his children young forever.

It was after midnight by the time William returned home. The briefing, if it could be called that, had been with Commodore Sus, Hornigold, William, and a handful of other officers from the *Dawnriser*.

It had felt more like a death sentence than a briefing.

Hornigold would not be captain.

William was given command of the *Lion's Whelp IV* and tasked with brining home the *Dawnriser* and Teach's head. The announcement of Hornigold's demotion had shocked them all. It would seem that when an ex-pirate loses one of the Royal Navy's most prized ships to his former first mate, people start asking questions.

William, however, knew his old friend had simply been bested. It was all part of the game. William understood this. Hornigold had driven the pirates to the edge of extinction. It made perfect sense that they would start getting desperate and the plain truth was that desperate actions sometimes worked. But men who fought with paper from behind desks could never see through the eyes of men who fought with steel.

Their shock had ignited into full-blown outrage when Commodore Sus told them their ship was being supplied and outfitted for their immediate departure the next morning.

William had refused the order outright.

"My men sailed a crippled ship half way across the Atlantic. I'm not taking them back until they're fully rested and have spent time with their families," William had argued.

The Commodore had threatened him with a court martial, but William had spent most of his life on the receiving end of threats. He knew when an empty shot had been fired.

William was a man of duty. He was also a man who followed orders. But keeping the men he commanded safe had always been his first priority. He was an officer of the people. And if he had to save them from a foolhardy order, so be it.

After further discussions, the departure date had been pushed back three weeks. It was enough time for his men to recover, barely. But William was happy to squeeze even that much time from his commander's grip.

The next morning found the Till family assembled in the courtyard. Ellie was keeping herself busy with the laundry. The sunlight danced across the linen sheets on the clothes line. They rustled and snapped in the gentle morning breeze.

Peter and Mara had their makeshift swords and were play-fighting under their father's care.

"Let him come to you, Mara," William called out. "When he overreaches, parry him off-balance, towards you."

Mara obeyed, giving ground as her brother advanced. Then, as William had anticipated, Peter's excitement at driving her back got the best of him and he leaned forward, reaching out to strike.

Mara struck as instructed, parrying toward herself rather than away. The added momentum tipped her brother off balance. He took a step forward to regain his balance – his focus shifting from Mara to his own unsteady footing.

Peter's misstep was all Mara needed. She simply rapped has hand sharply with the wooden sword.

"Ow!" Peter exclaimed, dropping his sword and scowling at his sister.

"I won!" Mara exclaimed.

"You won," William answered, applauding her.

"I've never won!" she yelled, running into her father's arms.

"Oh thankyouthankyouthankyou!" she yelled.

"Lucky shot," Peter muttered from behind her.

Mara spun around to face her brother, her hair whipping around her head a second behind. "Not true, Peter Till!" Mara yelled.

"Calm down, you two," William chided, placing his hands on Mara's shoulders and pulling her back a step. "Now Peter, she did beat you. You overreached and she took advantage of it."

"Just because you told her," Peter shot back.

"But she still executed the move," he replied. He smiled down at Peter. "Power can be clumsy. Strike smart, strike true. The second you become over-confident or emotional, you lose."

Peter kicked at a loose stone. "I get it," he said. "Losing stinks though."

"That it does," William replied, laughing. "That it does."

"Wanna have another go?" Peter asked, looking over at Mara.

"No, thanks," she replied, admiring her wooden sword as if it were an elegant blade. "I think I'll enjoy my day of victory."

William's first day home turned into a week, then two. By the end of the third week, the inevitability of his departure had doused all the joy brought by his homecoming. The two children had spent each day at William's side, every waking and sleeping moment. They had long since abandoned their own beds to sleep in their father's. Saturday brought the end of William's shore leave and the arrival of the all too familiar ache that accompanied goodbyes.

Back at the house, William had said his goodbyes to his own sister, Ellie, and then to Mara. William had held his daughter, her tears bleeding into his shirt. Neither Mara nor Ellie ever watched William sail away, the departure was too much for them.

Peter, on the other hand, always watched him leave from the docks. So, as was their custom, father and son walked the cobblestone street that led to the docks.

When they reached the ship, William knelt in front of Peter and unclipped a golden chain from around his own neck.

"This was your mother's. I gave it to her when we got married."

He drizzled the necklace into Peter's open hand.

It was a simple chain – bright golden links hammered flat. Peter had seen his father wear it for as long as he could remember.

"I want you to hold on to it until I get back," William said.

Peter gawked at the small chain, sparkling in the evening sun.

"Really?" he breathed quietly.

"Absolutely," William assured him. "Take good care of it, I'll be wanting it back. Now, I'll be back before you know it," he said. "Mind your aunt and practice your fighting but without sharps, I mean it. The last thing I need is to come back and hear you've impaled yourself."

Peter laughed at that. "Heh, I will." He smiled, wiping his nose on his sleeve.

"And lastly," William said, tilting Peter's head up to look into his eyes. "Take care of Mara. Don't pick on her. It's your job to keep her safe now. She's yours to protect until I'm back."

Peter straightened, shouldering the new responsibility.

"I will, father. I won't let you down," he said.

"Good man," William smiled, messing Peter's hair.

"Strike smart, Sailor!" Peter said, saluting.

"Strike true, Captain," William replied.

And with that, one of England's most renowned fighters tenderly kissed his son's head, turned, and boarded his ship.

SIX

The days that followed their father's departure were always the same. William's absence was tangible, as if the children's hearts had been ripped from their chests and thrown into the sea. And no amount of games or make believe could fill the resulting hole.

"You are my heart," William had often told Mara and Peter.

It seemed that William was as much a part of his children as they were a part of him. The tears lasted a few days then dried up. And dry eyes always led to a vacant sort of daze and no amount of fussing from Aunt Ellie could snap the two of them out of it. But after a week or so of sulking, the mischievous glint would return to Peter's eyes and Mara's laugh would slowly find its way out again.

"Peter?" Mara asked, one day, finding her brother on the front porch. "Will you spar with me again?"

"Ha! Why? Do you want to lose again?" he scoffed.

"If I recall, I beat you the last time," she said, prodding him with her foot.

"That's it," Peter said, "it's time to die."

The two ran to the courtyard and after a few minutes of wrestling over the same sword, each had armed themselves.

"Now, remember," Mara started. "Make sure yo–"

But Peter was already charging, hacking wildly at her with his short, wooden sword.

"I will have my vengeance!" he yelled, melodramatically.

Mara parried his attack, her clean, elegant style matching his fast, aggressive one. She ignored his verbal stabs, instead, focusing on his physical ones. She took his blows, drawing him in like her father had taught her. She stepped back, putting more space between them, and then Peter overreached.

Peter always overreached.

She twisted her blade in an attempt to wrench Peter's sword from his grasp, but as she pivoted to make the move, she tripped on a loose stone and fell backwards.

Peter lunged for her, but instead of the stinging rap of Peter's sword on her arm or side she expected, he grabbed her by the forearm, keeping her from hitting the ground.

He smiled down at her and winked. "Gotcha, sis," he said, grinning.

She pulled herself up, hurled the offending stone out of the courtyard, and readied herself.

"Another go?" she asked.

"Sure," he said, swinging his sword experimentally, nodding a ready to her.

She lifted her own weapon in salute and after a beat, the children began circling. This time their attacks were cautious, exploratory. Each knew the other's style intimately, so fooling the other took some work. Peter usually struck first, setting the tone and direction of the fight, but it seemed like he was changing his tactics this time. Their father had always warned them about the value of being unpredictable, and she knew Peter would much rather come out swinging with a killing blow. But maybe he was putting father's wisdom to the test.

He half-stepped forward, overemphasizing a wild, overhead strike. Mara brought her own blade up, held in a two handed grip, to block his typical attack. But this time, he shifted his weight, pivoted around her, and rapped her sharply on her backside. She whirled on him, her eyes alight with battle and a little fury. She took a step towards him, swinging her sword in a clearing arc, a clear message that the games were over; the spar was on.

Peter ducked under the blow, his eyes locked on his sister's as his father had always instructed him.

"If you see your opponent's eyes, you'll see their blade," William had said.

"But how can I see where he's attacking if I'm not looking at his weapon?" Peter had protested.

"Look at a man's blade and you see his actions," William had replied. "Look at his eyes and you'll read his mind."

This had been another one of William Till's many axioms that never really made much sense to Peter at the time. Regardless of his understanding of his father's words, he had learned to trust them. So he kept his eyes locked on his sister's as she kept hers locked on his – doubtless, the same lesson was running through her mind.

That was the problem when your trainer had also taught your opponent: the matches were always evenly matched.

Children though they were, under the gentle instruction of William Till, they were on par with swordsmen twice their age. What they lacked in strength and experience, they made up for in precision and form.

The two children continued to strike and riposte, parry and spin away, their skill and form mirrored in the other. Mara swung, a graceful figure-eight slash that zipped near Peter's stomach and face and sent him diving out of the way. He rolled toward the weapons rack and grabbed a short, wooden rapier to go with his longer sword. He ran toward his sister and attacked in a high, low, low, high pattern that put her on the defensive. Mara spun out of reach and slashed low, missing her brother but fully connecting with the ground. A cloud of dust puffed into Peter's face. He cried out, not in anger but in surprise. He backed away, dropping his rapier, and wiped his eyes clear with his now free hand.

"Clever girl," Peter thought.

Their father had taught them the reality of fighting. The honest truth was that when you fought for your life, the gentleman rarely walked away the victor. But while William showed them tiny glimpses beyond the gentlemen's sport of fencing, he always laced everything he taught with honor.

Dirt, however, was not a dishonorable tool. And while it might feel unfair to the blinded fighter, it didn't carry the same weight as gouging out one's eyes or lighting another on fire.

So Peter didn't protest. In fact, he grinned, knowing that his father's teachings were running through his sister's head too, and adapted to his new disadvantage.

He stumbled backward, giving the impression that he was off-balance. His watering eyes had already cleared most of the dirt, but he kept up the illusion that he was blinded. He scrubbed at his eyes and watched through half closed lids as his sister rushed toward him. She raised her sword to strike; clearly she was trying to end the match.

Peter waited.

Her strike seemed to move in slow motion. It reached it's full backward reach and began to move forward toward him.

He continued to scrub at his eyes.

Every fiber of his being wanted to block his sister's attack, but he had the advantage over her and he wasn't about to blow it on a simple parry. He wanted the win. At the absolute last second he sidestepped, allowing Mara's sword to pass harmlessly by him. He grabbed her by the sword hand, twisted the weapon out of her grip, and trapped her arm behind her, ending the match.

"Well struck!" Mara cried. "I thought I had you with the dust blind!"

"You almost did," Peter laughed. "But I could practically hear father's voice in my head," he said.

"Clear mind, clear strike," Mara said, raising her finger scholarly.

"Protect at all costs," Peter chirped.

"Wait, think, act!" the children said in unison.

"I do get tired of all his sayings," Peter said.

"But they're true," Mara said. "And I do miss them when he's gone," she ended, frowning.

"Aye," Peter said, a familiar pang of sadness filling his stomach as he remembered pleading with his father to stay. And his father's refusal. He chased the ill feelings away and decided that he would try to trust that his father knew best and that everything would be fine.

"Soon enough," he said. "With father leading the hunt, they'll be back home before too long."

"And maybe he'll have some new sayings for us," Mara giggled.

They both laughed as Peter put his arm around his sister and the two children walked into the house, quoting their father's favorite sayings in their best William Till voices.

SEVEN

William Till was dead.

The words made no sense to Peter. Somewhere in his mind, a switch turned and everything went gray and fuzzy.

He didn't really hear the crashing of his aunt's dishes on the floor or his sister's sickening scream as she ran from the room. Instead, he floated in the air, somewhere above and behind himself, and watched as a stranger told his family that his father was dead.

Benjamin Hornigold wasn't really a stranger, far from it. He had almost been like a second father to Peter for most of his life, but this man had let his father die and that was reason enough for Peter to disown him.

"Get out," Peter watched himself say.

Hornigold looked from Ellie to Peter, large tears pooling in the man's eyes. "I…I don't know what to say," he stammered, searching for words that didn't exist.

"Out! Take your lies and get out of my house!" Peter watched himself scream. He grabbed his chair and slammed it to the ground. The chair hit the floor and broke into pieces, splinters bounced under bookcases and into dark corners of the room. Distantly, he wondered if the chair could ever be fixed, and he wondered why he cared.

Hornigold spread his hands, his arms full of the guilt he carried.

"I'm sorry, son," he said.

"I'm not your son!" Peter roared and rushed the man, beating his clenched fists into the man's chest.

"Find him! Bring him back!" Peter cried.

Hornigold covered his mouth with one hand cradled Peter's head with the other.

Peter jerked away from his touch, rage burning in his eyes.

"This is your fault!" he accused, stabbing a finger at Benjamin. "If you hadn't lost your ship, he'd still be here!"

But before Hornigold could reply, Peter was gone, slamming doors as he passed through rooms.

"What happened?" Ellie whispered, lowering herself into a chair.

"A merchant ship came across wreckage," Hornigold sighed heavily. "The *Lion's Whelp's* nameplate was hauled aboard. There were no survivors, so we can't say if the crew was captured or," he paused, "or not."

"Well, what will be done?" she asked, leaning forward in her chair.

"My commission has been reinstated. The Crown never authorized my suspension in the first place, and despite the recent events, His Majesty still believes I am the only one who can bring Teach to heel."

"The poor children," she said, running her hands though her hair. "When do you leave?"

"Tomorrow," he replied. "Just before dawn. He turned toward the door through which Peter and Mara had left and lowered his voice. "Look, I don't want to get your hopes up, but it's possible that William is still alive. His reputation is renown and it would make sense for Teach to use him as bait. And if there is one thing that Teach respects, it's a skilled soldier, and William is certainly that," he said.

"Do we dare?" Ellie asked. "Do we dare hope?"

"I don't know what to think anymore," he said. "But what do we tell the children?" he asked.

"Nothing," she said. "If I know Peter, he'd do something foolish."

"What could he do?" Hornigold asked.

"Anything. That boy would do anything if he knew there was a chance his father was still alive," she replied.

"Well, I wouldn't worry too much about it. We leave at dawn," Hornigold replied.

Peter inched away from the door, letting the rest of the conversation fade away. He ran soundlessly over the floorboards to his room, skipping over the ones he knew creaked, and began to gather what few belongings he could smuggle with him onto a ship.

An hour before dawn, Peter noiselessly opened his window and followed his shadow out. He made sure not to rustle the bushes outside his aunt's room as he crossed under the window to get to Mara's room.

He quickly worked the pins out of the window hinges then painstakingly pulled the window down. He climbed through the open window and crept over to his sister's sleeping form.

"Mara," he whispered. "Mara, wake up."

She stirred but did not wake.

Peter rolled his eyes and carefully drew one hair from her head and gave it a sharp tug.

"Owmpf," Mara began to shout, but Peter's hand shot over her mouth, stifling her cry.

"Quiet," he hissed.

Her eyes widened but she made no effort to move.

"Listen, now don't say anything, just listen. Captain Benjamin's ship is leaving to search for Father in a few minutes and I'm leaving."

The question appeared in her wide eyes: *Father's alive?*

"Yes, there's a chance he's being held as bait for Captain Ben, so he's leaving in a few minutes to find him," he answered. "If you want to come with, we need to leave now. There's no time to stop me, so don't bother talking about that. Do you want to come with me and find Father, or do you want to stay here?"

Peter waited in silence for Mara's answer. Mara, unable to speak with Peter's hand over her mouth, simply nodded.

Peter flashed her a crooked smile and released his hold.

"Good," he said. "Let's go."

"But what about–" she began, climbing out of bed.

"There's no time for anything," he whispered, covering her mouth again. "We need to leave now, and we need to run," he said, handing her a pair of shoes and pushing her to the open window.

Mara slipped her shoes on as Peter climbed through the window. She gave one last look at her room and then followed him through the open window.

The clicks of their shoes on the stone street echoed around them as the two children raced headlong toward the docks.

"What are we doing?" Mara called to her brother.

"We're sneaking aboard the ship!" he answered.

"How?" she asked.

"No time. Hurry!" he called back.

They arrived at the harbor to find the docks in full swing. Peter and Mara sneaked from crate to crate being careful to keep themselves hidden. The two of them had spent more than enough time on the docks to be recognized by most of the workers and with the news of William's possible death, their presence on the docks would undoubtedly draw even more unwanted attention to them.

As they neared the ship, they could hear voices talking about final inventory checks and head counting. Peter looked out over the dock to the ship and found their way in – an open porthole.

"Climb in," Peter whispered. "Quickly."

Mara took a tentative step toward the ship and cast a nervous glance down at the empty air and black water that spanned the distance between ship and dock.

"Are you sure this is a good idea?" she asked, unease creeping into her voice.

"Mara, there's no time!" he replied. "Watch." And he leaped, crossing the distance and grabbing on to the edge of the hole. He crawled through, disappearing for a second, then reappeared, and leaned out offering a hand to his sister.

"See? Easy," he smiled.

"I don't know, Peter," she said, looking behind her. "Are you sure this is the best plan?" she asked.

"You want to find Father, don't you?" he said.

She looked back to him and nodded.

"Father told me to keep you safe, and that's what I'm going to do. Now jump. You'll be fine!" he called.

Mara turned back to the dock, took a deep breath and closed her eyes. She opened them and jumped. One hand met Peter's, the other met the edge of the porthole. Peter grabbed her other hand and pulled her in. They fell into a heap between two cannons.

Peter jumped to his feet, hands on both hips, and looked at their new surroundings. The sounds of heavy mooring lines thumping against the ship, farewells, and final orders could be heard outside.

Peter had spent his life up until this point watching ships depart so he knew the entire crew would be crowded on the deck waving and yelling. They had a few precious minutes to find a place to hide. They needed a place where they could stay hidden, at least until they were too far out to sea to turn back and bring them home.

"The armory!" Peter exclaimed.

"What?" Mara asked.

"We'll hide in the armory," he repeated. "They won't be needing weapons for at least a few weeks. We'll be able to hide there as long as we want!" he said.

They made their way together through the ship, searching for the armory. After a few minutes they found it.

"It's locked!" Mara exclaimed.

"Bloody locks," Peter muttered.

Mara slapped his arm. "Watch your mouth," she scolded.

Peter shot her a cold look then picked up a long wooden pole with a large sponge on one end.

"What's that?" Mara asked.

"A rammer," he said. "It's for loading cannons. You use it to push the charge down the cannon," he explained. "I'm going to use it to break the lock."

He swung the rammer and the wooden end connected with the lock. With a bright ping, the lock broke off the door and fell to the ground.

"Easy enough," Peter said, opening the door and stepping inside. Mara followed after picking up the broken lock and pulled the door shut behind her. In the span of three minutes, they had become stowaways.

The two siblings sat in silence. The darkness, combined with the steady rocking and creaking of the ship, quickly dissolved the adrenaline coursing through their veins, replacing it with slumber.

A deep voice hauled Peter from his sleep.

"In here!" the voice was yelling.

A glaring light was shining in Peter's eyes. He squinted against the brightness but couldn't make out the bodies silhouetted behind the light.

"Blimey! How'd you find us so soon?" Peter yelled, slamming his fist against the deck.

"My men heard snoring," a familiar voice replied. "I assumed it was a member of my crew ducking his duties. But imagine my surprise when instead I find children."

Captain Hornigold stepped into the light and stared down at them.

"Hi, Captain Ben," Mara said sheepishly.

A few of the men behind him chuckled softly until a glare from their captain silenced them. He turned back and addressed the pair.

"What in God's name were you two thinking?"

"We came to help," Peter replied. "We know how Father thinks. We're going to help you find him," he said.

"No, you're not," Benjamin said flatly.

"Well, we're not going back!" Peter spat. "We're not leaving this ship!"

"Well, that is something we agree on, because we can't turn back," Benjamin replied.

Peter smirked.

"Help me understand your plan, Peter, because I know this was not her idea," he said, pointing at Mara. "This ship," he said, indicating around himself. "Complements five hundred *men*, five hundred *experienced sailors*. This ship has supplies for five hundred hardened men who are hunting pirates. It is not a toy boat for children! So," he said, leaning toward Peter, "tell me, what was your plan for eating, sleeping, and surviving on this ship? What where you thinking?" Benjamin yelled.

Peter took the gold chain from around his neck and held it up to Benjamin.

"I was thinking about him," he replied quietly.

The golden chain twinkled in the lantern light the way William Till's eyes twinkled when he talked about his children, the way Peter's lit up when some new game sparked to life in his mind, the way Mara's did when she laughed.

For a moment, every eye stared at the golden chain wrapped around Peter's fist. Everyone in the armory knew William Till and the kind of man he was. Who could blame his children for trying find him, foolish as it was?

Benjamin sighed and shook his head.

"You do realize the position you've put me in," he asked.

"We do," Mara answered, coming along side her brother. "But we couldn't just sit at home if there's a chance he's still out here. We had to do something, even if it's just coming along," she said.

"What about your Aunt Ellie?" Benjamin asked. "She's going to go mad with worry."

"It's okay," Peter reassured. "I left a letter."

"A letter," Benjamin snorted, rolling his eyes. "Perfect!"

Mara looked from Peter to Benjamin, smiled, and nodded. "She'll know that we're safe with you," she said.

"Hunting pirates, " Benjamin added.

"Right!" Peter replied. "Hunting pirates."

EIGHT

A s luck would have it, having two children on board was not quite the nightmare Benjamin had predicted.

He had decided to bunk Peter and Mara in the galley's cellar but moved them into the captain's quarters after increasing reports of food going missing.

The children managed to serve as entertainment for the men as well. Evenings would find the two of them engaged in sparing matches with crewmen. And to the astonishment of the crew, the two children were impressively skilled.

Mara even managed to disarm a young midshipman, a few years her elder. The poor boy had had to live down the shame of being disarmed by a girl in the days that followed, and his shipmates had been quick to christen him "Sea Maid." The name stuck until Hornigold finally put an end to that.

A month had passed since Peter and Mara had stowed away on the ship. In that time, they had grown accustom to ship life.

Most mornings, Peter would rise shortly before dawn and make his way up to the crow's nest to join the night watch and wait for the sun to rise. But this morning, he climbed out of the crow's nest and out onto the yard.

"Peter! Get back over here!" the night watchman, Gale Brimble, yelled.

"Relax, limey, I've got my father's legs," Peter rebuked, steadying himself with rigging overhead.

As the sun began to rise, he stretched his arms out, both hands still gripping the rigging above him. He tipped his head back and closed his eyes.

He felt the ship beneath him, swaying. He felt the sun slowly growing warmer on his face. He felt the cool morning breeze and smelled the salt in the air. The ship seemed to disappear under him. He felt like he could let go of the ropes and float in the air, suspended next to the ship.

He let go of the rope for an instant and felt completely free.

It felt like flying.

An instant later, Brimble had him by the back of his shirt and was hauling him back on to the lookout stand.

"You trying to get yourself killed?" Brimble cried.

"Let go of me," Peter yelled, jerking his arm free.

"Get out of here, boy, you're crazy," Brimble shouted.

Peter rolled his eyes and began climbing down. He took one last look at the rising sun and followed the horizon until a small, black, speck caught his eye.

"What's that?" he asked, pointing at the dot.

Brimble's eyes narrowed and then widened. "Good eye, lad," he praised, his sour mood forgotten.

He reached for the bell and began ringing it.

"Avast ye! Ship on the horizon, all hands hoay!" he cried. "Best get to deck, Peter," he told him. "Capt'n'll want you at hand now," he added.

"Is it him?" Peter asked.

"Might be, off you go," Brimble replied.

Peter nodded and quickly descended the rope ladder to the deck.

The deck was a flurry of noise and activity.

"Is it him, Peter?" sailors were asking.

Peter could hear voices below deck and the scraping of cannon wheels grinding against the deck.

"Peter!" Mara called, running over to him. "What's this about?"

"I spotted a ship!" he said. "Brimble thinks it might be Teach!"

"How can he be sure?" Mara asked.

"Who knows," Peter replied. "But that old salt has spent more time up there than we've spent on dry land. If he thinks it's Teach, it's Teach."

Captain Hornigold's voice cut short their conversation.

"I want you kids in my quarters, now," he ordered. "We've got a lot of work to do and we don't need you getting in the way."

"Yes, Captain Ben," Mara replied.

Peter just rolled his eyes and followed Mara to Benjamin's cabin. Historically the captain's cabins were in the rear of the ship, but Benjamin had insisted on converting one of the forward storerooms into his own chamber to give his lieutenants more room.

"Well, that's that," Mara said, pulling the door shut behind Peter.

"That's that?" Peter asked. "That's nothing, help me find some weapons."

"Weapons? What for? You heard what Ben said," she replied, settling into Hornigold's bed and hugging a pillow.

"He said to stay in his quarters. Come on, help me find them. We'll make it a game," he said. "If you find his stash first, I'll let you have first pick."

Mara rolled her eyes and settled deeper into Hornigold's bed.

"We've spotted a pirate ship," Peter said, insisting. "Pirates," he repeated slowly. "Killers! How long will you survive an attack when all you're armed with is a pillow and your tears?" he said.

"Hmpf," Mara scoffed, then threw her pillow at him and jumped out of bed.

The pillow hit him square in the face, sending him sprawling.

He came up, smiling, to see Mara reaching deep into Benjamin's chest, pulling a short sword free from its sheath.

"How'd you know where they were?" he asked, incredulous.

"Silly boy," she smiled. "Captain Ben is always telling Father about the personal arsenal he always sails with." She tossed Peter a scabbard. An ornate dagger hilt protruded from the end.

"Bangerang." He smiled, admiring it. "All right," he said, unsheathing the dagger. "On guard!" he cried.

"You want to spar with sharps on a ship? You'll get us both killed," she scolded.

"Don't be such a girl!" Peter taunted.

"It's not happening. Someone needs to be the sensible one."

Peter put his dagger back in its sheath then walked over and patted his sister on the cheek. "Mara, you're going to make a brilliant grown up some day."

She glared at him and took his dagger.

"We know where these are, let's keep them in the chest for now," she said, ignoring his barb.

The two children spent the rest of the morning and afternoon trying to entertain themselves in the cabin. When all possible fun had been sucked dry from the small room, they stared out the window at the tiny sliver of ship in the distance. Sometimes it seemed to grow larger only to shrink away again.

Morning became afternoon, which became evening. Another dark speck appeared on the horizon. This one grew faster, expanding into the sky, widening across the horizon into a storm. The storm was nightmare black. It looked like a giant hand, reaching up out of the edge of the world. It flashed bolts of lightning and growled angrily at the two ships imposing on its realm, warning them to turn back.

Peter had seen storms before, but this was something new.

"Wow," Mara whispered. "Are we going in there?"

"Aye," a voice behind them replied.

The two turned to see Captain Hornigold staring out at the storm with them. He began to recite:

And now the storm-blast came, and he
Was tyrannous and strong:
He struck with his o'ertaking wings,
And chase us south along,

He looked down at the children. "An old sailor's song," he smiled.

"Dangerous things, storms. But I've seen worse."

Peter smiled nervously back at him before returning to look back at the storm.

"This'll slow us down a bit, and Teach, too. We've closed on him, though. We should be caught up to him by midday tomorrow," he said. "Why don't you try getting some sleep while you can," he suggested. "The storm may make for difficult sleeping later on."

"I wouldn't worry about that, Captain Ben," Mara said. "Peter can sleep through anything."

Peter shot her a dirty look and climbed into Hornigold's bed. Mara followed shortly after.

Hornigold smiled at them and closed the door behind him.

NINE

A loud boom jolted Peter awake. His heart stopped beating and hung in mid-air, until it, along with the rest of his body, slammed onto the cabin floor.

He wiped the grogginess of sleep out of his eyes with his hands as adrenaline replaced the blood in his veins.

"Peter? Are you okay?" Mara asked, sitting upright in bed.

"Yeah, yeah, I'm fine," he said, shaking his vision clear. He got to his feet and looked out the window.

They were buried deep within the belly of the black storm. Rain and wind rattled against the windows. The decking underneath them vibrated with the pounding of the waves.

"This is bad," Peter said.

"We don't know that," Mara reassured. "We've never been in a storm at sea," she said.

"Yeah, but still," he said thoughtfully, "this doesn't feel right."

"Why don't you try and go back to sleep," Mara insisted.

Thunder exploded overhead again. The sound rattled Peter's chest. He shot her a sidelong glance.

"Are you serious?" he asked.

"Maybe not," she conceded.

"Let's check it out," Peter said.

"What?" Mara cried. "You heard what Ben said, 'Stay in the cabin.'"

"That was before the storm, when we were on Teach's heels. But you heard him. We won't be caught up to them until midday tomorrow, earliest," he insisted.

"I don't know," Mara thought out loud. "It looks pretty dangerous out there." Peter peered out the porthole, the dark waves only illuminated when lightening forked down from an equally dark sky.

"Don't be such a girl," he said, making his way to the door. "We'll be fine."

He cracked open the door and a gust of wind caught it, blasting it wide open and slamming it into the wall. Peter jumped back out of the way of the swinging door, then gave it a tug, but the handle was buried deep in the wall.

Mara just looked at him.

"Well, now we need to get someone to help us close the door," he shouted over the gusting wind and then smiled sheepishly. "Come on!"

They walked out onto the deck and the reality of the storm's danger hit them. Ropes and loose rigging whipped around the deck. Sailors frantically ran to and fro, some tying down torn sails and other equipment they couldn't afford to lose while others hurled non-essential gear overboard.

No one paid them any attention; securing the ship was clearly foremost on their minds – which told Peter just how dangerous their situation was.

Lightning split the darkness, momentarily bathing them in bright, white light.

"Um, Peter?" Mara yelled to him.

"Yeah, good idea," he called back.

They turned around to go inside when lightning seared into the foremast, splitting it into pieces. The mast's yards spun wildly in the air, crashing into the captain's cabin.

The two children stood slack jawed staring at the ruined cabin.

"Maybe we should go below deck," Peter called.

Mara nodded numbly and followed him.

Carefully but quickly, they made their way across the deck as the boat rocked back and forth violently.

The shouts and cries of the crew, desperate to keep their ship afloat, nearly drowned out the sounds of the storm.

Peter lost his footing and slipped, sliding away from Mara, toward the gunwale and the edge of the ship.

"Peter!" Mara screamed.

He stopped himself and stood up again. He grinned at her and waved away her cry.

Suddenly, the ship slammed to a stop, hurling Peter into the gunwale. He scrambled to his feet as the ship pitched away from whatever they had hit. He swung his arms frantically as he struggled to regain his balance.

Lightning flashed above them, momentarily exposing a towering black rock face off the port side. Mara gasped at the sight of the enormous cliff. But her awe was short lived as the storm slammed the ship into the rocks a second time. She scanned the deck for her brother and spotted him struggling against the port railing.

"Peter!" she yelled, stumbling as she made her way towards him.

Another bolt of lightning blossomed overhead, hitting the mainmast. The mast exploded; wood and rigging rained down on the deck around them.

"Peter, look out!" she yelled again.

This time he heard her and looked up just as the main rig swung free and smashed into his face. He blindly reached out to steady himself, but his reach brought him too far over the edge of the deck.

"Peter, no!" Mara screamed, diving for him.

His arms waved uselessly around his body as he slowly tipped away from the ship. His eyes met hers and it looked for a moment as if he might regain his balance. But his momentum carried him off the side and into the dark waters. He was gone.

Mara shook with disbelief as an animal shriek bellowed from her chest.

First her father, now Peter.

The deck shook violently, as if mirroring her own grief and rage. It slammed her to the ground. Her head cracked hard against the deck. Blood flowed into her eye from a cut on her head. Sailors screamed in horror as the ship slowly rotated along its length toward the black cliffs.

Mara scrambled up the deck to the starboard rails, trying to wipe rainwater and blood from her eyes. The storm drowned the cries of the sailors who fell toward the cliff or into the rock-strewn waves. The mizzenmast fractured and split as the sea continued to assault the ship.

The ship slowly began to roll toward the cliff face. Mara climbed through the railing and knelt on the side of the ship as the storm crushed the deck flat against the rocks. The ship shuddered, shaking a few of the ill-footed sailors loose who had managed to join Mara on the ship's side.

The unlucky sailors slammed into the exposed keel before falling limply into the foaming sea.

Mara looked around at the sea and cliffs. The raging seawater meant instant death and the cliffs seemed to stretch to the left and right and up into the night sky forever. She strained to look up the cliff, trying to gauge the distance. Lightning flashed around, briefly exposing the cliff tops. They looked like the White Cliffs of Dover, only they were black instead of white.

Another wave brought the remains of the ship closer to the rocks again and she pressed herself to the cliff wall and tested the rock. Water trickled down the cliff in tiny rivulets. The jagged wall provided plenty of holds, but the glass-like rock was sharp. She tried to hold her weight on the rock, but the sharp stone nipped at her fingers. The words of her father broke through the storm and replayed clearly in her mind.

"Weigh your options then act, and think of nothing else but your task," he had said. His strong voice carried his smile even in her mind.

A large wave thundered against the ship, rocking Mara back to reality. She slipped, landing hard on her tailbone. Sharp pain flashed through her lower back. She got to her knees slowly and then to her feet. Reaching out to the wall, she stepped into a cleft and let her arms and legs take her weight. She immediately felt the wall's tiny black teeth bite into her hands and feet.

Sailors around her also tried to scale the cliffs, but the weight of the men proved too heavy for the needle-like stone. Sailors fell around her as she worked her way up. Weeping, she climbed. Torrents of rain beat against her back and the sharp rocks dug into her fingers, both willing her to release her grip. Water and blood poured into her eyes as she strained to see the top of the cliffs.

The indistinguishable sounds of ship's and sailor's bones being crushed against the cliffs followed her up as she continued to climb.

"Climb. Think of nothing else. *Climb*," she told herself.

Soon her hands were sticky with her own blood and her feet buzzed with numbness. After what seemed like an hour of climbing, her hand touched something soft. It was grass. With the last of her strength, she pulled herself up over the edge of the cliff and dragged herself a few feet from the ledge. She lay panting for several minutes as the rain continued to assault her before she began to crawl away from the cliff toward a line of trees. As she arrived she collapsed, her body giving out from exhaustion.

TEN

Mara opened her eyes.

The storm from the night before had left no evidence that it had ever happened. She pushed herself up, then winced as her burning hands brought the events of the night before back into the forefront of her mind.

"Peter!" she cried and scurried on hands and knees to the cliff edge. She looked down, frantically searching for any sign of her brother.

"Peter!" she shouted, but the distant sounds of waves crashing against the cliffs washed away her shouts. She called his name a few more times before realizing that there was no way he would have stayed at the cliff base. There weren't even any signs of the ship itself.

And if the ship was gone, then Peter... She shook the thought from her head. This was Peter. He would be fine. He had to be fine.

"Have you lost something?" a small, refined voice asked behind her.

The voice startled Mara, one hand slipping off the cliff's edge. But a sharp tug at her dress brought her back into balance.

She turned around and startled a second time, again bringing her dangerously close to the cliff's edge.

"Maybe you should move away from the edge," the voice suggested.

The voice belonged to what could only be described as a tiny, glowing girl. The girl, if the creature was, in fact, a girl, couldn't have been more than five to eight inches tall.

And she was flying.

She hovered right in front of Mara, a pair of semi-transparent wings whipping behind her. She was clothed in a plain, brown tunic with matching leggings that came down to her shins. A pair of sheathed daggers threaded through her belt and lay strapped against each hip.

"I..." Mara stammered. "My..."

The creature smiled. "Are you hurt?" she asked, pointing a delicate finger towards Mara's scabbed hands.

Mara held her hands out, looking at them as if seeing hands for the first time. She didn't speak but nodded dumbly.

The creature floated closer to her, smiling. She reached out and lifted Mara's giant hand with her tiny one. She held her tiny fingers over Mara's open hand and began to rub her own fingers together, as if sprinkling crumbs from her hand. To Mara's shock, something *did* fall from her fingers – a fine golden dust. The dust gave off the same golden glow that the girl did.

A gasp of surprise escaped Mara's lips as the dust touched her hand. It was warm and seemed to evaporate into her hand. The still-sharp burning in her hands began to ebb immediately. Her hands were still in pain, but the pain was significantly less than before.

"Do you have a name?" the girl asked, still sprinkling the golden dust from her fingertips.

"Mara," she answered, finding her voice but still staring at her hand.

"Nice to meet you, Mara," the girl said, still smiling. "I'm Siene. May I see your other hand?" she asked.

Mara nodded and offered her other hand to the girl.

"What are you?" Mara whispered.

"A fairy," Siene whispered back.

"How is that possible?" Mara said. "How are you a fairy?"

The fairy shrugged. "I don't know, it's what I've always been," she whispered.

"Why are you whispering?" Mara said, still whispering.

The fairy shrugged, "Oh, I don't know, you started it. I thought that's how you wanted to talk."

"Oh, sorry," Mara replied.

"These cuts," Siene said, inspecting her wounds. "Did you climb the cliffs?"

Mara nodded. "Our ship crashed into the cliff last night during the storm," she said.

"Be grateful for these wounds," she said, sprinkling dust into Mara's other hand.

"What do you mean?" Mara asked.

"You crashed into the Obsidian Cliffs, deep within mer territory," her eyes narrowing at the word *mer*.

"What's a mer?" Mara asked, her face wrinkling in question.

"Sea monsters," Siene replied, her voice suddenly turning icy. "Part man, mostly fish, entirely evil."

"Mer," Mara said, trying the word around in her mouth. "As in mermaid? I've heard that they're gentle, friendly creatures – in stories, of course. But they're not real. They can't be real."

"Oh, they're real," the creature spat, all traces of gentleness gone. "And they are nothing but deceivers. Even your stories are tainted by their deception. Harmless? Ha!"

Mara let the words sink in, or at least, tried to. She was having a very difficult time accepting the idea that mermaids were real. The fact was, she was having a difficult time accepting the idea that fairies were real, despite the evidence flying two feet from her face.

Siene continued. "It makes no difference if you believe me. There are things whose existence does not depend on our belief in them. Pray that the sea claimed your friends before the mers did."

"But what about my brother?" she asked. "What about Peter?"

"I'm sorry," the fairy said, elegance returning to her voice. Suddenly changing the subject, she asked, "What was your ship doing here at our island?"

"We were chasing a man," she started, "a pirate. He destroyed my father's ship and we we're trying to see if," her voice weakened and trailed off for a moment "if he killed him."

"I'm sorry to hear that," Siene said, her voice full of compassion.

"We were closing in on him when we hit the storm. Teach must have made it through because before we-" Mara started.

Siene's daggers were in her hand before Mara could blink. "Teach?" the girl interrupted. "Edward Teach?"

"Yes," Mara replied, cringing away from the now armed fairy. "Do you know him?"

"This island knows Edward Teach all too well," Siene replied. "Come with me, Adelaide will have questions for you."

"Who's Adelaide?" Mara asked.

"Our queen," she said. "Come quickly. If Teach is on the island, we won't have much time."

Mara moved automatically. Her head swam with thoughts of tiny flying girls and sea monsters.

And Peter.

She couldn't forget about her brother; he was all she had left. Peter was alive. He had to be. Mara knew that if her brother was dead, she would never make it off this island and certainly would never find her father. And she was going to find her father, so that meant Peter couldn't be dead. Peter was alive.

Siene led her through the forest, the fairy's tiny wings making soft whipping sounds. The sounds of her guide flying combined with the morning breeze whispering through the trees and provided a calming hum.

The pair moved silently through the forest for a few minutes more before Mara's thoughts began to wander to her brother again—wander, then race. Was he hurt somewhere? Was he trapped and was she the only one who could help him?

"We're here," Siene said, interrupting Mara's thoughts.

Mara looked up to see a waterfall. The water fell in sheets into a large pond, then churned about before splitting and flowing down one of the two rivers that forked out from the pond.

"Wow," she said, taking in the sight.

"This is your home?" Mara asked, looking around.

"Just about, yes," she replied.

Siene led Mara along the shore of the pond to a rock face at the base of the falls. She pointed toward a small path that led behind the water.

"Follow the path until you make it through," she said, then zipped away.

Mara made her way along the back wall of the cliff leading up and behind the falls. Mist soaked her as she picked her way over the slick, mossy rocks. She couldn't help but think that the wall was angling closer and closer to the water. Before long, she was pressed hard against the wall, the thundering falls right behind her. Thoughts of her experience from the night before flooded her. She began to wonder if this fairy could be trusted or if this island had somehow decreed that her fate would be drowning as well.

She came to the end of the path and a second rock wall jutted out in front of her – a dead end. Determined to see this through one way or the other, she snaked an arm, then a leg around the protruding rock. Water roared around her, threatening to pull her away and into the falls. Her arms screamed in pain as she once again, forced her body past their limits. With a great effort, she managed to get her head through the water and onto the other side of the rock. Her anxiety continued to swell with each passing second until with one final effort, she pulled herself free from the water's grip and fell onto the bedrock.

She laid on the ground, her head on her arms, greedily sucking air into her lungs. After a few moments, she felt a soft tickle dancing on her back.

"Welcome to White Falls," a familiar voice said.

Mara lifted her head and saw Siene standing on her shoulder. Then she saw the cave. She had fallen into a cavern behind the waterfall. But this was no ordinary cave, a city had been carved into every inch of the walls, which were like honeycombs.

Each space had little rooms built inside of them. They even had little windows and doors. She looked closer and saw that the sparkle came not only from the fairies, but from the walls themselves. The entire cave was lined with gold and shiny gems. She could make out rubies, emeralds, and diamonds. In fact, most of the tiny city's decoration seemed to be made up of the precious stones.

Both male and female fairies flitted throughout the cave. Some of them wore what looked like dark leather tunics with swords nearly as long as their bodies strapped to their back, between their wings. Others wore lighter, bright clothing and carried gems, food, and many other things that Mara couldn't pick out. The cave was buzzing with activity.

Mara was speechless. She gazed at the room around her. The walls shined like stars on a summer night. Each gem mirrored the reflections of the others creating so much light it dazzled Mara's eyes. The sight nearly brought her to tears.

"What is this place?" she asked, awestruck.

"Our home," a sweet voice above her answered.

Mara looked up to identify the speaker and her breath caught in her chest again.

Their queen, for this creature could be nothing else, drifted towards her. She wore a simple, white dress, but on her it looked anything but simple. Cascades of long brown hair poured from her petite, golden head. Her hair almost seemed to change from brown to a golden blonde as the dust moved throughout it. The golden dust that imbued every other fairy paled compared to their queen's white brilliance. She glowed with such intensity that Mara almost had to look away. Atop a perfect, tiny head perched a diamond-studded crown. And in one slender, white hand she held a golden staff.

Instinctively, Mara dropped to one knee and bowed her head in respect.

"I am Adelaide the Just. You are welcome here," the creature smiled angelically. She was the most regal being Mara had ever seen, but the fairy's brown eyes seemed disquieted by sadness.

"I'm Mara the…" she said, searching for a word, "the girl. This is your home?" she asked.

"This is our home," Adelaide agreed. "We've lived here for as long as anyone can remember. We don't have any recorded histories that place us anywhere but White Falls. We will show you our home—or the parts you can fit in, at least" she added with a smile. "But first, tell me what brought you to our island."

Mara told the two fairies everything that had led her to the island. She shared about her father returning home in Teach's wrecked ship, his promotion to captain, and his voyage that led his capture or…death. And finally, she told them about Peter and them sneaking aboard the ship that was ultimately shipwrecked on the island.

They spent the next few hours wandering through the cave sharing what they each knew about Edward Teach. Mara was surprised to learn that Teach had visited the island on several occasions. He had tried to curry favor with the island's leaders, the Grand Council. On his final visit, several years earlier, he had laid a trap for them and the results had been devastating. All but one Council member had been killed. The fairy king at the time, Tam the Wise – Adelaide's uncle, had been killed in the attack. With every other heir in the ruling family dead, the burden of leadership had fallen to Adelaide, a child at the time.

The chaos that followed the death of the Grand Council was crippling. Trust that had been built over centuries had been shattered. Teach's attack did more damage than he could have dreamed. Wars broke out all over the island. The only faction that had escaped the fallout of the attack were the mers. The fact that the only survivor of the attack had been a mermaid and that the mers had originally insisted on bringing Teach into the Council in the first place, made it clear that the mers had been working with Teach all along. After the attack, the mers disappeared back into the sea and Teach used the ensuing chaos that followed to launch an attack against the fairies in order to find their home. It seemed that in the end, all he wanted was their dust.

Adelaide sprinkled her fingertips the same way Siene had and the golden dust trickled from her fingers.

"It has remarkable healing abilities, as you know," Adelaide said, pointing to Mara's healing hands. "As well as many other uses."

"What about the mermaids now?" Mara asked.

"We rarely see them," Adelaide replied. "And when we do, they disappear as quickly as they're seen. They seem content to rule their underwater domain and anyone who has gone into, or even near, their waters have never returned. Now you can see how fortunate you are to have escaped their waters."

"Are they really that horrible?" Mara asked, still dubious.

The fairy queen smiled gently down at Mara.

"There exist," she began, "creatures of fairness, creatures of instinct, and creatures of treachery. The mers are dark—evil by the very nature of their existence. And where there is treachery, there can be no hope."

Adelaide's face softened and she opened her hands, palms up, to Mara.

"You would be wise to grieve the loss of your brother and move on. I'm so sorry."

ELEVEN

What's your name, boy?" the thick voice sounded in Peter's head.

"Ugh," Peter tried to talk but a weak moan was all he could manage. The sound of the voice reverberated through his aching head. He tried to lift his hands to his head but they didn't move.

"My hands," he muttered.

"They're bound. What's your name?" the voice asked again. "How did you get here?"

"Wh…Where am I?" Peter asked, squinting and trying to clear his vision.

"Leave 'im be, he's just a boy. He don't know anything," another voice said.

Peter sat up, slowly trying to get some sense of where he was. He was in a cave with ten or twenty men, that much he could tell. The men were all bound, like Peter, but the room was too dark to make out anything other than their silhouettes. The walls were dark, damp from floor to ceiling. Water dripped down the walls from the ceiling; the echo of the tiny "plink" of water dripping could be heard in all directions. There were no torches or lanterns to be seen, but the cave was lit well enough to see. The cavern walls seemed to give off a soft blue-green glow. As he looked closer, he could see that it was not the walls that glowed but something else. All around him he saw tiny glowing specs of dust. Their sizes ranged from grains of sand to that of small beads. The dust seemed to move on its own, a silent dance that almost seemed to mock his confinement.

"Where are we?" Peter asked again, his voice echoing a little stronger through the cave. His head was beginning to clear. "And why are my hands tied?"

"Quiet boy! They'll hear you," the thick voice barked.

"Who? What's happening?" Peter asked again, his voice becoming more frantic.

A guttural shriek echoed from deep within the cave. The sound bounced throughout the cave before shivering down Peter's back. His blood ran cold and before he could open his mouth to speak, a dark hand wrenched him off the ground and carried him away. He gasped in alarm and kicked instinctively, he made contact with something thick and strong. It was like kicking a stone wall.

"Ahh, help!" he cried out, trying to break free of his captor, but the iron grasp would not relent.

"Sssilence human!" his captor hissed. Peter went stiff with fear.

Moments later, the creature dumped him on the ground. The cool, smooth stone felt good against his still-throbbing head.

He moaned, rubbing his eyes with his bound hands, and looked up.

He was in a new room. The walls, stalactite-ceilings, and glowing dust were all the same, but the room was much larger. In front of him stood a ring of five stone-carved chairs. They seemed more like thrones than chairs. They had very high backs and the outside edges of the backs were pointed on the sides, swooping down to form a smaller point at the middle. The design reminded Peter of a pitchfork. For some reason that he couldn't understand, the chairs frightened him. But what frightened him more was the being who sat alone in the second chair.

She had the face of a woman with high cheek bones, a slender nose, and eyes that seemed unnaturally large for her head. She might have been beautiful had she not been absolutely terrifying. Her ashen-gray skin dimly reflected the light around her. She had thick wavy hair—oily, unnaturally black hair that was peppered with an assortment of beads, small bones, and some sort of fine green threads woven into her braids. She wore a patched tunic made from dark, coarsely threaded fabrics. The garments were heavily laden with beads and bones that matched those in her hair. But her most prominent feature was that from the waist down instead of human feet and legs, she bore a thick, dark-scaled tail.

The creature leaned forward and studied Peter. Her eyes glowed a luminescent blue that seemed to stare through him. Peter couldn't tear his gaze away from the creature.

"Where am I?" Peter managed, his voice cracking and filling with fear.

"You have come to free your companionsss, human," the creature said. Her voice seemed to catch on the "s" in "companions" the same way a snake hissed. Peter hated snakes.

"Wha–?" Peter stammered. "What companions? I don't even know where I am."

"You are untruthful," the creature interrupted. "I know for what you search. Man is ssso transparent. What is your name?"

Peter was afraid that if he gave her his name she would some how keep it.

"Peter," he replied, feeling himself answering against his will.

"Peter," the creature repeated his name. She rose and slowly began to move towards him, her tail snaking along the stones. "Peter of Man," she said, sliding across ground.

Peter instinctively tried to inch away, but his hands were bound to his feet. He frantically tried to twist his hands free, but the rope's dark green fibers bit deeper into his wrists.

The creature laughed at his feeble attempts, a wet, hissing sound.

"The weakness of man," she chuckled. "It is all over you, dripping, blackening you."

She paused, her large eyes shifting from blue to black. She bent down and seized him by his wrist bonds and lifted him up with one hand. His hands and feet rose awkwardly as she lifted him up to eye level with her.

Her eyes, those terrible black eyes, bore into his own. Peter stared back into them, unable to move, unable to think. It was as if nothing in the world existed but those eyes. They seemed to draw everything to them: sound, light, hope. Peter spoke almost automatically.

"I'm afraid," he confessed. "I'm afraid that everything I've ever known is gone and that I'll be alone."

"The weaknesss of man," she repeated, dropping him to the ground. "You are alone, Peter of Man. You are very alone," she said, circling around him, her scales scraping on the ground as she moved. "You are far from your ship, far from your brethren, far from that which you ssseek."

Peter blinked and shook his head, trying to clear his mind, but his thoughts were slow and thick. Your brethren? Did she mean the men in the other room? He didn't know what she was talking about.

"No," Peter said with an effort. "I don't know anything about those men out there."

"Unlikely," came the creature's response. "You are man," she continued. "Man has a single purpose for coming to our island and a single fate awaits him."

She was facing him again, staring at him with those eyes. She signaled to the guards in the doorway behind Peter.

"You share in their likenesss, Peter of Man, so you shall share in their fate."

The guard lifted him off the ground and carried him out of the large room, back to where he had woken up.

Peter was shaking madly as the creature deposited him back with the others. He fought back hot tears and massaged his aching wrists as best he could. One of the men leaned out of the shadow and asked, "Are ye all right mate?" It was the thin reedy voice from earlier.

"I, I don't know," Peter replied shakily. "What are those things?"

"They're mers," the man replied, shooting furtive glances to make sure their conversation was not being overheard. "Part fish and part human," he continued. "But not human like you or me. No, these creatures are all evil."

The man continued his nervous glancing as he spoke; he seemed to become more paranoid with every word.

"It's been said that if you look into their eyes they can steal your soul," he went on.

Peter listened intently, trying to put the pieces together as the man spoke.

"What's yer name, boy?" the man asked, changing the subject.

"Peter."

"I'm Rufus. Call me Rufe," he replied, extending his bound hands to Peter.

"How did you get here?" Peter asked, shaking the man's bound hand awkwardly.

"We don't know," Rufe replied, looking down, then away. "But enough about us, how did a small lad like yerself end up in on this island?" he asked.

"Our ship," Peter began, "we were looking for the pirates who attacked my father's ship, but a storm came and drove us into the cliffs," he continued, squinting slightly. "And I fell off the ship and into the water, and then I woke up here."

"Take heart mate," Rufe said, "I'm sure once–"

"Don't give the boy false hope," the thick-voiced man from the shadows snapped. "We're already dead and everyone knows it."

"I don't know what this place is, but I'm going to find a way out. I'm going to find my father and no creatures or caves or…whatever this place is, will stop me."

"It's Hell, mate," the voice said. "You're in Hell. And no one escapes Hell."

Peter leaned back against the wall as the man's words echoed through his mind. Gradually, he drifted into a restless sleep.

Peter opened his eyes and started. A small child was peering at him. The child cocked her head and smiled up at him, exposing a row of small, pointy white teeth.

The events from hours ago flooded back to Peter as he bolted up and tried to inch away from the child.

"Get away from me," he stammered. But the small child paid no attention, instead it moved closer, climbing up on his lap, still smiling.

Peter cringed as he felt the child's cold, leathery scales move across his legs. It sat motionless, looking at his face.

"How strange," Peter whispered to himself.

"Sstrange!" the small child chirped, grinning up at him.

Her shrill voice roused the other men from slumber; they looked at Peter and the small merchild in astonishment.

"Rufe! Grab her," the dark-voiced man hissed.

"Are ye mad?" Rufe scoffed. "And what then? The mers rip me to pieces? Capital plan, Pruner!"

"You fool," Pruner, the thick-voiced man, spat. "That child is our ticket out of here. We'll trade our lives for hers."

"She's just a child," Rufe said defensively. "Have ye no heart?"

"I'm not going to die down in this bloody cave and no fool is going to stand in my way," Pruner hissed.

He lunged for the merchild, but Rufe, having only slightly more sense than his shipmate, scurried in front of the man and tried to push Peter and the child out of reach.

The child shrieked and lashed out with her tail, striking Rufe hard in the face. Peter kicked, catching Pruner under the chin. Almost instantly, two mers materialized from the darkness and fell upon Rufe, while a third appeared and took the child away. The mers struck Rufe, slamming him hard against the cavern wall. The mer seized him roughly by the legs and dragged him out of the room before anyone could think.

"Fool!" Peter spat at Pruner, wiping blood from his lip. "You're going to get us killed."

"Hold your tongue, child, or I'll remove it," Pruner spoke, glaring at Peter.

"Take the child?" Peter nearly yelled. "What kind of plan is that?"

"Do not test me, boy," the man growled.

"No wonder they're going to kill us," Peter breathed heavily. "You're an animal."

"Pick your side carefully, child. Align with them and you'll receive the same treatment," Pruner hissed.

"Who are you people?" Peter asked, but Pruner just smiled and turned away.

The next couple of hours passed uneventfully. Peter drifted in and out of sleep, but the damp walls made for terrible sleeping. He spent most of the time wondering about Rufe's fate. There had been no signs or sounds of the mers since they had carried him away. Peter had no idea what time of day it was or how long he had been in the cave. All he knew was that he had to get out.

The next day, from what Peter could guess, brought no change in their situation. Rufe was still gone, and Pruner conversed with his companions in hushed tones. From time to time a patrolling mer would pass by, hiss menacingly at the group and move on.

Peter began to realize that despite the constant terror that gripped him, he was growing bored. He sat against the cave wall. His wrists ached from being bound for so long. He absently twisted his wrists in their restraints, trying to loosen them.

They appeared to be a plant weave of some sorts. He tested them with his teeth, faint hopes of chewing through them diminished as soon as he tested the fibers with his teeth. Whatever it was, it was strong.

He looked up from his bonds right into the glassy, blue eyes of the merchild.

"Get out of here!" Peter hissed, looking around to see if Pruner had noticed the child's return. He hadn't.

"They're going to take you," he tried to explain, turning back to the child. "Get out of here."

But the child paid no attention to his warnings. Instead, she laughed silently, shaking to herself and grinning up at him.

She produced a small fish and handed it to Peter.

"Sstrange!" the child chirped.

"Shh, shh! Quiet!" Peter nearly yelled, casting furtive glances at the shadowed men curled up against the walls.

Turning back toward the child, he spoke as slowly as he could.

"They're going to kill you. Do you know what kill means?" When she didn't respond, he took the fish and threw it down the cavern hall in frustration. Her curious smile melted into dejection as her bright blue eyes moistened and turned a sad shade of green. The child's shoulders sagged and she turned away to leave.

"I'm sorry," Peter started. "I didn't mean to–" but before he could finish his sentence, a hand reached out and yanked the small creature into the darkness.

Pruner.

The scarred man was wrestling to keep hold of the child. His bonds were cut. The little creature was going crazy, thrashing with arms and tail, while shrieking at the top of her lungs.

"Shut it, brat!" Pruner yelled, forcing an arm over hers and pressing a small, sharp stone against her leathery neck. "Now we get out of here, boys!" he cried.

The cave exploded with activity as mers poured into the chamber. Hissing and deep growls roared through the massive room. The hissing stopped suddenly and the crowd parted as the creature Peter had talked to entered the room.

"Return her and I will kill you quickly, pirate," she said in her snake-like tongue.

Pirate?

The word sent Peter reeling. These men were pirates?

"Nah," Pruner spat. "We leave, or she dies. Lead us to an exit, we swim up with the child, and when we're safe, we let 'er go."

The creature seemed unimpressed with his threat. Her hand flashed and something, thin and white blade, appeared in the throat of the man next to Pruner.

The man crumbled to the cavern floor, his final breaths gurgling in wet, raspy sobs.

"No more tricks!" Pruner boomed, moving the thrashing creature to cover his own neck and face. "Or I will cut her tongue out."

He increased the pressure of his sharp stone and the child stopped trashing. Black-red blood trickled down the blade as it pricked her leather skin.

"Eeeiii!" she shrieked.

"Quiet!" he ordered. "Out!" The man began to circle toward the room's exit. Some of his companions had managed to slip free of their bonds, while others merely hobbled behind.

Peter noiselessly watched the exchange as he quickly began sawing his own bindings on a stalagmite. The green ropes dug deep into his wrists as he sawed and twisted them. With a dull snap, he was free. He dropped low to the ground and slipped into the shadows.

He looked for a weapon. There was no way he was going to wander through the cave empty handed. He was convinced that no weapon existed that could help him defeat a single mermaid, let alone an entire room full, but still, he would feel better with something in his hand – anything. His hand fell upon a stone. It was a broken tip of one of the stalagmites that grew out of the ground. He picked it up, felt its weight, and moved on. It was better than nothing.

Peter crept through the shadows, stopping behind large stalagmites to catch his breath and try to convince his racing heart to slow down.

All eyes were on Pruner and the merchild near the center of the room. Peter crept past the standoff and made his way through the entry way and into the hall. Which way to go? He peered down both sides of the hall. Neither way seemed any better or worse than the other.

"*Left*," he thought to himself, shrugging.

He gave one final glance to the fools who had made his escape possible. They were inching away from the circle of mers with Pruner in the center. The coward was holding the child in front of him, using her as a shield.

She was terrified.

Peter could see her face now, and…blood? A thin vein of blood stained her neck and little tunic. Pruner would kill her for a chance to escape. Pirates were ruthless. There was no doubt in his mind that the child was moments from death.

"*Protect at all costs,*" his father had said.

Peter took a deep breath, looked down the hall one more time, then shook his head and slipped back into the shadows of the room.

He picked his way behind pillars and jutting rocks, careful not to disturb any loose stones. Pruner had his weapon pressed firmly to the child's throat now. One way or another, this mess was going to end soon. Peter crawled out of the shadows and sneaked up behind Pruner.

"*Well,*" Peter thought. "*Let the counting begin.*" And he swung the blunt end of his makeshift weapon at Pruner's head.

One.

The men who had joined with Pruner dispersed, seeing their advantage disappear as their leader fell to the ground. The runners quickly fell under the mer's retribution, their cries were cut short by flashing white blades. A handful of those still bound hopped clumsily toward the chamber's exit while others shrank back into the cave walls. The results were the same. The mers fell upon them, their long, greedy, white blades cutting down everyone in the room.

The mermaid Peter had met stared at him with blue eyes. He

stood behind the fallen form of Pruner. The merchild hid behind him, her arms wrapped around one of his legs. The mermaid advanced on Peter, her white lance clicking against the stone floor as she moved. She continued to stare at Peter, cocking her head as she considered the boy.

Pruner stirred at the Peter's feet, moaning pitifully. The mermaid killed him with one strike of her weapon, her eyes never leaving Peter.

Finally, she spoke. "Why?"

"I…I'm not a pirate," he replied, shaking violently. "I didn't want him to hurt her. I'm not a p-pirate." The bloody stone fell from his still-shaking hands.

"Perhaps not," the mermaid replied. "Come, Sarii."

The young mermaid scurried to the elder's side and nestled against her tail.

"Come," she commanded to Peter. He followed.

Peter's legs moved on their own, and he followed the imposing creature in a numb silence. For the second time in as many days, he had found himself on the knife's edge of death. And for the second time, he was surprised he was still alive. Somewhere deep inside, he knew that the mind could only handle so much strain before it came undone.

He tried to think, but his head was thick and foggy over what had just happened.

He licked his dry lips and stumbled after the mer, his clammy feet pittered and pattered against the cold stone floor.

"I am called Shiiklah of clan Nakkal. I am chieftess of the clan."

The mermaid looked down at the child, then back to Peter. "Sarii is my Shorttail," she said. "You saved her life, I am now indebted to you. Come."

TWELVE

Shorttail?" Peter asked, taken aback. "She's your child?"

The creature whirled on him. Peter gasped in surprise and stumbled backward, tripping and falling to the ground.

"She is not a child, human!" the mermaid hissed. "She is a mer, nothing like you, human!"

"I'm s-sorry," he stammered. "I didn't mean anything."

"That is the problem with Man," she spat. "You ssspend your small lives building monuments of arrogance and destroying things you do not understand."

"I…I don't understand," Peter repeated.

"Of course you don't. It is your curse. You wear it like a cloak, clothed in ignorance until death liberates you."

Her black eyes bore into his, then changed slowly to emerald. Finally, she looked away.

"Come," she said, turning back toward the cavern hall. "You require food."

Peter rose on shaky legs and followed the mermaid, careful not to step on the large tail that trailed behind her.

The trio passed through the narrow passage and into a cavernous room. The entire floor was spotted with large, round pools. The room echoed with the sounds of mers splashing in and out of the pools. Some were diving down into the dark waters, others were leaping up from them, their powerful tails propelling them out of the water.

The mers returning from the water carried bulging packs and proceeded to empty the packs in different piles. In one corner of the room were small piles of what looked like kelp. The returning mers would empty their sacks of kelp into the pile and then return to the water through the pools.

Other mers would then take handfuls of kelp and place them on smooth stone tables, then beat the kelp with large white clubs. From there, they took the beaten kelp and transferred it to large stone cauldrons where it was ground into a thick, green paste by mers wielding even larger white clubs.

Peter prayed this was not the food Shiiklah had mentioned. He watched the process with increasing curiosity but was startled as a wave of water suddenly splashed over him. A mer, returning from the ocean depths, landed next to him, hissing at Peter as it landed. A young, wriggling tuna thrashed in the mer's arms. He held the fish in two hands by it's tail and swung it hard against the wall. The wet fish slapped against the wall with a loud "thwack," then stopped wriggling. Satisfied, the mer dragged the fish to another corner of the cave where other mers were tearing off heads and removing guts from the fish with their claw-like hands.

Peter shuddered, remembering what those same hands had done to Pruner's pirates just minutes earlier.

A young mermaid, in her teens Peter guessed having no idea how the strange creatures aged, approached. She held a black tray with raw fish and a small pile of green paste, the beaten and mashed kelp Peter had seen earlier. She bowed low to Shiiklah, presenting the food to her.

Shiiklah nodded toward Peter and the young mermaid presented the tray to Peter.

The fish was raw. The head had been torn off and the scales removed. The idea of eating raw fish was anything but appetizing so he passed over it and grabbed a handful of the green paste. He sniffed it warily. It smelled fresh and green. He took a bite of the paste. It was definitely fresh. It was salty and soggy – it tasted like wet grass. A putrid juice oozed out of the paste as he chewed it.

He forced himself to swallow and felt the dense kelp slowly slide down his throat and drop into his empty, hollow stomach.

He smiled painfully at the mermaid, expecting her to turn away, but she continued to stare at him, still holding the tray up to him. Peter had the sinking feeling that she wasn't going to leave until he took the fish.

He had no desire to eat the raw fish, but he feared his captor's wrath more than the prospect of getting sick. He smiled weakly and took the cleanest and smallest looking fish from the tray. He nodded to the girl and held the fish in both hands. He let out a long, slow breath, closed his eyes, and bit into the raw fish. The wet, gummy flesh squished between his teeth. The sensation made his stomach flip. He fought the urge to vomit and quickly swallowed the raw flesh.

He breathed deeply and looked up to see Shiiklah looking at him, an odd look of amusement carved on her leathery face.

He nodded thanks to her and took another bite, this time a smaller one, and quickly chewed the gummy meat, pretending it was something he enjoyed.

"What is this place?" he finally asked, looking around.

"The Enclaves of Nakkal," she replied. "This chamber is where our food is brought in and prepared." Another young mermaid approached her and offered her food from her tray. She took a handful of kelp paste.

The young mer turned the tray to Peter, but he smiled and held up his fish and she turned away.

"What do you desire, Peter of Man?" Shiiklah asked.

"What do you mean?" Peter asked, taking another small bite from the fish.

"You are on our island," she explained. "Therefore you must desire something. And if you do not know of dust, then it must be something else. So tell me, what is it you seek?"

"My sister," Peter replied. "But how did you know I was looking for something?"

"We know," she said, then offered nothing more.

"I need to find my sister," Peter continued. "She was on the ship when I fell overboard. I need to find the survivors, she probably thinks I drowned."

"Your ship was destroyed," Shiiklah said. "The storm drove it into the cliffs. There were no survivors."

"How could there be no survivors?" Peter asked.

"Our scouts were in the water where the ship went down. No one survived."

"But, the storm couldn't have killed them all! Some would have made it to shore on the wreckage. We had lifeboats, it was a bloody frigate! There were over five hundred people on board, they couldn't all have..." Peter trailed off, the blood draining from his face. "You killed them," he said slowly, shaking his head in disbelief. "You killed the survivors! You murdered them!" he roared.

In a heartbeat, three white blades were at his throat, but he ignored them and glared at the mermaid chieftess.

The mermaid rose to her full imposing height; her large, over-sized black eyes stared unblinking at him.

"We liberated those ssailors, they no longer live under the curse of Man," she said slowly.

He said nothing.

"And I would gladly free you of that curse, but honor refuses me that pleasure. Had you not saved my shorttail, you would have died with the others, never forget that," she spat.

He ignored her and continued to glare at her.

"Did you liberate *her*, too?" he spat. "Did you murder my sister with the rest of them?"

"You were the only half-Man we found," she replied, waving a hand to dismiss the mers who still had their blades pressed against Peter's throat. "And the cliffs are too sharp for anyone to climb. The sea has claimed her."

"She's not dead. I have to find her," he said. "You're indebted to me. Let me go, I need to find her and your debt will be cleared."

A dark, gurgling laugh escaped the mermaid. "It does not work that way. In time, perhaps I will let you go. For now, you will stay. You are the first half-Man we have seen."

Peter sighed, crestfallen, the half-eaten fish in his hand forgotten.

"Come," she said, turning and moving again.

Peter closed his eyes and desperately tried to chase away the despair that threatened to seize him.

Mara was alive, she had to be. He couldn't live in a world where both his father and sister weren't alive, so she had to be alive.

"She's alive, Mara is alive," Peter said to himself, and repeated it until it became his reality.

"Do you always stay down here?" Peter asked, opening his eyes and changing the subject. "I mean, do you ever go on land?"

"No," she replied. "We no longer visit the dry."

Peter waited for her to explain but, again, she didn't. Instead, she kept on moving.

The boy, mermaid chieftess, and shorttail made their way out of the room of pools and into a long carved hallway. The stone had been hewn away ages ago, not like the naturally formed cave they had just passed through. The small glowing lights lit their way. They aimlessly floated in and out of the hall, each one moving independently of the other.

"What are those things?" Peter asked, tentatively reaching out to touch a cluster of glowing blue dust.

"They are Flora," Shiiklah replied.

"What are Flora?" he asked.

"They are all that remain of the first time," she replied.

"You're not much for answering questions, are you?" Peter asked.

"I have answered your questions," she replied without looking back. "Here," she said, pointing to a carved hole in the cave.

"What's this?" he asked.

"You will sssleep here. Ssstay here until morning," she said. "Do not wander."

Peter started to ask her why, but she turned and silently slid away, Sarii's hand held in her own.

The merchild turned and looked at him, her oversized emerald eyes crinkling as she smiled, then disappeared down the tunnel with her mother. The sound of leathery scales scraping stone echoed around him as he climbed into his quarters.

His room, or hole – it could not be described as anything else – was a shallow tunnel that was a foot deeper than Peter's own height. He lay motionless, starting at the damp rock in front of him. He felt like a cannon ball stuffed inside a cannon, waiting to be fired. The events of the last days washed over him; how close he had been to death. First by shipwreck and nearly drowning, then at the hands of these monsters. He found it ironic that all his luck in escaping death had led him to this tomb-like room.

His hands began to shake. Whether it was from the cold or shock wearing off, he didn't know. An animal-like sob erupted from deep within his chest like cannon fire and burst through the protective dam his mind had erected.

He rubbed hard at his burning eyes with his hands and buried his face in his hands and cried. He shook violently and wrapped his arms around his chest.

"Father," he sobbed. "Father, where are you?"

Far above him, through the thick walls of rock and water the sun was setting, dipping into the green sea. Back in the caves, Peter's cries bounced and echoed through the mer's stone labyrinth, searching for a way out, but finding none.

THIRTEEN

I'm dead," Peter said to himself. "I drowned in the ocean with the ship."

He stared unblinking at the rock wall in front of him, lit from the Flora floating around him. After the shock of the day's events had worn off, Peter had spent most of the night reeling as he tried to cope with his new reality—A reality where he had been pushed to the knife's edge of death and had slipped back. A reality where mermaids were much more than farfetched tales spun by bored sailors and were grounded in a deadly, terrifying truth.

Mermaids, or mers as they called themselves, did exist and they existed as the most terrifying force Peter had ever seen. It was a miracle that they hadn't killed him on the spot. When the other captured men – pirates – had risen up against their captors, Peter had protected the merchild Sarii.

The entire situation had been defused by Peter, then ultimately resolved by mer-retribution. Now Peter was the sole survivor and had found himself unwillingly in the graces of the mer chieftess, Shiiklah.

Shiiklah had said she was indebted to him. He wondered what exactly that meant and what sort of leverage he could employ. His actions must have been extraordinary in their eyes since every one he encountered seemed a breath away from killing him. Every mer except Sarii, Shiiklah's shorttail. The merchild seemed to regard him with a blend of curiosity and affection, the kind of affection one showed a pet. Still, all he had done was protect Sarii. Could that be enough to grant his freedom?

He had to escape and find his sister. And since it was clear the mers currently had no intention of killing him, there was a chance he might be able to talk his way out of this place. He decided that he would see how much latitude he had gained by being in Shiiklah's good graces.

Peter was pulled from his thoughts by the distinct sound of scales on stone. He looked out from his alcove and instead of the opposite wall he saw a well-muscled, scaly chest.

"Human," a slithery voice rasped, "come."

Peter crawled out of his hole, wiped himself off, and eyed the creature cautiously. This mer, a male, was clearly a warrior. While every mer he had encountered seemed more than able – and willing – to tear him limb from limb, this one seemed even more so.

"Where are we going?" he asked.

The mer said nothing but instead turned and began making his way down the tunnel in silence.

Peter squinted toward the creature, unsure if he should follow, but an angry hiss from the mer indicated that he should so he took off after him. Peter followed the mer through the winding tunnels that opened up into the room he had been carried into the first time he had encountered Shiiklah. He couldn't help but notice how different the two situations were. Originally, he was a hated prisoner, one wrong answer away from death. Now his situation was an odd blend of honor and disdain. His change in situation still confused him, but he was thankful for it none the less.

His mind was significantly clearer than yesterday. His mental defenses, while necessary at the time, had dulled his senses and thinking. But the shattering of that dam in the night brought new clarity. As unsafe as he felt, he was certain that if the mers were going to kill him, they would have done so already.

Peter's escort halted at the tunnel's mouth and indicated with another hiss for him to enter.

He entered the hall, this time on his own feet. Stepping on to the raised platform, he approached the row of black stone-carved thrones. The lone occupant, Shiiklah, again stood near the seat at the far left.

Shiiklah said nothing at first as she studied him with emerald eyes.

"Tell me of your home," she said without preamble.

"No," Peter replied, staring back at her.

The creature snaked toward him, her beads rattling as she moved closer. Most of Peter's new-found courage melted away, but he held fast.

"Answer my questionsss, human, or I *will* kill you," she hissed.

Peter's insides clenched themselves into hollow knots, but he kept his fear in his stomach, away from his face, and returned her stare.

"You're not going to kill me," he said with more confidence than he felt. "I think your debt to me won't let you. Just the opposite, I think." He paused, wondering how far he could push his luck.

He decided to press on.

"I think this debt means *you* have to protect *me*," he accused, stabbing a finger at the mermaid, then a thumb at himself.

"You assssume much, Peter of Man. More than is due you," she said smiling darkly. "You are correct that I will not kill you. We wish to learn from you," she continued.

Peter's fear relented its grip slightly. At last, he was getting somewhere.

Shiiklah continued, "You do not underssstand the place you are in. You have saved a mer from death. In doing so, our laws demand we grant you our highest honor: The Pan Hakki. If you were mer, we would have had a ceremony and a feast in your honor and would have given you a place of leadership in the clan with mer warriors under your command."

"Why haven't you?" Peter asked.

"You are also our enemy. A human has never left our enclave. A human has never spared a mer, and a mer would never take orders from Man."

"Okay," Peter admitted. "Sounds like quite the problem."

"Indeed," she replied. "Our instincts demand you be killed, but our honor requires that you live."

"*Which side will win?*" Peter thought, his unease returning.

"There are those who believe we should kill you and forget about the Pan Hakki," she continued. "While otherss believe that you should be spared and honored, regardless of your heritage."

"What do *you* think?" Peter asked.

"It doesn't matter," she replied.

"What?"

"Nothing matters," the dark creature said without emotion. "Nothing but blood. And hers is mine."

"*Sarii*," Peter thought. He had saved the chieftess' child.

Realization crashed into him. The full meaning of his father's words split through the stone walls of his head and burst in a colorful radiance of understanding.

"*Protect at all cost,*" he heard William Till saying.

Peter blinked as revelation washed over him, clearing parts of his cloudy vision. At last, Peter was beginning to understand his father's teachings. He had chosen to save a life, and in doing so, had saved two.

"What I think doesn't matter," she continued. "You have saved mer blood, sso you shall command mer blood, our laws require it. The Pan Hakki shall be yours."

"Is the Pan Hakki common?" Peter asked. "How many of you receive it?"

"Very few," she replied. "And those who do are usually dead. Only those who have received the Pan Hakki may become chieftains."

"So you've received it?" Peter asked.

"Yess," Shiiklah replied. "My full name is Chieftess Shiiklah Pan

Hakki."

"I think I understand," Peter said.

Shiiklah snorted, "No, you do not."

Peter shook his head, then changing the subject, asking "Will you answer my questions?"

The mermaid nodded.

"How many of you are there?"

Shiiklah paused, obviously reluctant to answer, then spoke. "I have ten score warriors in my clan."

"Are there other mer clans?" Peter asked.

"There are," she answered. "There was originally one united clan. But the clan was fractured when The Great Council was destroyed, and your actions will doubtless split our clans even further."

"What's the Great Council?" Peter asked.

Shiiklah shook her head. "Nothing for Man." As she spoke, her eyes turned black, then grew distant and stormy. Looking away, she said, "I have answered your questions, now you will answer mine."

"Seems fair enough," Peter shrugged.

"How did you find this island?"

"I don't know," Peter answered. "We got caught in a storm that drove us into the cliffs. We weren't looking for this place. We were looking for the pirate scum who destroyed my father's ship. We spotted his ship heading east into a storm. We followed him through the night, but the storm drove us against the cliffs."

"Through storms or stars, when morning calls, through Never's Gate appear." The mermaid spoke the strange verse almost as if in a trance.

"What was that?" Peter asked.

"This place is difficult to find," she replied. "It can only be found in two ways, one of which is through storms. That's how you got here."

"And the other is through stars?" he asked, not making sense of her words.

"The pirate's name," Shiiklah said, letting her words hang in the air, ignoring him. It wasn't a question, it was a statement that needed to be completed and for some reason he couldn't explain, he felt compelled to complete it.

"Edward Teach," he answered.

Shiiklah's eyes snapped from their neutral green to black. Her eyes seemed to suck in all light from around them.

"Edward Teach?" the mermaid snarled.

"Y-y-yes," Peter stammered, physically buffeted by her rage.

"That human is responsible for the slaughter of hundreds of merss," she spat. "This human is an enemy of yours?" she nearly shrieked.

Nearby mers ventured into the hall, alarmed by their leader's volume.

"He's an enemy to everyone," Peter replied, looking from the curious mers to Shiiklah. "He destroyed my father's ship and captured him."

Shiiklah rose to her imposing full height and let out a deep guttural roar that rattled Peter's chest so hard it felt like he was screaming along with her.

Mers poured into the cave.

The mermaid hissed and roared in her native snake-like tongue. The cavern hall was fully packed with mers now – all of them hissing and seething with fury as their leader spoke.

Peter backed away, tripping on the dais step and then crawling back behind one of the thrones to hide behind it. The sight of so many of the creatures in a frenzy turned Peter's blood to ice in his veins.

A loud, guttural, bark-like shout from Shiiklah wrapped the room in silence. Her speech turned slow and instructive – Peter guessed she was giving orders now. When she had finished, the mers stormed out of the cave. The rushing sound of hundreds of leathery scales on the obsidian floor sounded like a waterfall: an angry, violent waterfall – with teeth.

When the cave was empty, Shiiklah turned back to Peter. Her chest heaved as she caught her breath.

"Teach has been our enemy long before he was yours. He trapped and massacred the Council elders."

"What?" Peter asked, climbing out from behind the throne. "How?"

"With a single strike, he severed the unity of all mer clans. There has been instability ever since," she said. "Thiss enclave," she continued. "Was once the central seat of power for all mers. Thisss room was where we met." She pointed to the circle of stone chairs. "The five clan leaderss would assemble here and all of our race was united under a single leadership, a single ruling force."

Her eyes grew sad, as if she was looking far into the past and seeing a better time.

"But he tricked us into believing that he was different. There used to be an alliance between the three great races of this island, the Accord. But during Teach's great deception, all of the elders save myself were killed. I was the youngest elder at the time. Now I am the last. And now our own clansss have been reduced to quarreling and bickering between one another. We have long sssince given up on those who live in the dry. The men you were being held with were pirate scoutsss. Teach's pirates frequent this island and we've been waiting for the day when Teach returned. His blind thirst for dust bringsss him back here, even though every creature on the island wants him dead. Eventually he will return, and when he does, we will have our revenge."

"Not before he tells me where my father is," Peter said adamantly.

"If Teach has taken him, then your father is already dead," Shiiklah replied.

"Then I'll kill Teach myself. And nothing, not pirates or mermaids or, or anything, is going to stand in my way."

The mermaid watched him as he spoke, her eyes glowing blue, as if she was considering something.

"Teach's destructive arm reachesss further back in time than the death of your kin. There are many others who also have claim to his liberation," she replied. "I have sent my warriors around the island to search for Teach's ship." Shiiklah said. "We had hoped to interrogate the piratesss we captured – many pirates frequent our island; the dust draws them here."

"What's dust?" Peter asked.

She paused, considering, then answered. "It is the substance made by those hateful little pixies. Perhapss it's best if you didn't know. It drives men mad with greed and you would be better without another obsession."

Peter decided not to press the issue.

"So what now?" Peter asked.

"Now we wait for my sscouts to return," she replied. "Will you answer another question while we wait?"

"Yes."

"Good," she said. "Disarm me."

She threw a long dagger, hilt first, towards him, drew her own thin sword, and charged toward him.

FOURTEEN

We gather food from every part of the island," Siene explained. "Currants from the mountains, fruit from the forests and jungles, berries and wildflowers from fields like these," she said, indicating the field she and Mara were in. "But, bringing food back to White Falls is dangerous. To avoid discovery, we hide the food throughout the island. Then, when night falls, we make trips to bring it home."

"Why are you so worried about being discovered?" Mara asked.

The fairy stopped and turned toward Mara, then sprinkled her fingers. The fine, golden dust flaked off her fingertips, drifting to the ground.

"Oh, right," she said.

Siene sprinkled the dust into her palm, packed it into a ball and hurled it at Mara like a tiny snow ball. Mara coughed in surprise as the ball of dust hit her in the face.

"What was that for?" Mara asked.

Siene ignored her question and said, "Think Mara. What's your happiest moment? What makes you smile? When have you laughed the hardest?"

Mara tried to think, but the golden dust that bounced and danced around her, spinning around in silly little circles, made it difficult to concentrate.

"I," she started, "I remember my home, my family." She smiled. "And Peter. I remember making plans to sail our own ship one day," she laughed. "But we'd always end up fighting because we both wanted to be captain."

Then she stopped talking and looked at Siene.

"What does this have to do with anything?" she asked.

"Come with me," Siene said softly.

"Where are we going?" Mara asked, still confused.

"Up," was all she said.

"Up?" Mara scoffed. "Up how? I can't fly."

"You're already flying," Siene giggled.

"What?" she exclaimed, looking down.

Siene was right. Mara was no longer on the ground. Both she and the fairy were floating ten feet off the ground. Panic gripped Mara and she started flailing. Siene drifted away from Mara, keeping out of reach of the girl's thrashing arms and legs.

"Mara, calm down, you're fine!" Siene shouted.

The girl's commotion began to draw the attention of nearby fairies. They all gathered around the pair to watch Mara's maiden voyage. Some of them called out to help Mara, while others were content to just watch and laugh at the girl's efforts.

"Stop kicking!"

"Hold your arms down! Keep them at your side!"

"Now look what you've done, you're upside down!"

The advice continued and little by little, Mara gained control. She discovered that by dipping one of her shoulders and leaning, she could make her body respond and move in that direction. Furthermore, by arching her back, she could move forward and slouching forward would move her backwards. Except, it took more than the physical efforts. She also had to think where she wanted to go. After a few minutes, Mara was able to stop moving altogether. She hung motionless in the air, looking down at the fairies across the field.

"This is incredible," she said.

"Follow me," Siene said, getting Mara's attention again. The fairy shot away, daring Mara to catch her. Mara followed, willing herself forward and leaning toward the fairy. The trees turned into a green and brown blur as Mara flew past them. A score of fairies flew with her, some trailing behind, others flying dizzy circles around her. Tears squeezed from her eyes as she flew faster and faster, through forests, over fields and above lakes. The party flew all over the island. Throughout their journey, however, Mara's fairy dust would begin to wear off and she would find herself slowly sinking below the group. A fairy would have to produce another handful of dust and hurl it at her so she could fly again. On one occasion, her dust began to wear off over a lake and the fairies pretended not to notice she was falling away until after she had fallen into the lake

It was evening by the time the group returned to White Falls. The fairies trickled down through tiny hidden passages into the great hall. Mara, having only one option of entry, crashed through the waterfall and into the cavern hall. Laughing, she landed lightly, testing her weight as if remembering herself.

Siene and Adelaide flew over to meet her.

"So, that's why you're so sought after," Mara said.

"In part," Siene replied, glancing at her queen.

Adelaide nodded, as if answering an unspoken question.

"What is it?" Mara asked, seeing the exchange.

"Follow me," Siene said, hurling another ball of dust at Mara.

Siene flew up to the ceiling and Mara followed.

The ceiling looked like the bottom of a giant bowl. A wide, large stone basin had been carved out of the rock, with round portholes that lined the top of the bowl. The portholes were the only opening into the room, but smaller channels, also hewn in the stone ceiling, led down the center of every tunnel in the cave. The smaller channels had round holes carved in them as well.

"The channels are filled with dust," Siene explained as they drew closer to the central basin.

"So, you use the dust for light?" Mara asked, seeing the bright glow that shined from every carved hole.

"In part," Siene replied. "Watch."

They reached the main basin and Siene flew in through one of the large holes. The hole was plenty large for a fairy to fit though but only large enough for Mara's head.

She peered inside the basin and saw a large room with seven huge pools, all of them filled with dust. The dust ebbed and flowed in the pools like small oceans. Each pool was separated by a stone path. Each path seemed as wide as Mara's hand. Down the center of the basin was a wider stone path that was connected the rest of the paths. The main stone path reminded Mara of a spine, and the smaller connecting paths of ribs. Fairies were diving into the pools with empty sacks in their hands and coming up with them filled. The fairies would open their bags and inspect the contents. The bags were filled with dust, but instead of the bright, golden-colored dust Mara had seen, this dust was a richer gold – almost red.

"We store up dust," Siene explained, pointing to the pools. "And the shapers can create almost anything out of it. Anything but food."

"Like what?" Mara exclaimed.

"Fabric for clothes," she explained, indicating to her own outfit. "Metals for weapons. Gems. We also use dust to heal wounds."

Mara looked down at the gold and gems that lined the fairy city. "You made these?" she asked.

Siene nodded. "We store the dust in these pools to condense it. Complex things, like metals and gems are more dense, so we use condensed dust to make them. The dust at the bottom of the pools becomes more dense from the weight of the dust above it."

"So that's why Teach is after your dust," Mara concluded. "He knows you can create things with it?"

"We don't know the extent of his knowledge, but we know that he knows we can create at least simple items," Siene explained.

"How do you collect it?" Mara asked.

"Watch," Siene said.

The fairy landed in the middle of the main spine, where all the ribs connected. She knelt down and closed her eyes, then her entire body tensed. Her soft glow began to intensify. She glowed brighter and brighter until Mara could barely look at her. Siene's blinding white glow filled the entire basin. Then dust began to pour from every part of her body. It flowed from her hands and arms. Torrents of dust erupted from her legs and face. Then the dust subsided and her brightness dimmed. And Mara could finally see her clearly again. The fairy was on her hands and knees, panting. Tiny beads of sweat dripped off her face. After a minute, she rose on trembling legs, flexed her wings experimentally, then returned to Mara.

"That," she panted, "is how we collect it."

"Are you all right?" Mara asked. "What happened?"

Siene nodded.

"We're made of dust," she explained. "And if we concentrate hard enough, we can…" She pursed her lips, searching for the right word, "shed parts of ourselves. But the dust we lose regenerates."

"How?" Mara asked.

Siene shrugged. "All we know is that we're dust, we're created and we're special."

"Does it hurt?" Mara asked.

"No. But it's exhausting," she admitted. "And dangerous. If I did it for too long, I would disappear. But there are so many of us to take turns that we don't have to do it often."

"And that's why we can't let Teach, or any other pirate, find our home," Adelaide said, joining the pair. "If he knew how the dust came to be, he would capture us and force us to make it. But I'm sure you've had enough excitement for one day," the queen smiled. "Taylon, show Mara where she'll be sleeping."

Taylon came forward, his muscular frame suggesting that he was a warrior or a guard of some sort.

"This way, if you please," he said to Mara, and she followed him.

Golden dust trailed from him as he led her toward the far side of the great hall. He wore a sash that draped loosely across his chest and tucked into what appeared to be a kilt of some sorts. His manor of dress reminded her of ancient Roman centurions. On his right hip hung a small sliver of a dagger, no doubt a backup weapon, because what held Mara's attention most was the sword that hung strapped to his back. It was almost as long as he was tall. The blade was hung in a black leather sheath between his wings. The golden hilt was beautifully adorned with small gems, complete with a diamond pommel stone. Light flashed across the blade as Taylon moved through the air.

"If this suits you, you'll sleep here," he said, motioning toward a dark corner of the cave. "Some of our gatherers spent most of the day collecting moss for your bed."

"It's perfect," Mara said and smiled.

The wall and floor were lined with thick, soft moss. She climbed into the groove and sleep began to tug at her tired mind, but she still had so many unanswered questions.

Where was this place?

Did anyone else survive the wreck?

Was Peter alive?

A desperate reasoning switched on as her eyelids grew heavy: if she could believe that she had spent the day flying around with fairies then she had no problem believing that Peter had survived the shipwreck. He would be fine. Odds were, he was probably laying on a beach somewhere eating coconuts and going over his plans to find her.

FIFTEEN

W ait, what?" Peter exclaimed, catching the white dagger reflexively as his father's instincts spun him away from the mermaid's thrust.

"What are you doing?" Peter cried, dropping flat to the ground to avoid a second strike. Shiiklah ignored him. He rolled to his side as the mermaid's heavy tail slammed the stone floor next to him.

Peter jumped to his feet and stomped hard on the mermaid's webbed tail. But instead of crying out in pain, Shiiklah merely yanked the tail out from under his foot, pulling it forward and bringing him to one knee. Then the tail was coming at him, catching Peter square in the chest, forcing the breath out of him and sending him sliding across the floor.

He rose to his feet, gasping for breath as mermaid and boy circled each other. He said nothing but used the short moment to regain his breath and refocus.

"Strike smart, strike true," his father had always told him. "Recklessness will only get you killed. Think, then act."

He hefted the blade, feeling its weight and balance. The dagger seemed to be made out of a bone or coral. Whether it had been grown that way or carved, Peter didn't know. Either way, it was beautifully balanced. The foot-long blade felt surprisingly like his father's blades.

He knew how to handle his father's blades.

He looked from the dagger to Shiiklah. The mermaid had a long furrow of faded scars in the scales that ran the length of her right side, from her knee to her hip –if she had had knees or hips. The scales seemed like they had been burned or melted away.

He wondered if the pain that had come with that scar had faded.

He hoped not.

He charged, slashing toward her left side, intentionally making his strike look sloppy. Shiiklah shifted her weight to parry his attack. He slid to his knees and reversed his strike, letting the momentum of his swing spin him around. He swung as hard as he could and aimed the dagger's hilt towards the mermaid's scar.

But there was a reason Shiiklah was clan chieftess. She spun away, spinning her lance faster than Peter could track, and slammed the blunt end into the hilt of Peter's dagger.

The blow felt like a lightning strike. His dagger erupted into pieces in his hand. His arm went numb from the strike and he tried to pivot away, but the blow had thrown him off balance, turning his spin into more of a controlled tumble.

He came up crouching, throwing the dagger fragments in a clearing sweep around him. He looked up, but Shiiklah was upon him, batting the dagger pieces away in the air.

He feigned to her left, then her right, then struck at the right with a closed fist and connected with the scar. He might as well have struck the stone wall. His fist collapsed at the wrist, but he slid past her, driving his elbow into her side as he tried to put space some between them.

His elbow strike proved as effective as the punch and he felt himself quickly beginning to tire.

He raced up the steps of the dais, toward the door, but at the last second, leapt onto the central throne, turning and vaulting himself toward the perusing mermaid. He flew high into the air, arms and head back, willing himself higher, hoping he would have the speed to knock her off balance, praying he would never land and just keep flying.

He flew toward Shiiklah. She reached up and caught him with one hand, fully absorbing his momentum. She looked at him for a long moment, then deposited him roughly on the stone floor. He landed awkwardly on his feet but didn't fall.

"What was that?" Peter yelled at her, gripping his throbbing wrist and gasping for air.

"Another question," she replied, fastening her lance to her belt again.

Peter shook his head, resigned to the fact that he would never understand mermaids.

"What are those weapons?" Peter asked, looking from the fragments strewn about the cave to Shiiklah's lance.

"Coral," she replied, unfastening her lance and handing it to him.

"Are they all as brittle as the dagger?" he asked.

"No," she said. "Yourss was defective."

"Why?"

"I wanted to sssee," she replied.

Peter rolled his eyes at her ambiguities.

"The craftsmanship is incredible," he said turning the lance over in his hands. "How are they made?" he asked. "Do you fuse the coral together and then sharpen them?"

"Nothing so crude," she replied, then headed out of the room. "Come."

She led him out of the throne room and through the twisting labyrinth of tunnels and halls until they reached a dead end with a large, round pool in the floor. The water glowed emerald green from the Flora inside.

"What's this?" he asked.

"This is where our weapons are grown," she replied.

"Grown?" he asked. "I don't understand."

"No, you don't," she said. "Come." She slipped noiselessly into the water.

"But I can't," Peter started to tell her as she jumped. "Breathe under water," he said to himself after she had left. He took a few deep breaths and dove into the water.

The water was warmer than he expected and the large cavern he swam into was one of the largest he had seen yet. He swam down a few feet and looked around. Above him were a handful of pools like the one he had jumped through. He made a mental note of which one he had jumped through and made his way further down.

The cave could easily fit a full frigate inside with room to spare. Flora drifted through the water, bathing the entire cave in a soft green glow. The room's floor caught his eye; the entire floor was moving. It looked like a field of small, white snakes, swaying in the water's currents.

It felt more like he was flying and looking down on a field of wheat than swimming in a cave. He swam farther down, mindful of his breath running out, and saw that the swaying snakes were not wheat but were some sort of tubeworms growing on the white ground. The ground had to be coral. He could see dim figures – mers –moving through the coral fields, clearing the tubeworms away and exposing the coral underneath.

His lungs began to protest, so he turned and swam back toward the opening in the ceiling. He broke the surface of the water and the sound of his breath blowing out echoed down the tunnel.

He took a few deep breaths as he wiped the water from his eyes. He took another deep breath and plunged back into the water, this time swimming straight down, toward Shiiklah. He swam faster this time, covering the distance to the cave floor in a handful of seconds. The Flora seemed to help him move faster in the water. Before he knew it, he was at her side. She was hunched over a cluster of coral. It looked like a few of the pieces were inverted, growing into the stone floor rather than out into the water.

He frowned in confusion but watched as she took what looked like a tightly woven kelp basket and covered the inverted coral. She inserted a small tube into the basket and began blowing into it. She continued to blow until the basket ballooned, filling with air.

Peter felt his own air running out and began to leave for the surface again, but Shiiklah grabbed his leg and yanked him back. Air burst from his mouth in surprise as she pulled him back down by her side. A bubble of air gulped into the cave and floated up like a large jellyfish. She pointed to the kelp dome, then to the bubble of air, then to another dome.

Peter nodded and bent down, gently lifting the dome off of the rocks. He made sure to keep the basket level. He slowly raised it over his head, then let it drop on top of him. Inside the basket, the water level came to his chest. He let out his breath and inhaled cautiously, the cold air was stale and fishy, but it was air. He immediately pictured Shiiklah inflating the dome with her breath and shuddered, quickly pushing the mental image away. He took two deep breaths and slipped out from under the basket.

Shiiklah pointed to the coral that Peter's basket had been covering a moment earlier and made a pulling motion with her hands.

He knelt down and took the white stem in both hands and pulled. The coral came out with a scrape, and a few tiny bubbles escaped with it.

The coral tube had grown into a hole in the stone floor, into the solid shape of a weapon – a dagger.

He turned the weapon around in his hands, amazed at how dense and solid the coral had become. He turned toward Shiiklah, offering the weapon to her. She raised her hands and shook her head and pointed from the weapon to Peter before turning to swim toward the ceiling.

He stuck the dagger in his belt and followed her to the surface.

They broke the surface and climbed out of the pool. Peter

climbed out while Shiiklah merely leapt from the water and landed on the tunnel floor.

"Come," she commanded and headed back down the tunnel. Peter dutifully followed, drawing the dagger from his belt and inspecting it as he walked. Peter followed her into a room filled with weapons and animal hides. There were whale skins stretched on giant racks throughout the cave. Mermaids were taking dried skins off of the racks and cutting the thick leather skin into strips.

Shiiklah approached an old mer with skin as gray and leathery as the whale's skin bent over the workbench. His scales were scared and chipped and some patches were worn away completely.

Behind him, a row of white daggers in various stages of completion hung on the wall. They were all made of coral, like the one Peter had pulled from the ground.

Shiiklah motioned to Peter to give him his dagger.

He obeyed, removing the weapon from his belt and handing it to the old mer.

The mer hissed at Peter, snatching the weapon from his hands.

He inspected the dagger, turning it over in his hands. He fastened several long strips of leather to the hilt with some sort of black ring. Then, holding the weapon in his teeth, began to weave the leather around the coral. He started at the hilt and worked his way to the pommel, quickly entombing the coral in the black, shiny leather.

After a few minutes, the old mer finished his leatherwork and capped the pommel with a shiny black stone – the same obsidian stone that made up the caverns.

He finished his work and Peter stepped forward to receive the completed weapon, but a sharp hiss from the old mer sent him scurrying back to where he had been standing. The mer held the weapon by its blade, his ashen knuckles seemed to glow white as he gripped the blade. He presented the weapon to Shiiklah, hilt first.

She reached out and violently ripped the blade from his hand. Black-red blood spurted from the old mer's hand. He unclenched his fist, shook the loose blood from his hand and returned to his work, as if the wound was no more than a minor annoyance.

Shiiklah turned, presenting the dripping weapon to Peter. He stared wide-eyed at the bloodied dagger, even more questions etched on his face.

"It is an honor to be a weapon's first blood," she answered before he could ask.

"Okay," he said taking the weapon from her, deciding he didn't want to know any more.

He inspected it again, but this time, it was a work of art. He had never seen such craftsmanship, let alone such work done so quickly. The blade was perfectly level. Its perfect balance made the weapon feel weightless.

"It's incredible," he said, inspecting it, then handed it back to Shiiklah.

"The way we grow the coral condenses it," she explained, hanging the weapon on a rack. " Our blades become ssstronger than your steel ones after the coral has been treated and dried."

"Unbelievable," Peter said, bewildered. "What else do you do in these caves? Can I see more?"

Shiiklah nodded and led him out of the cave.

They spent the rest of the day touring the system of caves. The sheer number of rooms and the size of many of them were staggering. The caves were evenly split between underwater ones and dry ones. It seemed that this underwater city—for it could be called nothing else—was almost completely self-sustaining.

The mers made everything from their weapons to their food. Everything was harvested from the sea. As far as Peter could tell, nothing came from land, or, 'The Dry,' as the mers called it. And most things were made out of kelp. Peter never knew how universally useful the stuff could be. To him, it had always been seaweed, but to the mers, it was everything: the mats they slept on, thong ties, nets and baskets. They even ate the stuff. Almost everything they used depended on kelp in one way or another.

The days that followed were much the same for Peter. Some days Shiiklah would show Peter new parts of the enclave while other days he would be left to wander alone. When he would wander alone from cave to cave, often an angry hiss would send him on his way, letting him know when and where he wasn't welcome. Some of the mers were wary but curious about him, others regarded him with open hostility. And while he was necessarily tolerated by most, there was one constant: none of them liked him.

Some days when he was left alone, he would wander past the throne room to find Shiiklah and other mers engaged in heated discussions.

He thought more about what Shiiklah had told him about saving another mer. He was convinced that had he tried to escape rather than save Sarii, he'd be dead right now.

He thought about the Pan Hakki and wondered what it really meant in the mer society. Would he be given a command in the mermaid ranks? He thought about that and kind of liked the idea of mermaid warriors doing his bidding.

"Pan Hakki," he said to himself, nodding. He drew an imaginary sword. "Prepare to die! Mermaids, attack!" he cried, hacking and stabbing at imaginary enemies.

He kicked off the walls and spun and rolled, leaving no one alive.

"Ha-ha!" he cried, summersaulting backwards and spinning to his knees. "I am Peter Pa-"he stopped abruptly. In front of him stood Shiiklah and four ancient looking mers.

He stood up, sheathed his imaginary sword, and bowed.

"Good evening," he said, taking a guess at the time of day.

The foremost mer hissed in response and the party moved past him.

Shiiklah, who had been in the rear said, "We have decided to go through with the Pan Hakki."

"Great," Peter said, smiling at her.

"I have ssent scouts again to the search the wreckage. There were no signs of your kin. The ssea has claimed her."

"She's alive," Peter said emphatically.

"Sso you say," she replied. "None the less, a few days more and you'll be free to find her remains."

"You're letting me leave?" Peter asked.

"The ceremony will be in three days," she replied. "After that, you will be free to leave. Mers understand vengeance and lossss. Both are powerful things but together..." she trailed off. She stared at Peter and something akin to pity crossed her face.

"You have saved what matters most to me," she replied. "And your rage will ssserve us in the Dry better than it will here."

SIXTEEN

Peter felt ridiculous.

He was wearing a combination of bone, whale-leather, coral, and, of course, kelp. He had been yanked from his alcove while he was still dead asleep and had been subjected to countless rituals in preparation for the Pan Hakki ceremony. His arms were wrapped in leather strips and a heavy necklace made of fish bones and obsidian hung from his neck. He was given a sash with a half javelin in its sheath. He was led into a small, narrow room lit by torches. This was the first time he had seen fire in the caves. Looking at the wall, he could see names elegantly carved into the black, glass-like stone.

Peter heard the ever-disconcerting sound of scales scraping

against stone behind him. Turning, he saw Shiiklah. The mermaid was clad almost identically to him.

"What is this place?" he asked.

"The Hall of Eternity," she answered, touching one of the names carved in the wall with unexpected tenderness. "Every mer who has been named Pan Hakki is etched in these walls, forever becoming a part of our eternal linage," she continued.

"And the torches symbolize," Peter concluded. "Mermaids being around forever?"

"No," Shiiklah answered. "Fire is destructive, it kills and destroys," she said. She held a hand over one of the torches. The orange flame began to darken the scales on her hand, burning them away.

"The torches remind us of our place," she said. A thin reed of black smoke snaked up between her fingers as the flames burned her. The scales on her palm began to pop and snap from the heat of the fire.

"As long as there are forces that exist to kill and destroy, our clans will oppose them and stomp them out," she said removing her hand from the fire.

"You mean us, don't you?" he asked, but without fear in his voice. "You want to get rid of us." He laughed bitterly. "Well, if we're so bad, why didn't I let Sarii die?" he scoffed.

The mermaid ignored him. Instead she said, "Do you know how the ceremony will work?"

Peter rolled his eyes, growing tired of her ignoring his questions.

"Yeah, some old warrior gives me a weapon, gives me the title, and I give my first command as a Pan Hakki," he said. "What's the point of the command?" he asked.

"It is your first act as part of the clan leadership," she replied. "The custom is to order a week of feasting to celebrate the new Pan Hakki. All you need to do is command a week of feasting."

Peter nodded. "Seems easy enough."

The two of them moved from the Hall of Eternity into an enormous cave. The cave was the largest Peter had seen. The chamber was shaped like a giant water drop, with large curved walls that came to a point at the ceiling. The ceiling seemed a hundred meters high.

"Wow," Peter exclaimed, the magnitude of the hall's size surprising him.

"The grand hall," Shiiklah said, answering the question on Peter's face. "It is reserved for this occasion."

Peter's gaze ran from the ceiling down the walls and then froze on the room's inhabitants. The hall was packed with mers. Hundreds of mers.

"You said you had two hundred warriors," he stammered.

"I do," she replied. "Ours is not the only clan."

"Not very forthcoming," Peter mumbled.

"I have answered your questions just as you asked them," came her reply.

The growling din in the room died the instant Peter entered. An eerie silence filled the room as Peter and Shiiklah made their way to a raised platform on one end of the room. The platform was carved from the obsidian stone, similar to the one in the throne room, but much larger. Peter climbed the steps and walked up to an ancient looking mermaid.

The creature was terrifying.

Her scales seemed to cling to her old bones like a tattered canvas. Patches of her neck and arm scales were worn away, revealing leathery, cracked skin. The skin around her oversized, black eyes was pulled taut, as if straining to keep them from falling back into her head. Her eyes burned through him. She looked like she had seen every inch of the world and had concluded that it was a dark place that needed to be destroyed.

A wicked scar ran from her ear to her mouth, transforming her face into a ceaseless, hideous sneer. But the scars on her face were nothing compared to the rest of her body. Her tail was grotesque: a useless, mangled thing that bore deep scars that ran its entire length. Like all the other mers, bones and coral were braided into her thick, knotty hair. She wore a leather weave over her shoulders, similar to Peter's attire, and a white coral sword hung sheathed in a sash across a shoulder.

She barred her sharp, black teeth at him and hissed as he approached.

Peter's insides ran cold at the gesture and he wondered if he would make it though the ceremony after all.

"It would ssseem that honor has not completely abandoned Man," she hissed.

"What?" Peter asked, before he could stop himself. He couldn't have heard her correctly. Had this monster just complimented him?

"Uh, thank you," he stammered, trying to say something as to not offend the first mer who had shown him something other than contempt. True, Shiiklah had spared his life, but she had always seemed to be waging an internal battle between honoring him and tearing him to pieces.

But this mermaid didn't seem to have any problem with Peter in their midst, doing things like exploring their caves, eating their food, receiving their highest commendation.

The old mermaid barked twice, the noise blasting Peter's hearing and echoing through the great cave. The gathered mers fell dead silent.

At her nod, Shiiklah stepped forward and recounted the details of Peter's actions.

She told about the prisoner's uprising and how the cowardly pirate had seized Sarii and attempted to use her as a hostage to escape. And she spoke of the actions Peter took to bring down a fellow human for the sake of a mer.

After Shiiklah's tale, the old mer reminded the gathering that to act honorably is mer, to act sacrificially is Pan Hakki.

Shiiklah translated this all for Peter.

He stared out at the countless creatures staring–most of them glaring—back at him. Some were watching him with blank expressions, others were seething at his presence. He hoped that all of them were bound to the rules and honor that seemed to bind these creatures together.

"This human has shown honor and sacrifice far beyond what we thought his kind capable of," said the old mermaid as Shiiklah translated for Peter. "He hasss reached beyond the safety of himself, beyond the safety of his clan, even beyond the safety of his own kind. And in hisss reaching, has saved the life of a mer. We owe him nothing less but the Pan Hakki."

Murmurs began to ripple through the crowd.

"Do you find any reason to withhold this from him?" she yelled.

The mumming increased.

"Yesss!" a voice from the crowd hissed.

"On what grounds?" the old one asked.

"He is Man," was the speaker's response. "He is of *him*, of Teach!"

"No," she replied. "He issss not. We must judge him by his actions, not the actions of others."

"He is not one of us!" another voice cried.

"He is about to be," she answered. "And if you will not accept the title on him, then you will not accept it on me." She drew her thin sword and held each end, threatening to snap the weapon.

The room fell silent.

"She's a Pan Hakkii too?" Peter whispered to Shiiklah, who nodded at his question. "What did she do?"

"Another clan elder's son was eaten by a shark," she whispered. "Kinarah chased down the shark and allowed herself to be eaten as well. Then, she killed it from the inside, saving the son. It nearly killed her though. The child was small enough to avoid its teeth and was swallowed whole. But Kinarah…" she trailed off, her eyes running the length of the old mermaid's disfigured tail.

"Well?" Kinarah cried.

Slowly, the mers all began to raise their right arm, bent at the elbow, across their chest—a salute or pledge of respect, Peter didn't know which. After what seemed like an eternity, the old mermaid lowered her sword and sheathed it.

"So, she convinced them to support me?" he asked.

"No," Shiiklah replied flatly. "She reminded them that we serve honor, in all forms."

Kinarah turned and faced Peter. He swallowed hard. His chest swelled with pride and duty and a little shame that he was about to share titles with someone who had allowed herself to be eaten alive to save another. All he had done was knock out a man.

"Peter of Man," Kinarah said. "The clans of mer recognize your dedication to otherss above yourself. Your actions have saved a mer and in doing so you have aligned yourself with us. Honor has become you, the Pan Hakki has become you. You shall no longer be known as Peter of Man. For as long as you live, you shall be known as Peter Pan Hakki.

The hall echoed as every mer struck their closed fist against their chest.

Kinarah produced a white dagger and held it out to him, blade first.

Peter swallowed the knot that had been gathering in his throat, then squeezed the blade with his hand.

Kinarah ripped the blade away in a single, violent move. His blood splattered the ground and soaked the white blade.

"May this be the last blade that tastes your flesh, Pan Hakki," Kinarah said, handing the weapon to him again, this time hilt first.

"You are now Pan Hakki," she said. "You are now mer."

Peter could feel the tension in the room. It was a furnace of hostility that radiated from the others. Peter, a mere human, had received their highest honor and now was receiving their name.

Peter waited as his own warm blood dripped from his clenched hand, half expecting every one of the creatures in the room to rush him and tear him limb from limb.

But they didn't.

So he reached out with his hands and accepted the weapon.

It was the same dagger he had seen the old mer crafting, but the black pommel stone had been replaced with a bright, red jewel. Something else had been added to the weapon. Engraved along one end of the blade was the word 'Pan', and along the other side was 'Hakki'. The words were written in English, rather than in mer. Shiiklah had explained that each Pan Hakki weapon was specially crafted and designed to match the owner and that only the red pommel stone and the words themselves were the same.

"What are your orders?" Shiiklah asked.

Still holding the blade in two hands, Peter walked to the edge of the stage. He looked out at the ocean of mers staring back at him. He looked back over his shoulder towards the entrance of the Hall of Eternity and wondered if that was the exit through which his courage had fled.

"I command," he started. His voice squeaked and cracked under the pressure of so many sinister creatures staring at him. He looked down at the blade still clutched in both hands. He turned it over, reading the engravings on each side again; Pan on one side, Hakki on the other. It was an elegant blade, but not in a decorative way like his father's blades above the mantle back home. Those blades were displays of art, this was a tool of war.

War.

Peter had shipwrecked in the middle of a war that had been raging for longer than he had been alive. And now he was supposed to give a command for celebration? It felt wrong. Countless men, and who knows how many mers, were dead because of Teach. This was a time for finding the man who brought chaos everywhere he went.

"Edward Teach is a threat to both our worlds," Peter said, his nervous voice feebly ringing through the hall. "If he's not here already, he soon will be. I order that the week of feasting be replaced with preparations for war against Teach and his pirates!" he cried.

The room didn't exactly erupt in cheers or battle shouts. Each mer simply drew his or her weapon and stood where they were. A throaty voice chuckled behind Peter.

"Mer's are alwaysss ready for war," Shiiklah said, her own weapon in her hand. "But you've done a good thing, you've put the good of the clan first, a wise first command, Pan Hakki."

Kinarah addressed the assembly of mers again and the crowd began to disperse.

"What now?" Peter asked. Kinarah handed him a sheath and Peter put his dagger in it.

"You are Pan Hakki," Kinarah replied, handing him a bandage made of kelp. "We can no longer hold you against your will. You are free to go. It is evening though; if you wish to stay the night, we will bring you up to the Dry in the morning."

"How can you tell it's evening?" Peter asked.

"We are mer," was the response.

Peter turned and followed Shiiklah back through the halls to his alcove. Neither of them spoke as they made their way though the obsidian maze. They reached his chamber and he removed his dagger, leaned it against the stone wall, and climbed in.

"Night's peace," the mermaid said as she turned to leave.

"Night's peace?" Peter said to himself, shaking his head. He smiled to himself and waited for sleep to carry him to the morning.

And to freedom.

SEVENTEEN

Mara could see flickering lights from behind her closed eyes. She opened them and squinted toward the source. Fairies were flying to the center of the cave in hundreds. Mara rolled off of her moss bed and made her way with them to the center of the cave.

Bright, golden torches lined the middle, creating a ring around a fairy warrior. His right wing was missing and the other was horribly mangled. A pale fairy was propping him up, applying some sort of glowing salve to the place where his wing had been. Another was treating a deep slash across his chest.

Siene dropped down from above and landed lightly on Mara's shoulder.

"What happened?" Mara asked.

"Kites," Siene replied.

"The birds?" Mara asked, confused.

"Yes," Siene nodded. "They attacked a party of our scouts. We've been warring with them for months. Three were slain, and two made it back, including him," she indicated the fallen fairy with a nod.

"Will he be okay?" Mara asked, cupping her hands to her mouth. "Can't you heal him with dust?"

"No, his wounds are too great" she replied. "Adelaide is coming to resolve him."

"Resolve him?" she asked. "I don't understand. Is he dead?"

"No, not yet, but all is not lost," she began. "When one of us is near death, our queen can save us. It's called the Resolution. One fairy's essence can be transferred to another willing fairy by the queen. But it's a great sacrifice to both fairies. The wounded fairy is saved, but both of them are changed forever."

"How come?" Mara asked.

"The resolved fairy cannot live their old life once they have received another. He'll be a new being," Siene explained.

"Is it better?" Mara asked.

"Better," Siene repeated, cocking her head in thought and then nodding. "It's harder, but I've been told it's also better. Shhh, they're starting!"

Mara didn't know what to make of this. She watched as Adelaide made her way to the center of the room and knelt beside the wounded fairy and placed a hand on his chest. She said something to him and Mara could make out the faintest nod from the wounded fairy.

Then a second fairy, wrapped in a blue robe, his wings tucked inside, entered the circle.

"Kiert," Siene whispered, "He'll be resolving Lo."

Mara nodded her understanding but kept her eyes on the center of the room.

"But only Adelaide can initiate it?" Mara asked.

Siene nodded.

Adelaide turned to Kiert and asked him something Mara couldn't make out. Then turning, she addressed the crowd.

"Kiert has requested to resolve Lo," the fairy queen said.

Kiert laid down next to Lo, the wounded fairy. The spacious room was dead silent save for the dull growl of the waterfall and the soft whipping of thousands of fairy wings. All eyes were on Kiert and Lo.

Adelaide bent down and put her head between the two fairies and whispered something to them that Mara couldn't make out.

"What's she saying to them?" Mara whispered to Siene.

"Shhhh," Siene hissed. "It's not for us to know. Only the queen – or king – and those who have been resolved know the words."

"The words?" Mara asked.

"The ceremony is nothing without them," Siene explained. "The words are what change everything."

Then a bright flash filled the cave. Lo and Kiert went limp and Adelaide fell to the ground. No one moved to help her. Their queen, normally surrounded by aids and attendants, lay untouched in an awkward heap.

The queen was the first to stir. She slowly got to her feet, waving off the help of an aid, indicating that she did not need help.

Kiert was the next to stir. He groaned softly and sat up, a slightly bewildered look on his face.

Adelaide knelt besides him and helped him to his feet. "Welcome...Tolan," she said, smiling at him.

Adelaide turned to the silent crowd and smiling, she said, "This is Tolan, he was once Kiert, he has resolved Lo, both are no more."

The cavern hall erupted into cheers and tiny applause as all the fairies rushed Tolan to greet him.

Eventually the cheering died down, and the fairies retreated into the deeper parts of the city to celebrate Tolan. Mara returned to her bed, unsure of what, exactly, had just happened.

***

Morning found Mara lying on her bed watching three white-clad fairies wrapping up the dead form of Lo.

"He's being prepared for burial," a small voice next to her said, answering her unspoken question.

Mara started. "What is he being wrapped in?" she asked, looking up to see Siene above her.

"It's a transparent silk cloth we make for funerals," she explained. "It reminds us how thin the barrier is between life and death. One small step toward it, and you're gone."

When the white-clad figures had finished their task, one of them produced a small horn from her waist sash and blew into it. A single, thin note rang throughout the cavern.

Four warriors approached and gently lifted the wrapped fairy, resting him on their shoulders. Queen Adelaide led the procession out of the cave. The entire population of fairies trailed behind as their queen and the body of Lo processed through the cave.

Siene led Mara toward the back of the cave and up into a tunnel that had been carved out for air flow. Mara squeezed through the tunnel and found herself outside of the cave on top of the waterfall.

The procession moved into the forest and traveled for a short time before entering a clearing. Lo's body was brought to the center of the clearing. Other fairies began digging a hole in the earth next to him. Mara closed her eyes and took a deep breath. She smelled the flowers nearby and heard the sound of old trees creaking in the wind and the snap, crack of fallen branches.

The sounds and smells reminded her of England, reminded her of the old oak trees at home.

It all reminded her of Peter.

She opened her eyes and looked around, the funeral momentarily forgotten.

"Peter," she whispered to herself. "Where are you? I need you here."

Peter gritted his teeth, praying that the small cloud of glowing creatures hadn't heard the branch break under his foot. They had to be the pixies Shiiklah had warned him about. He had to get a better view. With painstaking effort, he rose from his hiding spot and crawled over to a tree. He waited a few minutes to make sure he hadn't been seen, then began to climb. He noiselessly ascended the tree, making sure his body stayed out of sight from the tiny gathering as he climbed. After minutes of climbing, he reached a large branch that reached over the clearing. He stretched himself along the top of it and peered down.

Mara!

Peter couldn't believe his eyes. Mara was alive! A prisoner no doubt, but alive.

"If those little monsters lay a hand on her, I'll tear 'em apart," he growled to himself.

A few of the pixies were walking around, putting something in the ground. Mara looked sad. Clearly she was their captive. But why had they brought her out here? To kill her? No they didn't seem to be paying much attention to her, they were all focused on what they were burying.

Peter inched back toward the tree, hiding himself in the leaves. He had already made up his mind to follow the party back and then rescue Mara when they weren't paying attention. They didn't seem to be paying attention to her now, but he knew he needed to know more before acting. The last thing he needed to do was get both of them killed. So he would wait.

Nearly an hour passed before the group headed back into the forest. As silently as he could, he made his way down the tree and then followed behind as they departed. The group slowly wandered deeper into the woods. Peter would move closer, then wait to make sure he hadn't been heard, then move closer again.

Their journey led them to a small pond and waterfall. He watched several of the creatures slip around the falls while others flew to the top of the falls and disappeared. Unfortunately, he hadn't seen where Mara had gone. Peter weighed his options: he could climb to the top and try to follow the creatures, or he could go behind the waterfall.

He waited a few minutes more, making sure the little monsters were gone, and then skirted along the shore of the pond to the waterfall base. With his back to the rock wall, he began moving behind the waterfall but almost immediately realized it was a dead end. A large rock angled out into the falling water. Scowling, he moved out from behind the waterfall and began to climb the cliff.

Getting up to the top of the cliff was an easier task than he had thought. Hand-sized rocks and deep cracks made for easy climbing. Before he knew it, he was on the top of the cliff, looking down the falls without having broken a sweat. He turned from the edge and began to look for any signs of the little creatures.

He kicked sticks and leaves around, looking for tiny footprints, then rolled his eyes after he realized that flying creatures wouldn't leave footprints. He did notice, however, a handful of large holes in the ground. There were five of them and all were roughly the width of a large bucket. The holes were partially hidden by brush and it occurred to Peter that these might be the entrances to the pixies' home. It also occurred to him that the holes might lead to something worse than pixies, like a fox den or something.

He had to find his sister, and these holes were as good a place as any to start looking for her. He took a few calming breaths and crawled in.

The air was surprisingly cool and fresh. The dirt was dry and hard packed, smooth to the touch. Trying to calm himself, he reasoned that if it were a fox's den, the ground wouldn't be smooth but would be covered with claw marks, tracks, and possibly the remains of other fools who had wandered into the hole in search of missing siblings. Peter focused on moving forward and tried not to focus on darkness or on foxes.

A few minutes later, Peter began to feel the air beginning to warm, and he thought he could see faint lights ahead.

"I'm imagining things," he said to himself.

But as he continued to make his way, the light grew brighter, turning into a soft, warm, golden hue that illuminated everything around him.

He crawled deeper into the tunnel until it split into two paths. One of them angled down, while the other stayed even. He decided that he'd rather be higher up, looking down, so he chose the even path and continued crawling.

The path went on for another twenty meters or so, then opened up into a huge room containing five pools filled with golden water. Once he entered the room, his dirt path became a stone one that ran to the center of the room like a spine, with ribs branching out to support the edges of the five pools. The room was circular, shaped like a giant bowl. Each pool had three openings on the outside wall, about the size of a man's head. He crawled up to the edge of one of the pools and saw that they weren't filled with water but with a fine, golden dust.

The gold seemed alive, pulsing and ebbing in the pools around him, some of the gold jumping up out of the pools to drift lazily back down.

Now he could hear voices coming from below the pools. With painstaking effort, he slowly crawled across one of the ribs and stretched himself out over one of the pools, trying to peer out of the openings.

The shimmering dust smelled sweet and he could feel the warmth from its glow as he held himself over the pool. He repositioned himself, stretching a leg on each side of the pool, then held on to the hole with both hands. With both arms and legs fully extended, he leaned to look down out of the portal when a small, glowing light flew into his face.

He gasped in surprise and felt his mouth and nose fill with dust. He sneezed instinctively, sending the light shooting back out through the opening. He lost his balance and tumbled into the pool of dust.

Panic gripped him as he lost sight of the ceiling and his vision was replaced with bright, yellow lights. He gasped in his panic and felt his mouth and the back of his throat become coated with the warm dust. He held the half breath in, not daring to finish it or let it go.

His feet touched the ground of the pool and he frantically felt around for a way up. But the smooth walls offered no holds.

Jumping, he tried without success to reach the rib's ledge. He tried swimming, treating the dust like water, but it gave no ground. He frantically moved along the wall, praying to find a ledge, a crack in the stone, but he felt nothing except warm, smooth rock.

His stomach felt hollow with fear as the realization set in that this was where he would die. He frantically thrashed at the dust around him as his lungs began to burn.

He moved faster, desperately clawing around him, while his lungs screamed for air. He continued, every muscle tensed with exertion, every fiber demanding oxygen.

He bit his lips, straining to keep his mouth closed, but his body's demand to breathe overpowered his own will power. His breath exploded out of his mouth and to his horror, he reflexively took a deep breath.

He felt the dust rush deep into his body, coating his lungs, throat and mouth with its golden brilliance. And with the dust came the last thing he expected: air.

The precious air filled his body as he breathed out, then inhaled again.

He was alive! Hope and joy gnawed at him and he rose a few inches off the ground. His feet touched the ground again and he pushed off, jumping with all his strength. He flew up through the dust and broke the surface. He reached out and felt the round opening of the window. With his other hand, he scrubbed the dust from his eyes. His vision cleared and he looked up into a pair of very small, very angry eyes.

Those small, angry eyes belonged to a small head that sat on a small, winged body that hovered in front of him. And the creature's tiny hands gripped a sword that was almost the same size as his body.

"Pixies," Peter said, positive that he had found the creatures Shiiklah had warned him about.

The creature narrowed his eyes at the term and without a word, struck Peter across the face with his weapon. The small blade slashed his cheek open and blood began to dribble out.

With a cry, Peter pushed off the wall, turned and found the main spine that ran through the room. Peter scrambled to his knees and headed for the tunnel as fast as he could.

He could hear the angry whipping of pixie wings as the creature chased after him. The pixie screamed and Peter felt a sharp pain in his calf. He spun around and lashed out with his foot, catching the pixie in the body and sending him flying into the pool of dust. Ignoring the pain in his leg and face, he turned back to the tunnel and crawled with every ounce of his strength.

He could hear the yells of more voices as he made his way back to the surface. He crawled faster than he thought possible, but he could tell the pixies were gaining as the tunnel grew brighter and brighter behind him. He could see daylight ahead. His knees burned with fatigue and his hands felt like lead weights as he crawled faster and faster.

What seemed like an eternity later, he burst out of the hole, an explosion of golden yellow sparks erupting behind him in pursuit. He scrambled to his feet, stumbling toward the edge of the cliff, but the pixies were gaining on him.

He hazarded a glance behind him. The leading pixies were close enough to strike as Peter neared the cliff. He felt the tiny sting of their small blades in his back as he reached the edge of the cliff.

"If I can just get to the pond," he thought. *"I can get underwater and maybe shake them."*

He reached the edge of the cliff and jumped with all his might, praying his leap would send him far enough out to land in deep water. He squeezed his eyes shut and waited for his body to hit the water. Wind rushed past him, increasing in speed. He squeezed his eyes tighter and waited for his body to slam against the rocks that lined the shore.

He opened one eye and gasped.

Instead of rocks and water, he saw trees and clouds. He was still well above the treetops, and they weren't getting any closer to him. He momentarily forgot about the pixies chasing after him and gawked at the trees whipping by.

"What?" he exclaimed, turning around to look behind him, and his heart stopped again. A cloud of pixies were ten meters behind him with the sun glinting off their silver weapons.

"Ahh!" he screamed in surprise and fell, crashing through the treetops and landing in a heap on the forest floor.

He lay on the ground, shaking with fear and disbelief.

But before he could think about what had just happened to him, the pixies started streaming through the tree canopy, descending toward him.

He scrambled to his feet and ran deeper into the forest. Fear clung to his heart as he tore through the woods, desperately trying to escape his pursuers.

He heard what sounded like rain ahead of him. He looked up and instead saw a second group of pixies crashing through the leaves toward him.

He cut to his left, stumbling through bushes and ducking low branches as he ran. The pixies dived at him from all directions, slashing at his legs, arms, and face. Tiny arrows began to bury themselves in his arms and back.

Peter screamed in pain and fell to the ground as more arrows found their marks in his calves and neck. He rose again only to trip on a fallen branch. He picked up the branch and swung it madly. A few lucky swings sent pixies flying into the bushes. But their assault only grew stronger. Peter's vision was filled with burning golden light as the tiny creatures surrounded him.

They gathered around him, collectively beating the branch out of his grip. He fell to the ground and scurried backward, kicking violently at the nearest fighters, but it was hopeless. They pressed in for the kill. Like a single wave, they swelled up and crashed toward him.

Sunlight burst through the canopy as a large form crashed though the top branches, landing hard on the ground between Peter and the mass of pixies.

"Stop!" a voice screeched.

The pixies immediately parted, flying harmlessly past him.

The figure ran through the thinning cloud of creatures and crashed into his arms, driving him to the ground again.

"Peter!" Mara cried. "Oh Peter, you're alive, you're alive!"

"Mara!" Peter blurted, his body rigid with shock. His shock melted away as hot tears welled in his eyes.

"You're not their prisoner?" he stammered.

Mara smiled through her own tears. "No, they're friends. Oh, Peter. I knew you were alive. I just knew it!"

Peter smiled. "Well, I wasn't sure I would be for a while, but it all worked out. But, what are you doing with them?" he asked, indicating the pixies still hovering near him.

"They're fairies," Mara said. "And that's a long story, too."

"Fairies?" Peter said, his fears confirmed. Then dropping his voice to a whisper, he said, "I don't think you're as safe as you think." His eyes darted around. "I was told they're dangerous."

"By whom?" Mara asked dubiously.

Peter lowered his voice and replied, "Mermaids."

The word had scarcely left his mouth when four fairies appeared at his throat, knives and swords pressed firmly to his flesh.

"Those sea witches sent him!" a female fairy screamed. "He's a spy! Kill him!"

"No!" Mara cried. "He's not a spy!"

"That will be enough," a small, commanding voice called out.

The ranks of fairies parted to allow an elegant, regal-looking figure into the clearing. This fairy seemed like the others, but instead of leather tunics and weapons, this one wore an elegant, white gown. And she seemed to glow more white than gold. Her tiny lips, pursed, wore a hint of red. The fairy's ice-blue eyes stared appraisingly at Peter's as she neared him. Her bearing suggested she was royalty of some sort. He resisted the urge to kneel, but noticed Mara inclining her own head respectfully.

"Ah," she breathed softly. "You must be Peter. I am Adelaide the Just. You have our deepest apologies. Pirates have been scouting our lands and have had children do their bidding in the past." She waved, dismissing the warriors at Peter's neck. "And lately, our relationship with the mers has been," she paused for a moment, searching for an appropriate word, "tepid, at best," she continued.

Peter smiled knowingly, "I think I understand."

"You must forgive Siene's suspicions," she said indicating the fairy who had accused him of being a spy.

"It has been a long time since anyone has left the '*hospitality*' of the mers."

"Well," Peter smiled. "It's quite the story."

"I look forward to hearing it," she replied, returning Peter's smile. "But I must insist we continue our discussion back in the cave. We are closer to the cove than I would like. Let us be off."

Fairies began to fan out and the procession began to move north, back toward the waterfall.

"Perhaps Mara can explain how you were able to fly so far after your jump from the waterfall," Adelaide called over her shoulder.

"It's fairy dust," Mara explained.

"Ah, so that's how they fly," Peter concluded.

"No, stupid, that's what their wings are for," Mara retorted.

"That makes more sense," he said, smiling sheepishly. "What is it used for then?"

"Everything," she replied.

"Well, it makes me fly," Peter said. And with the words still on his lips, he lifted off the ground and slowly started to flip forward. He abruptly fell on his face.

"Umpf," he sputtered, scrambling to his feet and shaking dirt and debris off of himself. Nearby fairies snickered at him. He glared back, but Mara just laughed.

"I'm so very glad you're safe," she beamed at him.

"Me too," he said, catching up to her again. "The mers are…interesting, to say the least. I'm very lucky I got out of there in one piece."

"Too lucky," Siene said under her breath, but loud enough for Peter to hear.

Peter glared back. "Maybe it's the pixies and their dust that can't be trusted."

A heartbeat later, the fairy's dagger was in her hand, her tiny white knuckles shaking with silent fury. A word from Adelaide sheathed her weapon and silenced her. But her angry little eyes continued to bore through him.

"So, this dust," Peter said taking another experimental hop into the air. "What else does it do?"

Mara explained how the fairies used it for almost everything. It had healing qualities, it was a light source, it could keep them warm, start fires and even, as Peter had learned, make you fly.

"It seems," Adelaide said, flying next to Peter. "You have been exposed to a very high concentration of fairy dust. You fell to the bottom of the pool?"

Peter nodded.

"The dust grows more dense the deeper you go. The effect should be temporary."

"I hope it isn't," Peter said.

"It's incredible that you haven't died or gone crazy," Adelaide said.

"We wouldn't know it if he had gone crazy, though," Mara said, giggling.

"Wait, what?" Peter said.

"Dust drives men mad with greed. And with the amount you've been exposed to," Adelaide trailed off, looking away.

"This could kill me?" Peter cried, scrubbing at his arms and neck furiously.

"If it were going to kill you, I think it would have by now. Still, it's odd that it's had such little effect on you. Maybe you're special," Adelaide said.

"Oh, he's special," Mara quipped.

"I think I feel it burning," Peter said, still rubbing his arms. "Burning is one of the effects, right?"

Mara rolled her eyes, ignoring him.

"I'm getting dizzy, too," he continued. "Yeah, definitely dizzy. And thirsty, boy am I thirsty. I've never been so thirsty in my entire life. Can you use the dust to heal me from the dust?"

An hour later, the party returned to the falls. Mara showed Peter the hidden passage behind the falls while the fairies repaired the tunnels Peter had damaged during his escape.

The siblings spent the remainder of the day telling each other about their adventures since arriving on the island. Peter was astonished to hear about Mara climbing the Obsidian Cliffs.

"You're sure no one else could have survived?" Mara asked.

"There's no chance of it," he said shaking his head. "The water was teeming with mermaids," he said. "The only reason I survived was because they had never seen a child before. They wanted to study me."

"So that means Benjamin…" Mara trailed off.

"Yeah," he replied.

"First father and now Ben," she began to cry. "Oh, Peter, what are we going to do?"

He slid closer to her and put his arm around her. "We've got each other. Father said it's my job to protect you, and that's what I'm going to do."

"That was before we stowed away, shipwrecked, and were almost killed by mermaids, fairies, and pirates."

"Well," he said. "At least they're not all trying to kill us anymore."

"I thought I'd lost you. I thought I was alone on this island," she said. "I wouldn't let myself believe it, or even think it. But I knew, deep down, that there was no way you could have made it. I thought you were gone."

"Never," he said. "I knew you were alive, too. I knew I had to get out of those caves and find you. I was ready to fight all those mers and the fairies to find you."

Mara smiled and wiped her tears away.

"And father's alive, too, I bet," Peter continued. "He's too fast, too strong. There's nothing that could stop him."

Mara laughed and nodded.

"Enough of that though," he said. "You'll never believe what happened to me down there."

"In the caves?" Mara asked.

"In the Enclaves of Nakkal," Peter said, waving his arm dramatically and jumping to his feet. "The tale of a brave English lad who saved a chieftess' daughter, united all the clans, and made mermaid history."

Mara rolled her eyes. "This ought to be good."

EIGHTEEN

A few days later, Peter and Mara were foraging for fruit—their new joint chore. Despite Mara's defense, most of the fairies still did not trust Peter. As far they were concerned, the mers had sent him to infiltrate their city, for, as they insisted, "Nothing good ever came from the sea."

So each morning, Peter and Mara would explore the acres surrounding White Falls in search of food. The fairies ate fruit and nuts exclusively. Since the two children could carry many times more than a fairy could, they had volunteered to join the gathering party. Today was their fourth day gathering, and in their first three days, the two had brought back so much food that the stores were completely packed.

Fairies were now having to work through the night to preserve the food by roasting or drying it with dust, which would preserve it nearly indefinitely. The dust seemed to stop the effects of time and decay on food.

"Can you still fly?" Mara asked as the two of them entered a meadow. Fairies, the other members of the gathering party, zipped around the field, their little wings making soft fluttering sounds as they passed.

"Yeah," he answered. "But I can't really control it." He rose off the ground and slowly started to flip upside down. He waved his arms to reorient himself but continued turning. Then, without warning, he dropped to the ground.

"Umpfh," he grunted, rolling over on his back.

"What a gift," Mara smiled, stifling a laugh.

He glared at her, but the look held no sting.

"Try concentrating, silly boy," she offered. "What are you thinking about when you try?"

"I'm thinking about not dying," he said.

A fairy flew by the pair, her arms wrapped around a strawberry. Her eyes could barely peek over it's green leaves.

"What do you think about when you fly?" Peter asked the passing fairy.

"Flapping my wings," she responded, sardonically, without slowing.

"Helpful," Peter replied, matching her tone.

"It's not just about thought," Mara suggested. "You need to act, too."

Peter got to his feet, then shrugged his shoulders, like a puppet being pulled off the ground.

Nothing.

"What were you thinking about?" Mara asked.

"Strawberries."

Mara rolled her eyes.

"Focus, Peter," she scolded. "If you're going to be like this forever, you might as well learn to control it. It could be a great gift."

Peter pursed his lips, considering. Then, closing his eyes and shaking his head as if to empty his mind, he raised his shoulders again and focused on a single thought.

Fly.

Nothing happened. He kept his eyes squeezed shut and thought harder.

Fly.

He remained on the ground.

His thoughts began to sneak back into his mind. He thought about the faint orange light he could see from the sun through his closed eyes. He thought about the warm breeze that whispered through his hair, hints of salt from the ocean. The smell instantly brought him home.

Home.

He thought about the raw joy he felt when his father retuned home after countless months at sea. He thought about the love his father radiated when he looked at him, a near-physical warmth that had buffeted Peter. He thought about Mara and her fierce loyalty to him, their endless hours of play-fighting in the yard.

"You're doing it, Peter!" Mara cried. "You're flying!"

His eyes snapped open. He was hovering several feet off the

ground. He gasped, then flashed a smile at his sister. Then, still holding on to his thoughts of home and family, he dipped his right shoulder and willed himself to move. He glided to the right. He leveled his shoulder and his movement halted. He lowered his left shoulder this time and began to move to the left. Again, he leveled it and came to a stop. Laughing, he put his arms out, and spun in a slow circle, gradually picking up speed before coming to a full stop.

He looked back at his sister, his face twisting into a crooked grin.

"Don't you dare," she said, recognizing the mischievous glint in his eyes. "Peter Till, don't you dare!"

But before she could run away or protest any more, she was in his arms and they were soaring above the trees, the meadow below shrinking into a small, green dot.

"Peetteeerrrr!" Mara shrieked as they shot straight up. He stopped suddenly and they hung in the sky. From this height, they could see the entire island. It stretched out for miles all around them. The eastern hills graduated into bluffs and eventually resolved into twin peaks. The mountains gave way to rocky wastelands with twisted trees before ending at the Obsidian Cliffs.

To the north, the forest grew thick, all they could see were the tops of the trees. The northwest corner of the island was rocky with what seemed to be old ruins just off the coast of the island.

To the west, the forest became a jungle, with white sand beaches along the shoreline that ran south to a cove. They could see a path that ran from the shore up to the surrounding rocks that lined one side of the cove. The path led to a cliff, where what looked like an old mansion stood, built on and into the cliff, overlooking the bay.

"Wow," Mara said, trying to take it all in, looking from the eastern cliffs to the western shore. But Peter had stopped scanning the island. He had eyes only for the southern cove – for the lone ship anchored in the bay.

"Look," he said, nodding toward the south.

"Is that it?" Mara gasped.

"Aye," he replied. "It's the *Dawnriser*. I watched them build her."

Peter adjusted his grip on his sister. He could feel himself starting to tire. It would seem that being able to fly didn't mean he could carry anything he wanted. Apparently, he still had limits.

He dropped his shoulders and thought, "*Down,*" and began to descend. He realized that flying was taking less mental effort the more he did it. The pair dropped to the ground lightly and Mara straightened her dress as Peter flattened his wind-blown hair.

"We should warn the fairies," Mara said.

The pair raced back to White Falls. Mara ran through the wildflowers and tall grasses while Peter bounded through the air in long arcs, practicing his control over his new ability as he went. They arrived at the pool. To save time, Peter took Mara up in his arms and the pair crashed through the waterfall. The two erupted through the falls and fell to the cave floor. Scores of fairies scattered as they sprayed the room with water. The recovering fairies drew their weapons and advanced on the intruders.

"Pirates!" Mara cried, out of breath.

Seeing that it was Mara and Peter, they sheathed their weapons. Those watching Peter moved more slowly than the others.

"Where?" Siene asked.

"In the cove," Peter answered for her, panting. "There's a ship anchored in the bay.

"How did you see it? The bay is over two leagues from here," Tolan demanded, coming along side Siene.

Peter rolled his eyes and lifted off the ground. "I can still fly," he said.

"Scouts," a regal voice commanded. It was Queen Adelaide, her retinue following in tow. "To the bay. Remain unseen."

Fairies from around the cave began to salute and rise to the ceiling to leave.

"I'm going, too," Peter said, turning to Mara, but speaking loudly enough for Adelaide to hear. The queen did not object.

Mara started to protest, but Peter interrupted her. "If it's him, I need to know."

Mara, apparently seeing the determination in her brother's eyes, merely nodded. "Don't you dare do anything foolish," she said, meeting his gaze.

Peter nodded, then ran to his bed, retrieved his white coral dagger and dived through the falls.

Peter arched his back, thought "*up*," and felt himself rise. He raised one hand above his head and realized that by doing this he could control his movements better. He lowered his arms to his side, his hands slapping against his thighs, and felt himself surge forward even faster. He smiled to himself; he was getting better at flying by the minute.

Fairies zipped past him, then ducked down into the forest to remain hidden from any birds above them. Peter, not having to worry about birds, opted to stay just above the tree line. He flexed every muscle in his body, willing himself faster, and again, felt his speed increase. A quarter of an hour later, he could see the forest give way to the beach. He slowed his approach and slipped under the tree canopy.

He flew from tree to tree, careful to remain hidden from view of the beach. The scouting fairy party began to arrive as well. Peter watched each of their glows wink out as they approached the sand. Peter frowned in confusion.

"It's how we keep from being seen," a voice whispered in his ear.

Peter jerked in surprise and saw a female fairy – Siene, he thought – landing on his shoulder.

The young fairy seemed to strain for a moment, her jaw clenching in effort, then her bright burning glow dimmed and then flickered out. She looked like a normal girl, in her late teens, except only eight or so inches tall and winged. She blew out a breath, then looked at Peter again.

"It takes a lot of focus, but it's worth it to keep us hidden," she said, jumping off his shoulder and flying toward the beach. Peter followed, continuing to duck behind trees as he went.

Finally, he came to the last trees lining the beach. Hiding behind one of them, he took a deep breath before curling his body around the trunk to peer out toward the ship in the bay. There was nothing there.

The ship was gone.

"Where is it?" a nearby fairy asked.

"I don't know," Peter said. "It was here less than an hour ago, and it was the *Dawnriser*.

"Liar!" another fairy spat.

"Why would I lie?" Peter snarled, spinning on the speaker, a well-muscled male fairy.

"Because you're half mer," the fairy replied, unruffled. "You even carry their weapon," he accused, pointing at the white dagger in Peter's belt.

"Do you trust Mara?" Peter said.

The fairy glared at him for a moment, then nodded.

"Then trust me," Peter snapped. "I'm sick of this half-mer nonsense. They almost killed me!"

"Enough, Tolan," Siene said, coming between the two of them. "Peter is right. He has no reason to lie to us about this. You're sure it was Teach?" she said, the last part directed at Peter.

He nodded. "Yeah, I would recognize that ship anywhere."

"Why would they come and leave right away?" Tolan asked, his temper subsiding.

"I don't know," Siene said. "But if it is Teach," she looked at Peter and he nodded at her, "then he's up to something. He hasn't returned to the island since the Great Betrayal."

Peter knew all about the Great Betrayal, as the fairies called it. Shiiklah had told him the tale of how Edward Teach had tricked the leaders of the mer, fairy, and kite clans. He had assembled them together under the guise of petitioning them to join their Counsel, then killed them all. Shiiklah, the youngest chieftess at the time, was the sole survivor of the attack. She had also been the one to recommend Teach's admittance to the Council. In the end, all the fairies, kites, and even a great number of mers had concluded that Shiiklah had conspired with Teach to kill the Council. The truth was that Teach had fooled her as well as rest of the Council. The Great Deception – as the mers called it – had become the single most defining event on the island. And it was all because of Edward Teach.

"We need to keep scouts in these woods," Tolan said.

There were murmurs of agreement from the other fairies.

"Agreed," Siene said. "Adelaide will doubtless agree as well. Tolan, stay here with a handful of scouts. The rest of us will return and report to the Queen. We'll add the bay into our patrol, and the next watch will relieve you."

Tolan saluted, then went about selecting his scouts.

"They seem to respect your opinion more than others," Peter said, as they departed. "Why is that?"

"Adelaide is my cousin," she replied.

Her glow flared back into its normal brilliance as they entered the cover of forest.

"When the council was killed, the crown fell to Adelaide. Since we are the last remnants of the line, I'm the heir."

Peter whistled softly. Siene looked at him, confusion written on her tiny face.

"It's hard to believe that one man could cause so much destruction," Peter explained. "I thought the people in my family were the only ones Teach really hurt. I mean, I need to kill him, I just never realized how many others needed to as well."

"You mean you've only seen how your own life is affected and not others? How very human of you," Siene said.

"Well, there is something you and the mers can agree on," Peter said. "The weaknesssss of Man," Peter hissed, mimicking the snake-like way mers spoke.

Siene smiled at him.

"My apologies," she chuckled. "Before Teach, we had not had any interactions with humans for hundreds of years. I'm afraid our dealings with him has made us bitter. Please, forgive me."

Peter waved her off. "It's nothing," he said. "He's a horrible man. He needs to die so he can stop ruining people's lives."

"On that, we can agree." She smiled at him.

"As long as I get to kill him," Peter said, smiling back.

"We'll see," she said and winked.

The scouting party returned to White Falls and informed the others what they had found, or rather, what they hadn't. Adelaide agreed that the bay needed to remain under constant watch.

She was hesitant to dispatch a large group of scouts to the bay as the kite threat was still very high. Instead, she assigned pairs of fairies to keep watch on the bay. And when Teach returned, one of the scouts would raise the alarm while the others continued to keep watch.

Peter had insisted on being included in watching the bay. He was paired with Siene since she was the only fairy who remotely tolerated him.

Night was falling and the cheerful aura that normally permeated the great hall had been routed by a man whose malevolence knew no limit. Peter lay on his back, one arm under his head, and watched the chamber grow more nervous with each passing minute.

Edward Teach was a poison, and this was one corner of the world that he would not be allowed to destroy. Sleep gradually won him over but before it did, Peter resolved that he would do everything in his power to stop him.

NINETEEN

Night patrols were awful.

Open sky patrols were even worse. Put them together and you were asking for trouble.

Siene had always hated them. It was hard enough to stay focused and keep watch for both kites and pirates, but at night, you had to spend extra effort keeping yourself from glowing, or you'd stand out like, well, like a fairy in the night sky. And with the kites varying their tactics, the fairies not only had to keep watch on the ground and tree-top levels, but also the open sky. This forced the fairies to patrol the skies at higher altitudes than they had done in the past – at the peak of their flying abilities.

"What do you think about the humans?" Tolan, her scouting

partner, asked.

"The girl seems trustworthy," she answered, her eyes still scanning the forest below. "But the boy," she started, "I haven't decided yet."

"I don't trust him," Tolan sniffed. "He came from the mers. No one leaves mer territory alive unless they're in league with them. We'd do well to be on our guard with him."

"Perhaps," she replied.

The pair continued their patrol through the night sky, both fairies keeping a tight reign on their glow. They crossed paths with another patrol, six fairies strong—the main night patrol.

"Do you think they could be involved with the pirates?" Tolan asked. "They've used human children before."

"Doubtful," was Siene's reply. "It wouldn't make sense to be in league with both mers and pirates. The mermaids would have sniffed that out right away."

"Hmm," he replied. "True, but wha–"

His response was cut short by a piercing cry that filled the night sky.

Both fairies turned to see the main patrol that they had passed minutes ago several hundred meters away, flaring into brightness – the signal that they were in danger.

Without a word, they shot toward the group. As they flew, Tolan unstrapped his long sword from his back, Siene unsheathed her twin daggers.

The patrol in the distance burned brighter, silently pleading for help from anyone in the area.

The pair pushed harder, concentrating all their energy on speed.

Their focus on staying dark forgotten, they erupted into light and streaked across the sky.

They could see the main patrol now, wrapped in a fight with three large kites. The birds' war cries could be heard echoing through the sky.

Two other patrols were arriving ahead of them, joining the fray. One of the kites seized a fairy in its talons, plucked the fairy's wings from his back and let him drop.

"Tol!" Siene cried, pointing with one dagger at the falling fairy. "Look!"

"Got him!" he replied. He sheathed his sword and dived toward the falling fairy. The fairy saw him coming and stretched out his arms and legs in an attempt to slow his own decent. The act was enough for Tolan to catch up to him. He crashed into the wounded fairy, wrapping his arms and legs around him in a bear hug. He maintained his speed but adjusted his course toward White Falls. Siene watched Tolan grow dark then flare into light, a flashing, dim–bright pattern that would warn the home watch that he was bringing in wounded.

Siene flew faster, coming up behind a kite. The bird's white wing feathers seemed to glow in the dark. She rotated her grip on the daggers, angling the tips down, raised her arms up, and arched her back to strike. She struck with all her might, screaming as she swung. The blow took the kite completely by surprise. The daggers bit deep into the bird's wing, severing the joint. The bird shrieked in pain, flapping helplessly with one wing as it tumbled out of the sky.

The other two patrols were engaged with the second bird. Four fairies had piled on the kite while a fifth was squeezing the creature's beak shut. Another two were wrestling its talons together. With the bird effectively defenseless, another fairy – this one from the original patrol – came from behind and began to cut the bird's pinion feathers.

The fairies placed ultimate value on life and though they were at war with the kites, they opted to remove the birds' ability to fly over killing them outright when possible. They released the clipped bird, and it began to drop to the ground. More of a controlled fall than a deadly plummet, the bird would doubtless live but would no longer be a threat to the fairies.

Seeing that the second bird was taken care of, Siene looked for the third.

The bird struck her from behind, knocking the daggers from her hands. The bird seized her, its talons wrapping around her entire body. Her vision began to grow dark. She began to see spots of light, and distantly, she realized that the lights were more fairies joining the fight. Behind and above, she could hear the cries of more kites joining in the battle.

The bird squeezed tighter and Siene felt her arms twitch and beginning to grow cold. She thanked the fates that she had been able to kill one of them before she died.

"Aaaaahhhhh!" a loud voice cut through the din of battle, this one much louder and deeper than a fairy's, but unlike any bird call.

Siene felt the talon's grip go slack and release her. Then another talon, no, a hand, plucked her out of the air.

It was the boy, Peter.

"Can you fly?" Peter was asking her, opening his hand, palm up, to allow Siene to stand. She stood up on cold, shaky legs and gave her wings a few tentative flaps. They seemed undamaged. She flapped harder, lifted off of Peter's hand, and nodded.

"Good," the boy said. He flashed a crooked smile, dropped suddenly, then flew straight into the cloud of birds and fairies. He swung and hacked, his white dagger weaving dizzy arcs in the sky. The kites, used to fighting creatures half their size, were completely taken off guard.

The battle ended almost as soon as Peter had arrived. The shocked birds abandoned their assault and retreated north, back into their territory.

The remaining patrols regrouped and assessed their damage.

"It looks like we lost two," Rike, the night patrol leader, was saying.

"Tolan caught one," Siene added.

"Good," Rike said, nodding. "One, then."

"Does this happen often?" Peter asked, panting. "The kites," he said, waving his dagger around him. "Do they always attack you like that?"

"Yes," Siene spat. "They either try to pick us off one at a time or come at us all at once. I… I thought I was dead, thank you."

"You took care of my sister," he said. "That makes us friends."

Peter turned back to Rike. "Will they attack again tonight?"

"Unlikely," the fairy replied. "They suffered heavy losses. And they've never seen a flying boy," he smiled. "They're slow creatures," he said, pointing to his own head. "They'll think long and hard about what happened tonight before acting again. I think you've bought us some needed time. Let's head back to the falls. Adelaide will want to know what happened."

When the patrol returned, they found White Falls fully awake, despite the late hour. The fairies from the patrol filtered down from the ceiling and Peter crashed through the waterfall, as was his way.

The fairies made their way to a section of the cave near the back that resembled an infirmary. There were five beds in a row and the rows went ten deep into the wall. The room's ceiling was high enough for a fairy to fly over it and not hit the top. At the end of the room was what looked like a workshop. There were a variety of tools, hammers, knives, and something that resembled a potter's wheel. A fairy with missing wings was laying on his stomach on one of the beds.

"One of the fairies brought him in just after you left," Mara explained, coming up beside Peter.

The fairy was obviously in agony but was doing his best to remain still. Healer fairies were tending his wounds, dabbing them with a glowing, golden paste.

"What are they doing to him?" Peter asked.

"You're about to see why the fairies are so sought after," Mara said. "This is it. This is the secret."

Peter said nothing but watched as an older fairy rushed to the workbench. Fairies from all over the cave flew up to the ceiling and into the reservoir like the one that Peter had fallen into. The old fairy sat down at a golden stool at the workbench as fairies began bringing in armfuls of dust and dropping it on the table in front of him. He held out his hand and made a sprinkling motion and dust trailed into his open palm. He rubbed his hands together and began working. Reaching into the pile of dust, he pulled out a glowing handful and began to knead the dust like dough. Instead of falling apart, it condensed, the ball of dust turning a darker shade of gold. He added more dust to the ball and kneaded it more, repeating the process until the ball had grown to the size of his head.

He stood up, examining the golden ball, then seeing something Peter could not, pinched it and pulled. A thin strand of dust stretched away from the ball. But instead of going limp like normal string, the golden strand stayed taut. He grabbed the end still attached to the ball and twisted it until it came away. Grabbing each end, he bent the golden rod until each end met, forming a ring. Placing the edge on the table, he hammered at it until it elongated into a what looked like a blade of grass.

"What's he doing?" Peter asked.

"He's making new wings," Mara replied. "The dust," she explained. "They can form it into anything they want: tools, weapons, diamonds. Even wings," she added.

Peter nodded absently, continuing to watch the fairy create a new pair of wings for his fallen brother. He was starting to understand the value others would put on the material's ability.

"Does anyone else know they can do this?" he asked, looking back at his sister.

The old fairy was repeating his twisting technique, only this time making shorter strands, pinching them and then attaching them to the main wing frame, like a spider web.

"The kites and mers do, of course, but now Teach does, too. He saw one of them create something once. He's never been in here, though," she said, indicating the cave's interior. "And it was something minor, a quill or something to write with, but he figures that dust can make more than simple writing tools."

"And he's right," Peter supplied.

"And he's right," she agreed.

"We can't let him find this place," she said. "Who knows what he'd do to them and what he'd force them to make. "This is more important than you and I trying to find a way home or even finding father. We need to make sure Teach never finds this place," she said.

Peter didn't reply. Instead, he stared at the fairies working.

"Do you think father is…" Peter started. "Do you think Teach killed him?"

"Don't talk like that," Mara scolded. "Of course not. He's William Till, remember? And everything we know about Teach tells us he would keep father alive."

"I don't know," Peter replied. "Those mermaids seem to know Teach a lot better than we do."

"Well, I know what father would want us to do," Mara said, adamantly.

"Protect at all costs," Peter said with a half smile.

"Exactly," Mara smiled.

"We're going to be on this island for a while, aren't we?" he asked.

"I think so," she said, looking at him.

The old fairy put his last strand into the wing, then picked it up, inspecting his work. Satisfied, he handed it to a second fairy who had just joined him. The second fairy, a male with long, black hair, held the wing out as the first gathered another handful of dust and began to rub it rapidly in his hands. Pressing his hands together tight, the second fairy slid the wing between his two hands. A third, this one a female with yellow hair, grabbed the end of the wing as it came through the other side of the pressed hands. She pulled the wing through, allowing the entire wing to pass through the old one's pressed hands. A thin, translucent film covered the wing as it exited the other side. She handed the wing back to the old fairy. He inspected it again, and satisfied with his work, placed it back on the table.

Finally, he took a long, thin dagger, grabbed a handful of dust with the other hand and covered the blade with dust. Painstakingly he cut the wing in half lengthwise. The wing split in two, creating a thinner pair of identical wings. Again he turned each wing over in his hand, feeling their weight and inspecting his work closely. Finally satisfied with his work, he brought the wings over to the fairies who were tending the injured one. He handed the wings to them, then retuned to his workbench and gathered a handful of dust. Packing it with his hands, he walked back to the injured fairy and placed the glowing ball of dust on the fairy's back where one of his wings had been. Then, taking one of the newly crafted wings, he placed its tip into the glowing ball. The yellow-haired fairy came alongside him, packing another handful of dust in her hands, and repeated the process, placing the ball on his back. A dark-haired fairy attached the second wing, then took a step back, examining his work. Together, they squinted and cocked their tiny heads, making sure the new wings had been grafted evenly.

Once they decided they were pleased with their work, they began to blow on the dust where the wings were connected to the back. The dust began to blow away until all that remained were the portions that touched both his back and new wings. Then they waited, watching the wings. At first nothing happened. The wings remained as rigid and golden as an iron statue. But eventually, the wings began to lose their glow and began to grow transparent. The fairy sat up and rose to his feet, no longer appearing in pain. He flexed his wings experimentally, clearly not trusting them yet but just as clearly eager to try.

"It worked!" Peter said in astonishment.

"Simple things are easy," Siene said, drifting between the children from behind. She pinched her fingers together and touched her palm and drew out a thin string like a magician pulls a cloth from their hand. "For those of us who have been trained, that is. But for something like this," she continued, pointing toward the group of fairies still inspecting the new wings, "well, that kind of crafting is left to master shapers."

"It's incredible," Peter said.

"Indeed," Siene replied. "Mallon will be grounded for some time while his new wings fully heal. But he'll be fine in a few days."

Mara shook her head in amazement. "You have a beautiful gift," she said.

Siene dipped her head, acknowledging the compliment. "Thank you," she said. "You should return to bed, though. Peter, our watch in the cove begins just before dawn. I'll wake you."

Peter and Mara returned to their beds, amazed at what they had just witnessed and yet frightened at the danger created by these abilities.

TWENTY

The sun was peeking through the dense treetops, painting an ever-changing pattern of light and shadow on the forest floor. Peter and Siene sat on a branch near the top of an ancient oak tree. The pair had spent the last hour discussing the finer points of fighting with daggers.

Peter had always favored the single blade, despite his father's own affinity with dual wielding. Siene, on the other hand, firmly believed in the philosophy that more blades meant more stabbing, which meant faster killing.

"But with a single blade, you stay focused on your target," he insisted. "Each strike has meaning."

"No," Siene said flatly, shaking her head. "With two blades, you have a net of death around you." She illustrated by waving her tiny arms above and around her body in a blur, then looked at Peter and held her arms out as if her example was argument enough.

"Well argued," Peter said, laughing and looking out toward the sea.

Siene smiled. "What did Teach take from you?" she asked, changing the subject.

"My father," he replied. But before he could expound, two ships rounded the southern tip of the cove, gliding into the bay. And there she was, the *Dawnriser*, in the lead with a second just behind it. The ships coasted to a stop and the distant splash of anchors dropping into the water could be heard.

Siene followed his gaze and saw the ships. "Two?" she gasped in surprise. "But—"

"I know," he said looking at her. "There was only one before."

"What does it mean?" she asked.

Peter shook his head. "I don't know, but look."

A single boat was being lowered into the water. It bobbed against the *Dawnriser* and a single man dropped down into it and pushed off from the ship. He settled himself down and began rowing toward the beach.

"We need to warn the others," Siene said.

"You go, you're faster," Peter lied.

She eyed him suspiciously, but Peter waved a hand at her.

"Hurry, go!" he urged.

"Don't do anything foolish," she warned.

"I won't," he winked.

She shot away from the beach and headed toward White Falls.

Peter watched her until she was out of sight, then turned back and watched the boat approach.

The craft nosed into the sand as the waves slapped playfully against its sides. The boat's lone occupant leapt from the bow and pulled the boat the rest of the way up the shore. He stood and studied the tree line, silently appraising the woods. The man knelt down and picked up a handful of sand, his face hidden from Peter. He sniffed at the sand, then let it sift though his fingers. The man looked up toward the trees. He removed his hat, wiped his brow and ran his hand through his wild, black beard.

Peter had heard enough about the man to immediately identify him. The ornate pistols that hung holstered from his chest, the gold chains that held gem-studded swords at his hip, the black leather boots, even the strips of red ribbon braided into his beard and hair – he could be no one else but Edward Teach.

From the upper branches of the giant oak, Peter studied the man his father hadn't been able to catch.

"I feel your eyes, slave!" Teach shouted, rising to his feet and wiping his hand clean on his leg.

"I'm no slave!" Peter retorted, then clapped his hands to his mouth when he realized he had answered the taunt.

"Why do you sulk about in the shadows, then?" Teach asked, his hands on his hips. "Free men have no reason to hide. Whom do I have the pleasure of addressing?"

"William Till," Peter shouted back.

"Ha!" the man snorted. "Unlikely. But I'd be curious to know how you came by that name."

Peter stepped off of the branch he was perched on and dropped noiselessly to the ground. Keeping the giant tree between him and the pirate, he quickly collected three fist-sized rocks.

"My secrets are my own, pirate," Peter spat.

And as quietly as he dropped, he flew up, returning to his spot in the tree.

"Fair enough," came the pirate's reply.

Peter carefully piled his rocks in the crook of a branch, then selected one and hefted it.

"Why are you here, pirate?" Peter called down to the man.

Teach spread his hands. "I'm naught but a merchant adventurer, seeking a quiet cove to rest my crew," he said.

"Unlikely," Peter replied and threw the stone. It sailed near the edge of the wood. Teach drew a pistol and fired, turning the stone to dust before it hit the ground.

"What is your real purpose, pirate?" Peter called. He collected his remaining two rocks and leapt from tree to tree, carful to remain out of sight. "No one just finds this place," he said, now on Teach's other side.

"Indeed, not," Teach replied, his pistol still in hand. "I ask the same question of you, or are you a mere spirit who haunts these woods?"

"You would be safer if I were," Peter said, his voice icy and determined.

He threw another stone. A second gun appeared in Teach's other hand. Again, the stone erupted into dust.

"This island is under my protection, pirate. I know what you seek and it is beyond your reach," Peter said, flying to another tree.

This time he crashed through the branches before hiding behind another trunk.

Teach's eyes snapped to the source of the sound. Peter threw the last stone, this time directly at the man. Teach didn't see this stone coming, he was still watching where the trees had moved. With what seemed like exaggerated slowness, he holstered his pistols and stared up at the moving leaves, seemingly unaware of the stone sailing toward him.

Peter couldn't believe it was going to be this easy. The stone was about to hit him.

With Teach unconscious, he'd tie him up, gather the fairies and mermaids, and let them decide what to do with him. Or better yet, maybe he'd just kill him himself and be done with it, after he found out where his father was.

The stone was less than five meters from striking Teach when the man drew a third pistol and fired directly into the path of the stone. He disappeared behind a cloud of dust as the rock exploded in front of him.

"I go where I go," Teach said, stepping through the cloud of dust, back into the sunlight. "I am not swayed by mermaids, or pixies, or spirits throwing stones. You have my name so you must know of my deeds. You have my assurance, spirit – the stories you've heard are but a diluted fiction to their cannon."

Teach turned back to his boat and began pushing it into the water.

"It is you who is warned," he continued, his loud, booming voice carrying up to Peter. "Leave me to my business and when I am gone, you may haunt these woods until eternity's end. But cross me and your name will be nothing more than a whisper in my storm."

Peter watched the man row back to his ship, then realized that he was shaking from the encounter. He folded his arms tightly across his chest. What was he feeling? Excitement? Anger? He closed his eyes, trying to calm himself and slow his racing heart. Then he recognized the feeling – dread. The pirate's words had struck home. The realization intensified the emotion and he began to shake again even more.

The battle for the island had begun, and Teach had just drawn first blood.

TWENTY ONE

The argument was in full swing.

It seemed that no one could agree on the best course of action against the pirates.

"We should attack, now," Tolan was saying, again. "Before they're ready for us."

"We can't afford a direct assault," Siene argued. "The kites grow bolder each day. They would wait for us to leave and then wipe out the remnant."

"Couldn't we just hide?" Mara asked.

"For how long?" a yellow-haired fairy asked. "Stay hidden and let them establish their own borders?"

Adelaide remained silent, allowing everyone present to voice their opinions.

"Our wisest choice is to strike from the shadows," Siene insisted. "Make the forest a place of death for any pirate who enters it."

"Yes," Peter replied, nodding. "But make it more than death."

"What do you mean?" Tolan asked.

"Teach called me a spirit," Peter replied. "He was mocking me for staying hidden, but it reminded me how superstitious pirates are. Use your abilities to lay traps and let them think that fairies are deadly, dangerous, evil creatures. Let them think the forests are haunted. Let them believe that taking a step in the forest means taking their final steps."

The party fell silent, considering his words.

"I agree," Adelaide said, speaking for the first time. "Edward Teach's greatest ally is fear. It stretches out ahead of him like a plague. We would be wise to employ it ourselves."

There was a general murmur of agreement from those gathered. Then their talk turned to planning the specifics.

Several days passed and in that time the fairies, along with Peter and Mara, tracked the pirate scouting parties that wandered through the forest. They seemed to be making maps of the island. The larger parties were left unmolested, but when the groups split up, the fairies would start to harass them. They never openly attacked them, but the pirates would discover that their water skins would be mysteriously empty, their rations would go missing, and other annoyances that, over time, would begin to play on the pirates' superstitions.

On a few lucky occasions, the fairies even managed to replace their carefully drawn maps with scrolls filled with indiscernible markings. When they had taken out the maps to make additions, they threw them to the ground, crying out and declaring their efforts cursed.

That's when the fairies knew they were making progress.

While the fairies harassed the smaller partiers, Peter and Mara would follow the larger groups, listening to their conversations and repeating sentences back to the pirates in raspy whispers.

The pirates, upon hearing their own words echoing back would freeze in place, then slowly look at one another, each one desperately hoping the sound had come from one of them.

The children would hide behind trees, cramming their knuckles into their mouths to keep their laughter from bursting out.

The game was tricky for Mara since she could only fly with the aid of dust and needed to be sprinkled regularly or she would slowly drift to the ground and have to hide until a passing fairy could sprinkle her again. Peter, on the other hand, showed no signs of his newfound abilities fading.

Peter's plan was turning out to be a success and now he wanted to take it one step further. He thought a more direct encounter might turn away the pirates for good. He wanted the pirates to see the 'spirit' that haunted the forest. Many of the fairies were concerned that allowing himself to be seen would undo all the work they had done, but Peter had confidence in his plan, so Adelaide agreed to it.

He waited above the tree tops, looking for his target. Mara bobbed in the air next to him.

"That group," he said, pointing to a score of pirates hacking their way through the thick forest.

"Are you sure?" she asked. "It's a large group."

He winked at her and smiled. "It'll be great, watch!" He dived through the trees, flying circles through the leafy branches around the party. He howled and shrieked, making all the sounds he imagined a haunting spirit might make.

The pirates scattered.

Drawing swords and pistols, they ran in all directions, firing blindly into the treetops and waving their blades around. Peter continued to fly through the trees, crashing in and out of the leafy canopy. It didn't take long for panic to fully seize the men. Several were wounded by flailing swords while others ran into trees. Those even less fortunate tripped over rocks and found themselves falling down hills.

Peter returned to Mara, laughing.

"You were right," she said, smiling at him. "It worked."

"Told you," he smiled.

"Whoa!" Mara exclaimed, slowly beginning to sink. "I'm going to head back to the falls before I lose flight completely."

She took off towards the falls, leaving Peter to his own tricks – a lone spirit haunting its forest. He surveyed the forest. Every scouting party that had entered the forest today had been turned back, even the large one. He slowly drifted toward the falls, but when he turned around, he saw a handful of pirates, thirty yards or so away staring right at him. He froze for a heartbeat, then smiled as another idea sparked to life in his head.

* * *

"Did you just see that?" the pirate asked.

"What, the flying boy?" a second man answered.

"Yes, the flying boy, you fool," the first replied.

"It's gotta be some sort of witchcraft, Barret," the second man replied.

"No such thing," the man, Barret, replied. Then, pointing to the flying boy, said, "That's dust."

He watched the boy fly lazy circles toward a waterfall in the distance and disappear behind it. He smiled. "You know what else? I'll wager two pieces of eight that the fairies live in there."

"In the waterfall?"

"Behind the waterfall."

"Well, what are we waiting for, then? Let's go tell Teach."

"Stow that gab," Barret said. "We show Teach the location, he'll give us a pat on the back. We hand deliver bags of dust and dead fairies, he'll give us a command of our own."

"Okay, what's the plan?"

"There's five of us. I say we sneak into that waterfall and see if we can't slay us a few fairies."

"Good plan, chief!"

The pirates made their way around the small pond and to the base of the waterfall. They followed a narrow path that led behind the falls, but it dead ended at a flat stone.

It seemed like there was just enough room for them to squeeze between the water and the stone.

"We gotta be quick," Barret said. "We can't be going one at a time. Here, take my wrist, I'll go through and we'll each pull each other in, quick like."

The five pirates all held hands and on Barret's word, drove themselves through the wall of water. The five men all slipped around the stone wall and fell in a heap onto cool ground. None of them had known what to expect, but nothing could have prepared them for what they saw once the water cleared from their eyes.

Barret looked up, straight into the angry eyes of a small boy. His hands were on his hips and thrust in his belt was a white dagger. And he was flying. He hovered in the air at their eye level, and he was surrounded by walls of diamonds, gold, and hovering fairies.

"You're not supposed to be here, pirate," the boy spat.

"You're not supposed to be flying, boy," Barret retorted as he slowly drew his cutlass. He pointed the weapon at the boy and said, "And me thinks that pixie dust I've heard so much about might have something to do with it. "

The boy didn't move, instead he just looked at the sword in Barret's hand.

"You're not going to need that," he smiled mockingly.

"And why's that?"

"Because dead men don't need weapons," he replied.

The rest of the pirates drew their swords.

The boy drew his own dagger and pointed it at the pirate next to Barret.

"Die!" Peter yelled. And the man fell to the ground, dead.

The remaining pirates gasped in horror, looking at their dead comrade, then back to the boy.

"I'm a magic boy," he said, showing teeth. "You shouldn't have come here."

The pirates took one last look at their dead mate and then dived into the waterfall.

Barret hit the water and swam toward the shallows with all of his might. He, along with two other pirates, reached the shore. One hadn't survived the fall. Without giving their missing mate a second thought, they ran headlong into the forest.

Peels of the magic boy's laughter seemed to echo all around them.

The pirate to Barret's left fell to the ground, gurgling and clutching his throat.

He ignored the man and ran faster. Blood thundered in his ears as he sprinted.

"Split up!" he yelled.

And the other pirate crossed behind him and ran left.

He turned right and pushed even harder through the forest. A few seconds later, he heard a guttural scream that turned his blood to ice and he knew he was the only one left. He ran a little farther and then dived into a grove of thick lilacs. He desperately tried to slow his breathing, but his lungs demanded more air than he could give them.

He could hear rustling in the trees above and the faint call of the boy.

"Come out, come out, wherever you are," the boy called.

He heard another voice laughing, a girl's, maybe.

He closed his eyes, pressed his hands to his ears, and focused on catching his breath.

* * *

"Come out, come out wherever you are," Peter called.

"Stop it!" Mara laughed.

The two of them flew through the tree tops, scanning for the remaining pirate.

Four fairy warriors searched with them – the same warriors who had fired poison-tipped arrows into the throat of the pirate in the cave.

The theatrics had been Peter's idea. His thought had been to lead them to the falls, then have the punishment for finding it be so severe that no one would ever dare return. The ploy had worked marvelously, and now four of the five pirates had died believing the fairies were ruled by some sort of bewitched child.

Peter had wanted to leave the last pirate alive to tell the tale. Letting the man get away to warn every other pirate would ensure that no one would ever try and enter the forest, let alone White Falls, again. The fairies, however, were not convinced that Peter's plan would work. Fear would protect them for a while, but the pirates' greed would eventually lead them back to White Falls. And after seeing how the Pirates reacted to Peter's ability to fly – envy rather than fear – she ordered that no other pirate see him fly. Their greed would doubtless eclipse any fear they felt. The less the pirates knew about what dust could do, the better. Everyone was in agreement.

"Let's spread out," Peter called as the six of them searched the woods for the final pirate.

Peter perched atop an oak branch and listened.

Nothing.

Then he heard the snap-crack of a branch breaking underfoot, accompanied by a man swearing. Peter whistled sharply and dived down to the forest floor.

The snapping increased as Peter dropped down to ground level. Then he saw the man. He was clad in tattered black pants and a purple silken shirt that had seen better days.

The man looked back over his shoulder, his eyes widening as he saw Peter.

Peter smiled, waved at the man, then drew his coral dagger.

The man drew a pistol and fired it.

Peter ducked behind a tree, dodging the shot. The shot buried itself deep in the trunk. He came out from behind the tree and flew past the man, tripping him up as he soared past.

The pirate lost his footing for a moment but regained it and started to run again.

A single fairy streaked down from the sky like a fired bullet, dust trailing her small body. She landed on the pirate's calf and buried her daggers into the man's leg.

The man roared in pain and slapped his leg with the broad edge of his sword. The strike sent a puff of dust into the air and the fairy went limp and fell to the ground.

"Help!" the pirate called. "Fairy attack!"

"Oh, no you don't!" Peter said, coming around for the attack.

He landed right in front of the man and struck at him. The pirate parried his strike, then riposted. Peter dodged it, rolling away as Mara landed, catching the strike on her own blade.

"To arms!" the pirate called, aiming a kick at Mara. She flew backwards, the bottom of the man's boot barely grazing her stomach as she dodged backwards.

Three more fairies flew into the clearing, swords drawn.

Peter struck again, this time for the man's chest, but he leaned away to avoid it as Mara struck at his legs. She connected, slicing into his thigh.

The man howled, seemingly more in anger than pain and spun his sword around him, clearing the air.

The fairies disengaged and armed their bows.

The lead fairy drew his bowstring to fire, then exploded into a brilliant golden flare as a gunshot roared a few feet away.

The two remaining fairies fired. Their arrows found their mark, deep in the back of the man's neck.

Peter jerked his head in the direction of the gunshot to see three pirates running toward them, weapons drawn, smoke trailing from the leader's blunderbuss.

"Mara, run!" he cried, turning to escape. But instead of trees and freedom, he saw the butt of a rifle. The weapon smashed into his face, sending him sprawling. He hit the ground hard and tried to scramble to his feet, but a second blow sent him crumpling to the ground.

He heard two more guns discharge as his vision began to go dark. He tried shaking his head in an attempt to clear his vision, but his throbbing skull ignored his attempts to move.

The last thing he saw was his sister. She was curled up in a ball a few meters from him, unmoving. And as he fell into blackness, he heard the dying pirate's final words.

"The boy," the man rasped. "He can f–"

TWENTY TWO

Wake up, brat," a cruel voice was saying.

Peter's head buzzed with pain. He opened his eyes, half expecting to see Sarii perched in front of him, offering him more raw fish. But as his vision cleared, he wished he was in the mer's caves again. Instead, he was standing, tied to a huge, round beam. The smell of wood and a gentle rocking motion told Peter he was on a ship.

"You're going to tell me a few things, boy," the voice said again.

Peter squinted up at the man.

He was ugly--ugly and huge. The fact that he was overweight suggested that he held a high enough rank to make less-fortunate men do most of his work.

He had a gruesome scar that dug across his right eye. The eye still seemed to be in there though – shriveled and nasty looking. Although Peter couldn't imagine the eye did the man any favors anymore.

"Where am I?" Peter asked, still groggy, but feigning a little more of it than was true.

He looked around. The room was big. Barrels dotted parts of the room he could see, but the room was dark. The only light came from the handful of lanterns that swayed from the ceiling and the dim moonlight that peeked down through the crisscrossed boards that covered the hold.

"I ask questions, you tell me what you know, that's how it works, okay?" Slit-eye replied.

"Now," the big man continued. "I'm a simple man, but seeing that Barret was the only one to make it as far as he did, and from the three dead pixies we found in the woods, I'll wager that poor ol' Barret managed to find Pixie Hold," he said.

"What's Pixie Hold?" Peter asked.

Slit-eye slapped him hard across the face.

"Not finished, laddie," he chided, shaking a finger at Peter. "Where was I? Pixie Hold. I'd bet your big toes that poor ole' Barret found out where those pixies live. And since they were fighting him and you were fighting him... Are you ready for it?" he paused, clearly enjoying himself immensely. "You must know where the pixies live."

Peter smiled up at the man, "Sorry, mate, can't help you."

"Wrong answer!" Slit-eye yelled, punching Peter hard in the stomach. Then, squatting down to Peter's eye level, he said, "Would you like to try again?"

Peter mumbled something the man didn't hear.

"What was that?" he asked, leaning closer to Peter.

Peter gathered a mouthful of blood and spat it into the man's face.

The man laughed heartily and slapped him hard across the face again.

"There's spirit in this one!" he said, wiping his face.

"We'll try again after you've had some time to wonder why you don't hear that pretty little girl you were with," he said, patting Peter's cheek.

"Don't you dare touch her or I'll kill you!" Peter screamed at him.

"There he is," the pirate cheered. "I'll see you in a bit."

The man turned and walked up the steps.

Peter jerked at his restraints. They were thick, heavy ropes—the kind used to tie ships to docks. They were wrapped around his body several times, pinning his arms and legs in place. He tried flying up, but the ropes were way too tight.

The room was dark, which meant he was most likely in the lower hold of the ship – which also meant he was probably tied to the ship's mainmast.

He wasn't going anywhere.

Peter had no concept of time in the dark of the hold. He may have fallen asleep or passed out a few times, but eventually, the door opened again and a pair of gangly legs danced down the steps.

A wiry-looking man ducked and bobbed toward Peter. The man moved as if he were dodging obstacles that only he could see.

"Hello, Rogue," the man said.

"What?" Peter said, "I'm not Rogue."

"Of course, you're not!" the man snorted. "I am! Hahahahaha!" he laughed. "Oh no," the man gasped, suddenly. "There's something on your face!" He produced a long red feather and began tickling Peter's face with it.

"Itchy, itchy!" the man sang crazily.

"Stop it!" Peter yelled.

"What is it?" the man asked, looking hurt. "Don't you like, Little Kite?" he asked, holding the feather out for Peter to see. "I got him from Big Kite. But I ate Big Kite."

The man patted his stomach, remembering the meal.

"Big Kite," he sighed. "So tasty."

Peter narrowed his eyes at the man. "Big Kite didn't happen to be a bird, did he?"

"Why yes he was!" the man exclaimed.

"A Red Kite?" Peter asked.

"My, my, how did you know?" he asked. "Were you there, too? Wasn't he delicious?" the man asked, nodding vigorously. "Yes, yes, he was," he said, answering his own question.

"Lucky guess," Peter mumbled.

Footfalls on the steps drew Peter's attention, and he looked up to see Slit-eye returning.

"Ah, I see you've met Mad Rogue," Slit-eye said, patting the other man on the back.

"Mad Rogue had a little pearl diving accident a while back," he explained. "He stayed underwater a bit too long. Left most of his… sensibility on the ocean floor. Ango went down, Mad Rogue came up."

"So, he's insane," Peter said.

Mad Rogue was at his face an instant later, the sharpened tip of Little Kite pressing into Peter's throat.

"Mad Rogue is not insane, boy," the crazed pirate spat.

"All right, Mad Rogue, why don't you head to the deck. I think I hear Little Kite," Slit-eye said.

"Ooo did you hear that, Little Kite?" Mad Rogue said to his feather. "We've got to find Little Kite!" and with that, he turned and scampered up the stairs.

"It's all about misdirection," the man smiled, pulling up a stool to sit opposite Peter. "Now, shall we start over?" he said, looking up at Peter. "Where is Pixie Hold?"

Peter said nothing, but returned the man's stare.

"Maybe I'm making this too difficult. Let's start with something easy. How about your name?"

Again, Peter said nothing.

"Look, boy, you don't need to die. Your sister – as I gather from your earlier reaction – doesn't need to die. All you need to do is answer a few simple questions and you get to go home. How about we give and take a bit, eh?" he said, rubbing his hands together.

"I'll go first, my name is London."

"But your Irish," Peter said.

"My parents had a sense of humor," he replied. "Now," he continued, "what's your name?"

"Peter."

"Marvelous!" he said clapping his hands together. "Now, Peter, how did you get on this island?" he asked. He drew a dagger and began cleaning his fingernails with it.

The dagger was exquisite. The hilt was wrapped in oily, black leather. The silver blade perfectly reflected the lantern light. The pommel was inlaid with gold and capped with a large, green emerald.

Green like his eyes.

Green like his father's eyes.

This was William Till's dagger.

Peter's blood ran cold as the realization gripped him. William Till would never have let another man take away his weapons. Seeing his father's dagger, he immediately felt both closer to and further away from his father.

Peter stared at William Till's blade, a detached calmness settling on him as the reality of his father's fate worked its way into his mind.

"I came here to find answers," Peter said without emotion, shifting his gaze to the pirate's. "I found them. And now you're going to die."

"Big words," London said. "We'll see if you've spirit enough to deliver on 'em."

He sheathed the dagger, then punched Peter with his full strength, knocking him out.

"Now," the voice was saying again, "let's start over."

Peter raised his head and groaned. It hurt.

"Tell me about this dagger, Pete," London was saying. He was inspecting Peter's coral dagger, the one Kinarah had given him.

The man turned the dagger over in his hands, brushing his fingers over the words engraved in the blade.

"What's a 'pan,' Peter?" he asked, holding the weapon up to Peter so he could see it. "Are you a pan?" he asked.

"Wake up, Peter Pan," a crazed voice called from the darkness.

Mad Rogue bobbed and ducked into the light, singing and chanting as he moved, "Peter Pan, Peter Pan, time for wakey, Peter Pan."

"Rogue, fetch Peter Pan some water; I think he's thirsty."

"Peter Pan needs some water! Hello, Mad Rogue, the boy is thirsty!"

Mad Rogue disappeared up the stairs and returned a minute later with a wooden pail. He carried it to Peter, the water sloshing as he danced about.

"Are you thirsty, Peter Pan?" he asked as he emptied the freezing bucket of seawater on him. Laughing uproariously, he put the pail on his own head and marched back up the stairs.

"Drink up, Peter Pan," he cackled from under the bucket.

Peter shivered as the cold water soaked him, his teeth clacking together.

Suddenly, London held Peter by his face, clenching the boy's mouth shut.

"Now, hear this," he hissed. His breath was hot and stale. "You're going to *tell* me how you got here, then you're going to *tell* me what you're doing with those pixies and finally, you're going to *tell* me where Pixie Hold is." He emphasized each "tell" by slamming Peter's head against the mast.

Peter felt blood, warm and sticky, dribble down his neck and back.

"And if you don't give me those answers, I'm going to have to take your sister apart in front of you," he said. "I don't like violence," the pirate continued. "Many pirates do, many of my pirates do. But pain is a tool, not entertainment," he said. "I may be captain of this ship, but I report to someone, too, and he won't be pleased if these questions don't find answers."

"Rot," Peter whispered, then felt pain rip through his body as London's knee slammed into his stomach.

He grabbed Peter by the face again and squeezed. "You're making this very difficult for yourself."

Peter tried to scream, but the man's hands forced his mouth shut. "Answer my questions and it all ends. You go free, your sister goes free," he shouted over Peter's muffled screams "the pain ends!" he said.

Peter felt the bones in his cheeks buckle and crack. He shrieked in agony and tried to jerk his head out of the pirate's grasp, but his grip was unrelenting. He squeezed harder and harder, until Peter's brain decided that enough was enough, and he passed out.

White hot pain erupted in Peter's legs.

"Aaaggrrhh!" he screamed, jerking back into consciousness.

"You didn't think you could get away from me that easily, did you?" London's voice thundered. "You can end this, Peter!"

"It's time to die, Peter Pan!" Mad Rogue sang from somewhere in the darkness.

Peter heard a loud snap, then his body erupted in pain again. He tried to focus his eyes and saw the strands of a whip flying towards him. He jerked upright, screaming as the tendrils made contact with his legs.

"It only gets worse from here, Peter" London yelled.

The whip snapped again. This time his arms exploded in pain.

He had to think of something fast.

Snap.

Think, then act.

Snap.

"The cliffs," Peter whimpered. "The black cliffs, to the east," he muttered.

"The Obsidian Cliffs?" London scoffed. "Sending me to my death? Let the mermaids deal with me? I'm afraid that'll cost you, mate."

Snap.

"I don't think you realize what you're doing, Peter."

Snap.

"It doesn't end when you die."

Snap.

"You're just setting your sister up for the same treatment."

Snap.

Peter faintly heard London saying something to Mad Rogue, heard the skittering foot steps and the sing-song voice of the crazed pirate as he left.

"Peter Pan is thirsty, Peter Pan is thirsty."

Peter braced himself for the rush of cold water. The agony that lay in anticipation was almost as excruciating as the stinging of the whip, or the heartbeat he felt in his broken cheeks.

He waited for what felt like an hour with his eyes squeezed shut, but the water never came. He let out a small breath.

"Thirsty!" the crazed voice yelled as Mad Rogue dumped the pail of water on him.

He gasped as the freezing water hit his body, then screamed as the water's salt discovered every wound on his body.

Once again, his brain decided he had had enough and unconsciousness welcomed him.

"I've had enough of this boy's insolence," London barked.

"Are ye going to kill him?" Mad Rogue asked, clapping his hands together. "Are you gonna kill Peter Pan?"

"Soon enough," he replied.

Laughing, he cut the ropes that held Peter to the mast and let him collapse on the floorboards.

Peter's vision refused to focus. Instead, he lay on the floor, bloodied and feeling more broken than when he had first learned his father might be dead.

"Think, then act." His father's words played through his head like a mantra. *"You will live or die by those words,"* William had always said.

And in this moment, Peter couldn't believe how absolutely right his father had been.

"Think, then act."

Think? Peter couldn't even see, much less think.

But he could hear.

He squeezed his eyes shut and listened. He could hear the waves slapping against the ship's hull. He could hear Mad Rogue as he shuffled throughout the cabin. And he could hear the distinct sound of steel scraping against leather as London sheathed his father's blade.

"Think, then act."

Peter opened his eyes. Blinking away blood and water, he stared at the grains of wood on the deck, willing his vision to focus.

London grabbed Peter by the hair, forcing the boy to his feet.

Peter blinked again.

His eyes were good enough.

In one fluid stroke, Peter slipped his father's dagger from London's belt and plunged it deep into the man's side. Before the man could cry out, Peter had the second dagger, his own coral dagger, free from the man's belt, and slammed it into the man's chest. He pulled the first blade free as the pirate fell to the floor. Mad Rogue leaped from the shadows, brandishing his sharpened feather, his face creased in a wild grin.

Peter pivoted away from him and swung the dagger, striking Mad Rogue's temple with the blunt end of the weapon as hard as he could. The man went sprawling and crashed into the wall, moaning and muttering to himself.

Grim faced, Peter turned and advanced on the fallen form of London.

"Spirit enough to kill a murderer," Peter spat.

The pirate's eyes began to cloud over as death took him.

"Hear my father's song," Peter said, standing over London. "May it carry you to Hell's gates."

Peter knew that the next, and last, thing the pirate heard was William Till's blade singing.

Peter wiped the daggers clean, then unfastened his father's belt from London's waist. Putting his foot on the man's stomach, he heaved with his remaining strength and the belt pulled free. He secured it around his own waist as two pirates, doubtless drawn by the commotion, rushed down the stairs.

They pulled their swords them from their scabbards and advanced on him. He stood stone still, his arms hanging loosely at his sides. He took several slow, deep breaths, finally able to breathe fully again. His hands tingled as blood and feeling found their way back to his fingers.

The two pirates were less than ten paces from him when he sprang.

His left hand flashed and the blade zipped across the room, forever silencing the first pirate.

Peter flew toward the second man, his hand landing over the pirate's mouth. The man's eyes grew wide with shock as Peter's coral dagger seemed to grow from the man's chest.

Peter lowered the man to the ground, retrieved his thrown blade, and staggered toward the stairs that led out of the hold.

He had to find his sister and escape.

He felt close to death and knew that he had just spent his remaining strength killing London, Mad Rogue, and the two guards. He could hardly stand, let alone run, and if it hadn't been for his ability to fly, the two guards would have killed him for sure.

Leaping, aided by flight, he took the stairs in one bound and crashed headlong into another pair of pirates.

Peter fell backward down the stairs. He scrambled to his feet and tried to free his blades from their sheaths, but the pirates were too fast. The two men fell upon him. The first, a thick-bearded man, kicked him hard in the stomach. The blow knocked him to the ground, slamming his head against the deck in the process.

Light exploded in his head as he desperately attempted to dodge their strikes. His weapons forgotten, he focused every effort on avoiding their hungry blades. He somersaulted backwards, narrowly avoiding a slash aimed at his stomach.

The second attacker, a dark-skinned man with gold rings in his ears, dropped to one knee and struck at Peter's legs.

Peter kicked both legs avoiding the blade, but the bearded pirate struck from above, timing his attack with his shipmate's. The man's cutlass sliced into Peter's swollen cheek before cutting a furrow down his chest.

Peter screamed and stumbled backward, falling into a half crouch, one hand to his face, the other fumbling to draw his dagger. They took a step forward and then paused as if silently confirming their intent with each other. Then, as one, the two men advanced.

Time seemed to slow as they moved toward Peter. The lantern light gleamed off their blades as they swayed to a rhythm of their own in the dust of the hold.

Peter shook with silent, futile anger, his eyes burning into the two men.

He couldn't fly. Flying would only give them another reason to find the fairies and their dust, he knew that now. And then they would tear the island apart looking for it. And he knew the only pirates who had seen him fly were dead.

With the last of his strength gone, he stood no chance in beating these two, and revealing the location of White Falls was not an option.

Still, if he was going to die, he would make sure these two remembered the day. He drew the other dagger and readied himself as best he could.

The pirates closed in, their weapons raised to strike.

"Hold!" a gruff voice commanded.

The speaker walked down the staircase, his heavy footfalls reverberating the floorboards with each step. He descended the stairs, dragging Peter's sister roughly behind him. The man's scabbard chains jingled with each step he took. His curly black beard was unkempt and twisted.

"Let her go, Teach!" Peter spat.

"You will tell me the location of the fairies' home," he said ignoring Peter's demand.

"I should have killed you on the beach," Peter said, his face twisting in rage.

The man smiled in recognition. "You should have heeded my words, spirit." He stopped at the bottom of the stairs. "Tsk, tsk. What a mess," he said, his face growing thoughtful. "Now tell me where the fairies live," he said, his voice calm, almost pleasant.

"I can't," Peter said softly, staring at Mara.

"You will tell me," Teach said, drawing a long, serrated dagger. "You will tell me, or the girl dies."

"No!" Peter cried, stepping forward, but a kick from the dark pirate sent him sprawling.

"This situation is simple," Teach said, testing the dagger with the tip of his finger. "You have something I want, I have something you want," the man shrugged. "Simple."

Peter and Mara exchanged looks, silently communicating with each other.

"Don't do it!" she screamed at him.

Teach raised his hand then slapped her hard across the face.

She fell to the ground but brushed her hair out of her face with her bound hands, her eyes pleading a single word to her brother.

Leave.

Hot tears pooled in Peter's eyes and he shook his head.

"No," he said shaking his head adamantly. "I won't."

Teach sighed heavily. "I'm rarely wrong, you know. I thought threats would loose your tongues. I see now it will take something sharper. We will find the fairies with or without your assistance, and we'll burn this island to the ground if we have to!"

Teach raised the dagger above his head.

"Fly, Peter, fly!" Mara shrieked. "If you don't warn them, they'll die!"

The pirate plunged his dagger into Mara's stomach.

"No!" Peter screamed, diving toward Teach.

The bearded pirate stepped in front of Peter, blocking his way and punched him in the stomach. The breath left him in a painful gasp as the kick sent him careening into the wall, then dropping to the floor.

Peter, nearly unconscious, rolled to his side to avoid the boot that stomped down next to his face. He scrambled to his feet and tried to run, but his knees buckled under him as Mad Rogue, conscious again, leapt out from the shadows and drove him to the ground.

He clambered away from the insane pirate, running out of places to retreat to.

He glared at Teach but the man just smiled back.

"You've got a choice," Teach said, sounding bored. "I've seen what that dust can do. And I'll bet her life," he said, pointing the bloody dagger at Mara's crumpled form, "that they can save her. Take me to them and she lives, or stay here and you both die. Either way, I will have my prize."

Peter stood on porcelain legs, afraid that the slightest step would leave him broken on the ground. Blood and sweat dripped from his body and began to pool at his feet. The dry floorboards happily soaked up what Peter thought might be the last contribution he would make to the world.

He said nothing.

The blades trembled in his hands as the two pirates readied their weapons again. They paused for a moment, then struck.

The bearded man was upon Peter, hacking and slashing at him. Then the second man advanced, this time swinging at Peter's chest. Peter leaned back to avoid it, but that's when his legs buckled. He staggered back, his balance lost. The pirate seized the opportunity and kicked him hard in the chest, rocketing him backwards.

His daggers flew from his hands as he slammed into the mast. He crumbled to the ground, coming to rest on his back. He stayed there, motionless, staring up as the moon watched him through the slats in the ceiling.

"I suppose we won't be needing this anymore," the dark-skinned man laughed, picking up his father's dagger and tossing it out the port hole into the sea.

"Or this one," the other man laughed, finding Peter's coral dagger and sending it out the same hole.

"I think our friend's usefulness has run its course, would you agree, Cap'n?" the bearded pirate asked, turning his head toward Teach.

Teach looked toward Mara, moaning on the deck, and then back to Peter and nodded.

Painfully, Peter rolled over to his stomach and looked up to find his sister staring at him.

"I'm so sorry, Mara," Peter said.

"Go!" Mara croaked.

Every muscle in Peter's body tensed as he gathered what he hoped would be enough strength to fly.

"I love you, Mara. I'll come back for you, I promise," he sobbed.

The two pirates raised their weapons to strike when Peter shot up into the rafters.

The deck blasted into debris as Peter threw himself through the ceiling, screaming like a banshee.

Pirates scattered in all directions as the near-dead, flying boy ripped through the ship, bursting through sails and riggings as he departed. Pirates screamed in terror as he soared into the night, the sky thundering his departure.

The thunder subsided, wrapping the ship in an eerie silence. The only sounds came from the rigging and wood that splashed into the cove.

And then the crazed voice of Mad Rogue: "Peter Pan can fly?"

TWENTY THREE

P eter continued to fly up. Somewhere, a small part of him knew he should stop or at least slow down. But the part that was in control seemed stuck on a single word.

Fly.

He puffed through the clouds, continuing deep into the night sky. The wind squeezed tears out of his squinted eyes as he continued to pick up speed. Finally, he stopped. His vacant eyes stared at a moon that looked close enough to touch. He reached for it, but his eyes rolled back into his head and everything went black.

* * *

"If you're not moving, you're dead," Siene remembered Rike telling her. He had been referring to a patroller's eyes – moving eyes were effective eyes.

So Siene remained all-seeing, scanning the forest below, the sky in front and behind her.

After the last kite attack, the fairies had began patrolling the absolute apex of their flying abilities. At these heights they could see the entire island and much of the surrounding sea; White Falls was the merest speck far below.

Patrols at this altitude were especially dangerous. Strong gusts of wind threatened to knock even the most controlled flyer out of the sky.

Most kites rarely risked the winds this high up, which was exactly why Siene's patrol was here.

A movement above Siene caught her eye.

"There!" she said, pointing to the dark object.

"That's no kite." Rike said. "Too large."

The dark object was picking up speed. Rike was right, it was too big for a bird. Realization rocked her small frame.

"It's Peter!" Siene cried, recognizing Peter's limp form. She took off, flying toward him.

The party followed her as she chased after him. She caught up to him and began tugging at his shirt, trying to slow his descent.

"Pull," she urged.

The six fairies strained against Peter's weight, pulling at his legs, shirt, hair and arms.

"He's too heavy," Siene gasped. "We need help," she said, flaring into golden brilliance.

"Are you insane?" Tolan shouted. "He's not worth alerting every bird on the island."

"Yes, he is!" she yelled back.

Tolan didn't respond but added his own glow to Siene's as the other fairies ignited. Fairies from all parts of the island began streaking toward the group, taking up positions above and below Peter. But the group continued to fall. Peter's tattered clothes snapped in the wind as they plummeted toward the black water below. More fairies joined in on the group, but still he fell.

"Get him over land," Tolan yelled. "He'll drown if he falls in the water."

"He's dead either way if we can't slow him," another fairy yelled over the roar of the wind.

Several fairies moved to Peter's side and began to push. Slowly, his body angled toward the beach rather than the open water.

Hundreds of fairies continued to pour up from the forest, taking hold of his hair, parts of his clothing, and limbs. Finally, the boy began to slow.

Then the birds came.

The flock fell upon the glowing mass of fairies like a black cloud, swallowing their light. They slashed and pecked at the fairies, inflicting as much damage as they could, not caring about who they targeted.

The fairies, their attention now split between defending themselves and saving Peter, found themselves with no good options. Peter began to pick up speed again. Some turned to fight, attempting to drive the birds away, while others stayed with the boy, dodging wing-strikes and slashes from beaks and talons.

Still, fairies continued to stream into the chaos-filled sky. Another large group of fairies, warriors rather than scouts, slammed into the ranks of kites.

"Keep pulling!" Siene ordered her scouts, as the warriors began trading places with the scouts. Again, Peter's free fall slowed.

A few of the birds, recognizing Peter from their last skirmish, started to attack him directly. They dived towards him, slashing with their talons as they flew by. A bold kite dived from above the pack and, landing on Peter, locked his talons deep into the boy's side.

Siene released her hold on Peter, drew a dagger, and severed the bird's leg with a single swing. The bird screeched in pain and released his remaining talon, then disappeared back into the fray.

The chaotic battle grew more intense as they grew closer to the ground. More fairies swelled around Peter, slowing him even more. They neared tree height and Siene hoped against all hope that they had slowed Peter enough to save him.

The entire mass of fairies, kites, and Peter hurtled into the sand, the impact sending kites and fairies flying in all directions.

Peter, still unconscious, lay unmoving on the sand, a peaceful contrast to the chaos that stormed around him.

Fairies, stunned from the impact, began to find their bearings and returned to Peter's side. Siene tugged at the severed talon that still clenched his side, but it wouldn't budge.

"Lift!" she yelled.

Peter began to rise. The fairies half carried, half dragged Peter though the forest toward the falls. The tradeoff between fighting kites and moving Peter made the journey seem endless but they eventually reached the top of the falls. The fairies dragged Peter through the same tunnel he had sneaked through weeks earlier. They pulled him through the passages and down to the floor of the great hall.

The fighting moved from the open skies to the cavern interior as the kites followed the fairies through their once-secret entrances.

Every fairy in the cave poured into the great hall, throwing themselves at the intruding birds.

Queen Adelaide was among them, armed with a long, golden staff. The staff blurred as she twirled it around herself, spinning away from talon-strikes and using it to shatter any beak foolish enough to come within range.

The battle had become a free for all. Fairies and kites alike began to drop to the ground. The fairies' normal bright glow flickered into darkness as they died, while the kites merely crashed into the stone floor, twitching in the throes of death.

The birds kept coming, and Siene's resolve was beginning to wane.

She caught her cousin's eye. The queen clearly read the uncertainty and fear on Siene's face. Adelaide gave her a nod as she wiped blood from her eyes.

Siene raised her head, feeling resilience starting to rekindle inside her. The message was clear. If tonight marked the end of White Falls, they would make the kites pay dearly for it.

Siene exhaled, selected her next target, and prepared to strike when the waterfall erupted, showering the room with water as seven dark figures burst through the falls.

Mermaids.

With the traitorous Shiiklah in the lead.

Apparently the villainous creatures wanted to bear witness to their final moments as well.

So be it.

Siene's blades had hungered for mer-scales long enough.

This would be a fitting end.

To her astonishment, though, instead of attacking the fairies, the mermaids formed a circle around Peter, shielding him from attacking birds. Then they began raking kites out of the air with their hands and tearing them apart. Others chose to impale the birds mid-flight with their thin coral blades and javelins. Regardless of their method of attack, one thing was consistent – they all avoided injuring the fairies.

A few minutes later, the fight was over.

The last remaining birds had fled, and those left wounded on the ground were being finished by the mermaids. The wounded fairies, however, they left untouched.

"What do you want, traitor?" Adelaide yelled, pointing her staff at the mermaid chieftess. "Have you come to finish what you began?"

"Hold your tongue," came the mermaid's sharp reply.

The remaining fairies rushed forward toward the mermaids. Shiiklah bared her sharp teeth and hissed at the oncoming cloud.

But Adelaide raised a hand and the cave fell silent; the charging warriors instantly stopped in mid-flight.

"What's your business, mermaid?" Adelaide demanded. "Have you brought pirates to our sanctuary as well?"

"The Pan Hakki is wounded, we have come to mend him," she replied, ignoring the fairy's insult.

"What did you call him?" Adelaide gasped, shock etched on her tiny face.

She looked from Shiiklah to Peter, but the mermaid ignored her question.

"A human? The Pan Hakki? Impossible," Adelaide pressed.

"We do not expect you to understand our wayss," the mermaid spat, her black eyes reflecting the glow of every fairy in the cave.

The cloud of fairies parted as she moved through them and bent down over Peter.

"He reeks of dust," she hissed, recoiling in disgust. "What have you done to him?"

Adelaide circled Peter and Shiiklah, her head cocked thoughtfully as she considered her response.

"He fell into the reservoir," she said, her eyes looking up to the glowing openings in the cave ceiling. "He's been able to fly ever since."

"And he's alive? He hass not gone mad?" Shiiklah asked, looking into Adelaide's eyes.

Adelaide shook her head. "No," she replied. "He's different. But you already knew that, didn't you, mermaid?"

Shiiklah looked up at her but said nothing. She began inspecting Peter's wounds. She gingerly felt his swollen cheek, then reached one hand inside his mouth and gently began to coax his cheek bones back into place. She ran her hands down his arms, feeling for breaks in the bone. She began filling his cuts with a black and green tar-like paste that she pulled from a pouch tied around her waist, then wrapped the injuries in strips of kelp. She removed the claw from his side, tossing the dead thing across the cave.

"His legs," Adelaide offered.

Shiiklah finished her inspection of his upper body and moved to his legs. His purple and black legs were filled with splinters and bruises.

"This is sship decking," she said, carefully lifting a leg and inspecting it more closely.

Marria the Healer drifted down toward Peter's leg but retreated when Shiiklah hissed at her.

"We can remove the splinters easier than you can," Adelaide insisted.

Shiiklah looked from Peter's wounds to the fairy then grunted in agreement.

A score of fairies cautiously descended on Peter and began tugging the wood from his legs and sprinkling dust in the wounds. The fairies worked around Shiiklah as she continued to work on his other, more serious, injuries.

"How did this happen?" Shiiklah demanded.

"We don't know," Siene replied, joining Adelaide's side. "We saw him falling out of the sky, near the cove. Peter, his sister, and a scouting party had chased pirates out of the falls," she said sorrowfully. "When none of them returned, we feared the worst and have been searching for them ever since. How did you know he was here?" she asked.

"Even a blind scout can see a thousand fairies in the night sky," Shiiklah replied.

Shiiklah pointed a scaly arm toward Peter's wrists. "He's been bound," she said. "Piratesss," she hissed.

"That must be where Mara is too, then," Adelaide added. She snapped her fingers softly in Tolan's direction.

"The cove," she mouthed to him.

He quickly assembled a patrol and departed through the ceiling.

As if in response to his sister's name, Peter stirred, choking and coughing out blood.

"Mara," he sputtered, trying to sit up.

"Don't move," Shiiklah ordered. "You're wounded."

"We've got to save Mara!" Peter croaked. "She's hurt, Teach stabbed her. She sent me to warn you. He's going to burn the forest to find White Falls."

He coughed again, spitting more blood from his mouth. "We need to save her."

"Where is she?" Adelaide asked.

Peter told the fairies and mers everything that had happened from the time they had left the falls to Peter's escape to warn the others.

"We've got to get to her, if we can bring her back, the dust can heal her. If we have a small party, we can sneak in and rescue her," he said, trying to rise again.

"No," Shiiklah said, pushing him back down to the ground.

Fairies began landing on him, weighing him down until he was pressed firmly against the stone floor.

"Get off me!" he cried. "She's dying, we need to save her!"

"No," Shiiklah said, shaking her head. "I will not endanger mers for a human."

"Blood matters!" Peter yelled, finally managing to sit up. "And hers is mine!"

The mermaid stopped, obviously considering his words. She turned to a few of the mers in her party and hissed something to them. The mers began to melt back into the waterfall until only five remained. Shiiklah turned back toward Peter.

"Blood matters, Pan Hakki," was her final response.

Peter looked to Adelaide. She nodded and a handful of fairies, broadswords still in their hands, drifted out of the crowd and toward him.

Peter struggled to his feet and began pulling off his kelp bandages.

Shiiklah moved to stop him.

"You are too injured to go," she insisted.

He limped toward the waterfall. "There's no way I'm staying here," he said.

"Shiiklah is right," Adelaide agreed. "You can hardly walk, how can you fight?"

"I don't need my legs to fight," he snapped and lifted off the cave floor. "See?" he said, turning back to face them. "I-" his voice trailed off.

Siene watched as Peter saw the carnage for the first time. Mangled kites and the gray ashen bodies of dead fairies littered the entire cave. Large parts of the cave walls – the dwellings and chambers that had been carved into the stone and adorned with glass, gems and gold – were smashed and ruined.

"What happened?" Peter whispered. "How did this happen?"

His mouth crumpled into a frown as he tried to piece together what had happened.

"How did I get here?" he asked.

"We saw you falling," Siene said. "We managed to slow your fall enough to land you on the beach, but the kites saw us and attacked. We carried you back here, but they fought us the entire way. We had hoped they'd leave once we'd gotten you inside," she said, indicating around her, "but they followed us down."

"They would have gotten us all, if they hadn't shown up," she admitted, nodding towards the mermaids.

"All this because of me?" Peter whispered.

He landed softly, but his legs gave out, forcing him to sit.

"You saved me?" he said, looking from the fairies assembled to the mermaids. "All this because of me?" he asked, looking at all the bodies.

His eyes grew wet and then he began to cry.

"I'm so sorry," he sobbed. "We should have never come here. We should have stayed at home," he said, shaking his head in disbelief. "This is all my fault," he said, putting his face on ground. "Please forgive me."

Siene landed lightly on his shoulder.

"Our actions are our own," she said.

"How can I ever repay this?" he cried.

"We chose to save you," Adelaide's gentle voice said. "Any price is ours to bear, not yours."

"No," Shiiklah said. "Teach."

Siene twisted around to look at Shiiklah, surprised that the mermaid had shifted the blame from the fairies to Teach.

The mermaid held her gaze for a moment, then looked away.

Peter's sobbing had turned to heavy, laborious breathing. He rose on trembling legs, but they gave out, sending him to the ground again. Instead, he lifted off, giving up on walking and opting to fly instead.

"Shiiklah's right," he said, wiping his eyes. "Teach has brought chaos and death from the moment he entered your waters. He turned all of you against each other. His plan has been your destruction, and it's working."

He looked out across the cave again, then turned back to Shiiklah. "Are you ready?" he said.

She dipped her head in acknowledgement. "To the *Dawnriser.*"

"He's moved her," an exhausted-sounding voice called.

Siene looked up to see Tolan and his patrol returning. The fairy, drenched with sweat from his flight, panted heavily as he forced out his words.

"They're all worked up over Peter's escape. Teach moved Mara to the mansion. We should find her there."

"What mansion?" Peter demanded.

"On the cliffs, at the edge of the cove," Siene replied. "It's been abandoned for ages."

"Thank you," Peter said, then flew through the falls and into the black night.

Shiiklah looked back to Adelaide and took one final look around White Falls before slipping into the falls with her warriors.

TWENTY FOUR

Peter flew.

He half-closed his eyes against the wind as he pushed himself faster. His path was dimly lit by the small group of fairies flying around him, straining to match his pace. Their light glinted off of the mer's scales as they glided noiselessly just beneath the water's surface.

The old mansion came into view – a huge old house built into the cliff wall. Peter maintained his speed and aimed for the main door.

He closed his eyes and slammed into the door. His shoulder erupted in pain as the door exploded off its hinges, slamming into a group of pirates playing cards in the middle of the room.

Siene and Tolan zipped from man to man, hacking and stabbing with their tiny blades. The men screamed in terror. A few tried to flee, making it as far as the doorway only to impale themselves on coral blades as mers came rushing in.

But Peter had eyes for none of them. He continued into the next room – a narrow room lined with rows of bunks – but there was no sign of Teach. He soared past pirates in their beds, blankets and pillows flying in the air in his wake.

The next room was empty and dark. Peter stopped and looked around, his already battered body buzzed with numbness from breaking down the door, but he pushed it from his mind and tried to focus.

The sounds of pirates fighting for their lives grew louder and louder behind him as the mers and fairies fought through the bunkroom.

Peter started to think that he had come to a dead end when his eye caught light coming from the corner of the room. He flew near it and found stairs leading down into a well-lit room, probably a cellar. He flew down the stairs and found them: Mara and Teach.

The pirate was dragging Mara toward the far wall.

"Teaaaach!" he screamed and flew toward the a man.

The man started and turned to see Peter careening toward him. He drew a pistol and let go of Mara, then sprinted toward the wall. He fired blindly behind him as he ran, a wild shot that hissed harmlessly past Peter. Teach reached the wall and turned one of the stone bricks.

The wall grumbled and mouthed open. Teach dived through the opening as the hidden door slammed shut.

Peter was at Mara's side immediately, holding her head up, ignoring the pirate's escape.

"Mara, I'm here, we're going to get you better," he said.

"No, Peter," she said weakly.

"Yes!" he cried. "You're going to be fine. You have to be fine."

"It's okay," she said. "It's okay."

"No, no, we're going to get you back to White Falls and we'll get you patched up," he nearly shouted. He looked around the room for something, anything to help move his sister.

"Peter," she said, grabbing his hand and pulling him back to her. Her hand felt cold in his.

"You need to be strong," she said.

Peter shook his head; hot tears began to pool in his eyes.

"You can't blame yourself for this," she continued. "Don't you dare."

She coughed hard, and her breathing was labored as she tried to continue.

"You saved the others, you warned them. It's okay. Father would be so proud of you."

This was too much for Peter. He spun on Shiiklah and the fairies who had descended the stairs.

"Why aren't you doing anything?" he spat. "Use your bloody dust, get her out of here!"

Siene looked down and away.

"We are too late," Shiiklah replied.

He turned back to Mara, her face looked ghostly white in the dark room.

"I love you, silly boy," she whispered. "It's okay, it's okay."

"You can't go," he whimpered, shaking his head. "You can't leave me. Please, please don't leave me."

He held her cold hands in his, willing his own warmth to save her. He stared into her eyes, begging her to stay.

She smiled weakly and stared back, her eyes filling with love, then sadness, then nothing.

An animal sob choked out of Peter, then a groan that grew into a tempest. It screamed out of him in a rush of anger and grief and it grew until he was screaming at the top of his lungs.

He flew to the wall that Teach had escaped through and clawed at the stones, trying to find a way in.

"You're a dead man!" he screamed. "You are a dead man!"

He flew back to his sister's body and cradled her head in his arms.

"Mara," he sobbed.

Then he was on his feet again, a mad light in his eyes.

"We've got to get her back, we can still save her," he said.

He took a step toward the group, but his leg gave way and he dropped to a knee. He tried to rise, but the room began to spin and fold in on him. He stumbled to the ground and slipped into unconsciousness.

TWENTY FIVE

Peter sat alone on the beach.

Alone.

Siene had told him that Shiiklah and the rest of the mermaids had carried both Peter and Mara back to White Falls after they killed every living thing in the mansion. Teach had been the only one to survive the attack.

There had been no sign of him since he disappeared into the cellar's hidden passage.

Peter had alternated between unconsciousness and sleep for three days, and in that time Shiiklah and her mers had worked tirelessly with the fairies to mend him.

His physical wounds would heal – many of them were already

healed. The combination of the mermaid salves and fairy dust was astounding. Who knew the two would work so well together? It seemed they could heal almost anything.

Almost.

Waves rumbled up from the ocean's deep belly and rolled toward the shore, each wave hurling itself onto the white sand, losing its strength, then draining back into the sea leaving no impact, no sign that it had been there. The waves hissed at him, a mocking song that reminded him that nothing he did mattered.

He picked up a handful of sand and watched it run through his fingers until there was nothing left. He picked up another handful and felt the grains fall away. Each time he was left with nothing.

It seemed that fate would strike his heart with every pain it knew: the dull, ever-present sadness of never knowing his mother, the shocking stab of having his father ripped from his life, and the frantic tearing he felt as he watched the life fade from his sister.

He looked at his hands. Mara's blood still stained the creases of his palms and crusted under his fingernails. A fresh ache in his heart made its way to his stomach and he wanted to retch.

"Keep her safe," his father had told him.

"Keep her safe," he repeated aloud, turning his hands over to hide the blood.

His father had charged him with protecting his sister. The orders had filled Peter with pride and duty. He had basked in the approval that his father had thought him man enough to protect his family.

Now, months later and a thousand miles away, he was just a stupid boy on a beach with blood on his hands.

He thought about his mother. He imagined what she might have looked like. He imagined her cursing the boy she had birthed.

He thought about his father and the shame he would feel if he knew how terribly his son had failed him.

And he thought about Mara. He thought about her cold, lifeless body wrapped in a death shroud, laying in a cave.

She would have to be buried. But putting her in the ground meant accepting that she was gone forever and he couldn't do that yet.

The fairies wanted to bury her in the forest, in the clearing where they buried their own. Shiiklah wanted to bury her in the coral fields, in the underwater cavern. There her body would eventually nourish new coral that would be grown into weapons – weapons that would kill pirates.

Peter wanted to trade places with her.

"Mara," he whispered, "I'm so sorry. I love you with all the broken pieces of my heart."

The soft whipping of tiny wings faintly registered as a fairy landed beside him. It was Adelaide. She settled on a fist-sized rock next to him and sat. The normal retinue that surrounded her was gone.

Neither of them said anything. There were no words that could comfort him because grief was unnatural. And words had no power against something as alien as grief.

The pair sat, silently staring out at the sea.

Another wave broke on the shore and then Shiiklah was in front of them. She melted out of the waves the way only a mermaid could and moved noiselessly through the shallows. She said nothing but sat supportively, if not awkwardly, on Peter's other side.

Peter was the first to break the silence.

"It's pointless," he said after a few minutes had passed. "Everyone is dead, and for what? Nothing."

Minutes passed as the question hung in the air.

"When is the last time a mer hasss sat on the beach with a fairy?" Shiiklah asked, finally responding to him.

Adelaide smiled sadly. "Many years," she replied, still looking out at the sea. "Peter," Adelaide started. "The impact you and your sister have left on this island is greater than you know. Mers and fairies worked together for the first time in many years."

She paused, considering her next words, then continued.

"Mara's sacrifice was anything but meaningless. Her refusal to give up White Falls saved every fairy on the island and undoubtedly the island itself. But moreover, it showed us that honor has not completely abandoned Man."

Her last words got Peter's attention. His eyes widened, remembering Kinarah, the old mermaid who had been present at his Pan Hakki ceremony. She had spoken those exact words to him as well.

"Anger will only keep you from seeing that," Adelaide continued.

"Still," Peter said, the brief moment of whatever it was he was feeling – purpose? – faded away.

"It won't mean anything while Teach lives," he said. "This island will never be safe while he's alive, and I need my anger to kill him."

"Yes," agreed Shiiklah.

"No," Adelaide said, speaking at the same moment as the mermaid.

"What would Mara want?" the fairy quickly said, before Shiiklah could say any more.

Peter closed his eyes.

He thought of Mara and her smile that would explode across her face. He thought of the way she always managed to ground him in reality – if only momentarily. He thought of how she always had enough room in her heart for one more person. He thought of her love for Siene and Adelaide and all the fairies. And he knew that it was love that made her sacrifice herself for them.

Love and sacrifice were Mara. She choose those she loved over herself.

Mara's death had been her sacrifice, not Peter's mistake. He knew that, and yet, he also knew that her death was still his fault. And he knew it would take him a long time to wrestle through what that meant.

"What would Mara want?" he repeated.

***

Siene sat hugging her knees and stared at the thin embalming veil that separated her from Mara's body. That thin veil was all that seemed to separate her from death and Mara from life.

A tiny question had worked its way into Siene's mind. It had started as a quiet whisper of a thought that inexorably grew into a single, burning question: could a human be resolved?

The question had consumed Siene for nearly two days. For a fairy, a Resolution had to be completed before a fairy's essence faded. She wondered if the human essence might take longer to fade since they were so much bigger--if humans even had essences.

She knew that Adelaide would never approve of this kind of thinking. But she couldn't help it.

Mara's brief time on the island had brought the two of them very close. Mara had become something of a sister to her. And she couldn't let Mara slip away into oblivion.

Siene blinked, surprised at how made up her mind had already been. Swallowing hard, she got to her feet, drew her glow in around herself as to not be spotted by others, and quietly ran toward her friend's body.

She climbed the veil that wrapped around Mara's legs, then scurried up to stand on her chest. She looked around to make sure no one had noticed her, and then turned back to Mara.

Siene had seen the Resolution performed countless times. She knew Adelaide's lines by heart.

"What is your wish concerning this fairy?" Siene could almost hear her cousin's voice.

"I wish to resolve her," the Resolver would respond.

Then Adelaide would announce the Resolver's intention, whisper the Words, the light would flash, and then it would be done.

Siene bit her lip thoughtfully.

"Okay," she said, thinking aloud. "Siene, what is your wish concerning this," she almost said "fairy," but caught herself. "Human?" she said.

"I wish to resolve her," she said, answering herself. "Now what?" she wondered. "What could the Words possibly be?"

She had no idea what passed between Queen and Resolver. Was it some magical command that unlocked something inside of the fairies? Maybe it was... Siene sighed heavily. She had no idea what it was that brought the Resolution.

"I'm a fool for thinking I could invoke it at will," she chided herself.

She released the hold on her light and flared back into brilliance.

"I'm sorry, Mara," she whispered.

She kissed her hand, bent down, and gently touched her palm to the white veil.

"Goodbye, my friend," she said, slowly rising and turning to leave.

As she turned, she bumped into something – Tolan.

"Are you okay?" he asked, making sure his blade hadn't cut her.

"Yes, I'm fine. What are you doing here?" she asked.

"Adelaide ordered that we add the Falls entrance to our patrols, just to be safe," he said.

"Because of the mers?" she asked.

"Or pirates," he replied. "Or just to keep us from going mad while she figures out what to do," he smiled. "What were you really doing here?" he asked.

"Just saying goodbye," she replied, avoiding his eyes.

"She was surprising, wasn't she?" Tolan said, looking down at Mara's shrouded body.

Siene looked up at him.

"She's not how I remembered humans," he continued. "Mara made me feel like there might be hope for them."

"Still, it's a pity," he said, looking from Mara back to Siene and resting a hand on her shoulder. "This isn't the ending I expected," he said. "For either of you."

Siene went rigid with fear. Had he heard what she had said below? Would he turn her in? What else could he mean? She quickly looked away again.

"I…I don't know what you mean," she lied, her mind racing.

"Siene," he laughed softly, shaking his head, "you're a terrible liar."

He leaned toward her, kissed her cheek, then whispered in her ear.

***

"We need to find Teach," Peter was saying.

"Peter…" Adelaide started to say.

"No, no, no," he said, waving her off. "Mara died so White Falls wouldn't be discovered, but the island is far from at peace. Teach is the chaos that destroyed your peace. You were united before he came. Now, all your time is spent fighting each other. It was him and only him, not Shiiklah, who's responsible for the death of the elders. He's the enemy, not them," he said, pointing out to the water.

"But, had Teach not first deceived us – me – the Council would ssstill be in tact," Shiiklah countered. "The shame is mine to bear. The pixies and sky fish are correct in their rage; it is I who should bear their retribution."

"Still," Adelaide said thoughtfully. "Our ire may be best directed toward Teach, rather than by Teach."

"Good," Peter said. "We need to show him that this place is off-limits to pirates. We need to show them that our island is not tame."

"We kill Teach," Shiiklah said flatly.

"No. Death is too good for that scum," Peter said. "He's renowned among pirates. Look at all the ships he's amassed! We'll use Edward Teach to send a message to the rest of the world. We make this place a nightmare for any pirate who sets foot on it; if you land here, you never leave."

"How will we accomplish that?" Adelaide asked.

"We sack the fleet," Peter replied. "We'll let one, maybe two ships escape to tell the tale."

"The entire fleet?" Shiiklah asked.

"They'll never expect it," he said. "And with our combined forces, we'll have a chance. Then the island will have peace."

"Shiiklah," Peter said, turning to the mer chieftess, "how many warriors can you get?"

She paused. "It will take sssome time to assemble and convince the clan chiefs, if they agree to it at all."

"Tell them Peter Pan Hakki commands them," he said.

"That may just make them more angry," she snorted. "There are still many who protest it."

"Well," Peter said, "blood matters." He smiled and held up his scared palm to her. "And I'm mer."

"Indeed," she grumbled.

"Adelaide?" Peter asked, turning to the fairy queen.

She considered.

"Perhaps it is time to put an end to the pirate-led harassment of our island," she said, finally. "But what about the kites?" she asked. "We're still at war with them," Adelaide said. "They've been attacking us since," she paused, glanced at Shiiklah, then continued, "since Teach killed the Council elders."

"Hmm," Peter considered.

"We've located their new nesting grounds, so we know where to strike, but we can't justify wiping them out just to be rid of them. Still, they're stubborn creatures," she said.

"Maybe we can use that fact, and the prospect of a new enemy, to redirect them," Peter offered.

"We don't need sky fish," Shiiklah sniffed.

"It's worth a try," Adelaide said, ignoring Shiiklah. "Although, I don't think sending fairies to Kite Nest would go over well. They're simple creatures. I don't know that they'll believe that Teach was the one behind the elders' death and not Shiiklah."

"Who is their current leader?" Peter asked.

"Kite Grath," Adelaide replied. "In fact, it was his talon Shiiklah dug out of your side," she said, pointing at his still-bandaged torso.

"Well," Peter considered. "Since sending a group of fairies would end in fighting, and mers can't climb trees, it seems like I'm the only one left to talk to them. I'll visit their nests and talk to Kite Grath and see if we can't sway them. We can't move–"

Adelaide held up a hand to silence him, then turned toward the forest, frowning.

"What is it?" Peter asked.

A pair of lights shot out of the forest and onto the beach.

"Majesty!" the leader, a scout, cried.

"What is it?" she asked.

"It's Siene," he said. "Something's happened."

"What?" the queen demanded.

The scout hesitated, glancing sidelong at Shiiklah.

"Ssspeak," the mermaid said, a dark smile creasing her face. "We are allies now."

The fairy's eyes widened in disbelief. Shiiklah's grin broadened, no doubt enjoying the fairy's shock.

"What is it?" Adelaide asked again, drawing the scout's attention back to her. "What's happened to Siene?"

"She's," the scout started, searching for words. "She's not Siene."

"Take me to her," Adelaide said, rising into the air.

"Shiiklah, we–" she started to say.

"We will ssscout the bay and alert you when Teach surfaces," the mermaid finished.

Minutes later Peter and Adelaide were in White Falls, standing in front of a pair of fairies – Siene and a fairy dressed in a white gown.

"Evee, what's going on?" Adelaide demanded.

"We're not sure, Majesty" the fairy in white, Evee, replied. "She hasn't answered any of our questions."

"I don't understand," Peter said, stepping up to the fairy. "This is Siene."

"No, it isn't," Adelaide said sternly, staring at the fairy. "Siene has been resolved."

"Resolved?" Peter asked.

"When one of us is near death," Evee said, "we can merge ourselves with the dying fairy. Both fairies lose their identity and become someone new."

"So who did she...resolve with?" Peter asked.

Then his eye caught his sister's shrouded form.

"What? No, what?" he exclaimed. "You didn't... Mara?! Is, she? Are you? Someone tell me what this means!" he said, growing frantic.

"She needs to be named," Evee said, ignoring Peter's hysterics.

"Belle," Adelaide said, without hesitation. "Tinker Belle. I imagine you will have great difficulty not interfering with things best left alone."

"It was the only way to save her," the fairy, Tinker Belle, said.

Adelaide's tiny chest heaved with a sigh.

"Something tells me you're going to give me grief for a long time," she said.

Tinker Belle shrugged. "Who can say?" she smiled.

"Are you Siene?" Peter asked, approaching her.

"In a way," she said, then squinted her eyes in thought. "But, no."

"Do you have Siene's memories?" Peter asked.

"Not in the way you're thinking, but yes," she said, still smiling. "But she's not the one you're really asking about."

"Okay," Peter admitted, taking a deep breath. "Are, are you my sister?"

"She's..." the fairy began, searching for the right words. "You're not alone."

"What does this mean?" Peter asked, looking from face to face. Grief and hope and confusion all mixing together inside him. "I don't know what I should feel," he said. "I, I don't know who you are."

"I know this is strange," Tinker Belle said. "I'll make it easy."

She reached out and extended her hand. Peter shook it cautiously with a finger.

"I'm Tinker Belle," she said. "And we're going to be great friends."

Peter smiled at her, as the emotions warring inside him began to tip ever so slightly from grief to joy.

"Now," Tinker Belle said. "Don't we have some pirates to kill?"

"Unfortunately, yes we do," Adelaide answered. "Peter, see if you can convince the kites to join us," she said. Then her gaze slid back to Tinker Belle. "And take this one with you. I want her out of the way while I find out who aided her in the Resolution."

"Good luck," Tinker Belle winked.

TWENTY SIX

Built between three giant trees deep in the heart of the northern wood, Kite Nest was a mass of branches, dirt, and debris that looked more like a fortress than a nest: a giant bowl suspended high above the ground and filled with hundreds of smaller nests. The bastion of the red kites was an impressive sight to say the least.

Peter, with Siene--or Tinker Belle, or whoever she was – at his side, flew toward the nest.

He kept sneaking glances at the fairy when she wasn't looking. She still looked like Siene. Maybe this Resolution thing wasn't all the fairies thought it was. Other than a weird new name, Tinker Belle seemed exactly like Siene to him.

"I can see you looking at me," the fairy said, looking sidelong at him. "Silly boy."

Peter quickly looked away. "I was just looking at that tree," he said, pointing to the forest as his face reddened.

Tinker Belle smiled.

"Come on," she said. "Let's get this over with."

Peter landed in the center of the nest with a crunch, sending dirt and broken twigs flying in all directions. A cloud of birds erupted out of the nest, taking to the skies. Their angry caws echoed throughout the forest as they flew. A moment later, Tinker Belle landed lightly on his shoulder, her hands hovering above the hilts of her daggers but not touching them.

Peter stood with his hands on his hips and stared at the lone large Kite that seemed unruffled by his arrival.

Instead of joining his brethren in flying dizzy circles around Peter, this one watched Peter with cold, dangerous eyes.

"Can he speak?" Peter asked, looking at Tinker Belle.

"He's a bird," she said, her brows raised. "No, he can't speak."

"Well, you exist," Peter said defensively. "I figured talking birds wouldn't be much more of a stretch."

The large raptor flapped once and rose to hop on its single remaining talon. Red and black feathers covered his meter-wide wings. The dark colors covered his entire body then graduated to white with black spots at his neck and head. He had yellow eyes that were dotted with black pupils.

"Lose something?" Peter asked, pointing to the bird's stump.

The bird's eyes grew stormy. It might not be able to speak, but it sure seemed to understand everything Peter said.

Peter produced the severed leg that Shiiklah had removed from his side and unceremoniously tossed it in front of the bird.

The bird's eyes widened and it squawked in surprise as it stared at its own dead limb. The narrowed eyes looked from the leg back to Peter then back to the leg. The Kite took a tentative hop toward it and nudged the still-clenched talons with his beak before turning to screech and clack angrily at Tinker Belle.

"It wasn't me," Tinker Belle said, a mischievous smile tugging at the corners of her mouth.

Technically, the fairy's statement was true since it had actually been Siene who had cut the leg off, not Tinker Belle. But Peter, who still didn't understand – or even fully believe – the Resolution, wasn't about to try and explain it to a bird.

Peter sat down, folding his legs under him.

"Are you sure about this?" Tinker Belle murmured, stealing glances at the still-cawing birds that circled them.

"Trust me," Peter whispered.

The bird clacked his beak at Peter, taking another hop toward him.

"We've come to talk, Grath," Peter said.

Adelaide had explained that with the death of the Council elders, the Kites experienced a leadership void, similar to the one Adelaide and her fairies had gone through. Grath Kite, young and inexperienced but well-respected, quickly ascended to power. Almost immediately upon assuming leadership, Grath sought out someone to blame for the death of their elders and they poured out their fury on their nearest neighbor: White Falls.

The bird twisted his head back and forth in what Peter took as head shaking.

"You know, we could have come in force," Peter warned.

The bird spread his wings and rose to his full height, an obvious effort to intimidate Peter.

"Ooo, scary bird," Peter taunted, waving his arms around in mock fear at the bird's gesture. But if he were being honest with himself, the bird was indeed quite terrifying.

"How many Kites live in the ground colony?" Peter asked, forcing thoughts of imminent doom away.

Whenever possible, the fairies would abstain from killing the birds in favor of cutting, or pulling out, their flight feathers. As a result, those who managed to return home after being rendered flightless were forced to live together on the forest floor. The population of birds there who were unable to fly and therefore unable to fully return home nearly outnumbered those who could.

Grath looked away from Peter.

"And how is your war with the fairies going?" Peter pressed.

Grath looked back at Peter with eyes that were less angry then they were a moment before but were instead filled with a sad resolve.

"Ah," Peter said to himself, as understanding clicked in place for him.

"Kites are creatures of honor, but they're growing desperate," Tinker Belle whispered. "The fact that they had openly assaulted White Falls is proof enough of their desperation. But surrender isn't a possibility for Grath. To surrender would mean great dishonor and shame for the Nest. Grath would maintain the honor of the Nest even at the expense of its own existence."

"Well, that's comforting," Peter whispered back. "Maybe we just need to nudge Grath in the right direction and let him maintain his bird-honor."

"I want to tell you a story," Peter said, returning his full attention to the bird.

Peter went on to tell the story of the Great Deception, not as the kites knew it, but as it had really happened, starting with Shiiklah's unwitting involvement in Teach's plan.

He explained how the death of the Accord Elders had brought just as much turmoil to the mer clans and fairies as it had to the kites.

After the attack, an injured Shiiklah had returned to her waters and was almost immediately accused of conspiring with Teach to murder the now-dead clan chiefs. Many were convinced that this had been her ultimate intention since it had been Shiiklah who had first proposed that Teach's appointment to the Council be considered.

With the six of the seven clan leaders dead, Shiiklah had been in a unique position to disband the clans and attempt to consolidate the them under a single leadership – hers.

She had never had any intention to do so, but before Shiiklah could defend her innocence, a civil war broke out. Spurned by grief and anger, the clans had turned on each other. Mer clans fought other mer clans for the first time in history. Sub-chiefs tried to wrest control of the clans from each other.

But after months of infighting, the quarreling began to subside and older, wiser voices began to be heard again.

In an effort to reestablish unity among clans, a once-forgotten tradition had been revived. Mers who displayed acts of great self-sacrifice, putting the needs of another mer above their own, were given a high honor. In addition, they were given a role of authority over all mers, regardless of clan.

This title, the Pan Hakki, slowly began to reknit the fabric of unity that had been torn by Teach's actions. Gradually, the clan lines had started to blur and mer-unity began to replace clan-unity.

Peter left out the part of the story where the most recently named Pan Hakki, himself, may have undone some of the unity that had been restored.

That story was for another day.

"The fairies, the kites, and the mers," Peter concluded, "every group has suffered because of Teach. Punish Teach, not each other. We need your help to stop him from destroying the island."

He finished speaking and waited for Grath's response.

The bird rocked on his remaining leg, considering Peter's words, then squawked angrily and waggled his stump towards Peter and Tinker Belle again.

"It's hopeless," Tinker Belle muttered. "The fighting did too much damage."

"Maybe not," Peter wondered aloud. "What if you could have your leg back?" he said, speaking to Grath.

The bird looked at the severed leg, then up at Peter.

"A new leg," he said.

The bird stared at him.

"Come with me," Peter said, lifting off the ground.

"What are you doing?" Tinker Belle demanded.

"We're going back to White Falls," he replied.

"We're what?" she demanded.

"If you want this to end, then you've got to make a gesture. A big one," Peter said.

"He was just in White Falls," she protested. "You saw what they did. He even tried to kill you!"

"Do you want to end the fighting?" Peter said, as the trio cleared the treetops. "Then give him his leg back."

"This isn't going to go well," Tinker Belle said.

She was right.

Upon entering the falls, the entire host of fairies had descended on Grath. It was only Adelaide's command to stop that saved the bird. And after a few moments of tension, the crowds dispersed, leaving only Peter, Tinker Belle, Grath, and Adelaide's willingness to try and set aside arms for the sake of peace.

An hour later, Grath was standing on two legs, inspecting the fairy's handiwork. A minute later, he was flying up through ceiling tunnels, then was gone.

"So… are they going to help us?" Tinker Belle asked. "Or am I going to have to cut that leg off again?"

"I thought that wasn't you," Peter said, winking at the fairy.

"Time will tell," Adelaide said. "We've done what we can to put an end to the fighting. It's up to Grath, now."

* * *

Days later, Adelaide, Tinker Belle, Peter, and Shiiklah met in

White Falls to discuss their plans for war.

"We have sspotted Teach," Shiiklah was saying. "He sneaked aboard his ship late last night."

"Good," Peter replied. "For this to work, we need him on his ship. The other captains look to him, and when we crush him, the others will falter."

"There are sseven ships anchored in the cove," Shiiklah added. "We felt the latest arrive this morning."

"Do we know how many ships are expected?" Adelaide asked.

"There are talks of one more, but not everyone is convinced it will come," Shiiklah replied.

"Peter, any word regarding Kite Nest?" Adelaide asked. "We haven't seen so much as a single bird in days."

Peter shook his head.

"Nothing," he said.

"We do not need ssky fish," Shiiklah added.

"Who's the eighth captain?" Tinker Belle asked, changing the subject.

"We do not know," Shiiklah said.

"It doesn't matter," Peter said. "A pirate is a pirate."

"Do we all understand the plan?" Peter asked, looking from person to person.

Everyone nodded in agreement.

"When do we begin?" Shiiklah asked.

"After dark," Peter said. "Everything is scarier at night."

TWENTY SEVEN

Wakey, wakey, Sommers!" Mad Rogue said, teasing the tip of his red feather on the sleeping man's nose.

The man, Sommers, woke with a start, his snore catching in his throat as he fell to the deck. Laughter erupted from all of the pirates within view.

"Rogue!" the pirate bellowed, swatting at the feather as he tried to get to his feet.

"Hahaha!" the crazed pirate laughed, placing the feather on the ship's railing. "Asleep on the railing? You're supposed to be on watch. Do I need to report you to Little Kite?"

Mad Rogue's eyes slid from the man to the red feather now resting on the ship's railing.

The man reached for the feather, trying to grab it before Mad Rogue could get to it. But the insane pirate was too quick. Just as Sommers' fingers brushed the tip of the feather, Mad Rogue snatched it away. And just as quickly, Mad Rogue drew a dagger and slammed it down on the man's hand, pinning him to the railing.

Sommers shrieked in pain, fitfully tugging at the buried hilt to free his hand.

Rogue danced behind the man, then leapt onto his back.

"No one touches Little Kite," he hissed into the man's ear. "No one."

"All right, Rogue," a voice from the crowd said. "I think he gets it."

"Did you see what he did, Captain Two?" Rogue protested, turning to face to the speaker. "Little Kite," he said, cradling the feather in his hands. "He...he touched him."

His name wasn't really Two, but after the flying boy had killed Captain London, the *Royal James* was in need of a new captain, and now the first mate was wearing the hat, making him the second captain – Captain Two. Mad Rouge had given him the name, and the crew had taken to it almost immediately.

"I know, I know," Two said. "But why don't you take Little Kite below deck and make sure he's okay."

Mad Rogue saluted and started to leave, then turned back as if remembering something. He reached over to the rail and yanked his dagger free of the wood, both unpinning the man and eliciting a fresh round of anguished cries.

Rogue sheathed his dagger and grinned, waggling his feather above his head as he walked away. The movement of the feather drew

Rogue's attention and the pirate looked up.

"Hmm. More stars out tonight," he said absently, then headed below deck.

The pirates within earshot looked up at the night sky.

"Look, a falling star!" a pirate exclaimed.

"Sink me, another one!" someone else said, as a second star fell out of the sky.

Then a third.

And a fourth.

Then all of the stars fell.

"Begad," Two whispered.

The night sky seemed to collapse as countless stars fell toward the cove, brilliant, golden light trailing them as they fell. They grew larger and brighter as they neared the ship, bathing the crows nests and then the masts in bright, golden light.

The captain's eyes widened as the stars grew closer.

"Raise the alarm!" he screamed, drawing a pistol with one hand and his sword with the other.

He took off at a dead run toward the quarter deck where the alarm bell was.

"Not stars! They're not stars!" he cried.

The stars flew straight down into the unsuspecting pirates on the upper deck. Cries of pain and terror filled the night sky as fairies – for they could be nothing else – rained down on the ship.

The captain bobbed and weaved around pirates. Some of the men flailed about with drawn swords, while others blindly fired guns in the air. He heard a fluttering sound behind him, then sharp pain blossomed in his neck. He swatted behind him with his pistol just as his calves erupted in white-hot agony. He stumbled but managed to stay on his feet and took a few more steps until that same burning pain erupted in his back and shoulders. The pain drove him to the deck, right at the base of the stairs leading up to the quarter deck. He rolled on his back, hoping to trap a few of the creatures beneath him and was relieved to feel several squirming lumps under him as he lay gasping for breath.

He tried to scramble to his feet, but his legs gave out under him. The light from the fairies behind him cast dark, eerie shadows on the steps in front of him. He crawled up the stairs after his shadow until the light from approaching fairies scrubbed it from the deck completely.

He was almost totally covered in fairies, each one of them stabbing or cutting. Despite the golden lights around him, his vision began to darken and he wondered if Captain Three, would last any longer. But just before everything went dark, he saw it – the alarm bell.

He stretched out his arm, aimed his pistol, and fired.

The last thing Two heard was the bright, clear tolls of the alarm bell as it echoed throughout the cove.

"Well, they know we're here," Peter said to Tinker Belle as they sat perched in the trees that lined the cove's shore.

The pair watched as nearly every fairy on the island rained down on the ships in golden brilliance.

The only sound that could be heard was the faint tolling of a bell from one of the ships.

"The mers are next?" Tinker Belle asked.

"Yup," Peter replied. "While they're all looking up, the mers come from below."

"And when do we go?" Tinker Belle asked, clearly itching to put her weapons to use.

"Well," Peter said. "There aren't any boats on the shore, so no one is on the island. So our job here is done."

"That was easy," Tinker Belle shrugged.

"The next part won't be," he said.

"Teach?" Tinker Belle asked.

"Teach," Peter confirmed. "Our job is to get close and wait for him to appear, then let everyone know where he is. The mermaids will be sabotaging most of the ships and then sneaking aboard from the lower decks to 'liberate' – as Shiiklah put it – as many pirates as they can."

"Heh, liberate," Tinker Belled snorted, "I like that."

Peter shook his head.

"Let's go," he said.

Tinker Belle dimmed her glow until she was completely dark, then climbed up onto Peter's back, and held on to the back of his shirt.

Peter stepped off the tree, then flew toward the ships.

As they drew closer to the fleet, Peter could hear thunderous booms as the mers slammed their muscular tails against the ships. The tails smashed though rudders, snapped keels, and weakened portholes. The reverberations traveled up the ship, unbalancing pirates. Sometimes the shaking was just enough to throw off their aim as they fought the fairies, while other times it was enough to send them tumbling overboard where they met foes more deadly than fairies.

Peter, with Tinker Belle still on his back peering over his shoulder, hovered near the *Dawnriser* and waited for signs of the pirate leader.

Just off of the *Dawnriser's* starboard side, another ship drifted aimlessly, its anchor chains snapped, its rudder floating uselessly on the water's surface. The two ships bumped into each other, scraping side by side. The collision wasn't bad enough to damage the ships badly, but it did send every man on board sprawling.

Peter circled the two ships in an effort to get a better look at the *Dawnriser.*

All around, fairies continued to battle with ambushed pirates on the upper decks – dodging gun fire and sword slashes while zipping in to strike at hands, backs and throats. But the initial shock of being taken unaware had begun to fade and the pirates were recovering.

A large group of fairies were harassing a smaller group of pirates on the *Dawnriser* near the captain's quarters when the door flew open and Teach emerged from the cabin.

His huge, curly black beard covered most of his face, coming up to his eyes. It was twisted in parts and tied with red ribbons. He wore a long, black coat with large gold buttons. A pair of jewel-crusted hilts peeked out of the scabbards that dangled from his hips. Around his shoulders hung slings with three ornate pistols in holsters like bandoliers. And in each hand was a pistol. The pistols were connected by a length of red silk that draped in front of him as he held the guns aloft.

Teach roared in bloodlust, firing his pistols above the heads of the pirates in front of him. Each shot found a fairy and turned it into a burst of golden dust.

Peter dived toward the man just as Tinker Belle flared into light and drew her daggers. Peter screamed as he drew his own blade and slashed at Teach. The pirate caught the strike on his pistol, then swung the other pistol like a club at Peter's head. But before the gun could connect, Tinker Belle flew into Teach's arm, redirecting the blow into the banister instead of Peter's head.

The pirate dropped the two pistols and drew one from his holster. He raised his arm above his head to shoot the fairy, but before he could fire, Peter had him by the wrist, pushing the gun away from Tinker Belle.

Peter dropped his own dagger and grabbed Teach's wrist with both hands, then began to fly, pulling the man into the air with him as he went.

Tinker Belle caught Peter's dagger in mid-air, carrying it out of Teach's reach. Teach lashed out with his knee, catching Peter in the stomach and knocking the wind out of him and sending him tumbling to the ground. Teach landed hard on the ground, but Peter landed harder. The pirate rolled to his feet, and fired at Peter, but instead of hitting the boy, the shot connected with a passing fairy. The fairy erupted in a bright flash, golden dust showering both Peter and Teach.

Teach reached out his hand, letting the dust fall into his open palm. He squeezed his hand into a fist, then smiled as he dropped his pistol and slowly drew a sword.

"So, the Spirit has come for me after all," Teach said, smiling at Peter. "Have you come to join your sister in the afterlife?"

"Hardly," Peter spat, as Tinker Belle returned his weapon to him, then landed on his shoulder. "I came to finish what my father started."

"Your father? Ah," Teach said, recognizing the dagger in Peter's hand. "William Till had a family." Teach smiled. " Well, your sister already has company then."

The pirate's sneer turned into a cruel grin.

"What I mean to say is, aye, your father is dead."

Rage and pain and disbelief ignited inside of Peter.

"A shot and a swim, lad," he winked. "That's what he got. London knocked him cold when we ambushed the *Lion's Whelp* , so it seemed fitting to give one of your daddy's fancy blades to him, which I gather is how you came to it," he said, pointing to Peter's dagger. "Well, we tied ol' Till to the mast, that mast," he said, pointing to the mast behind Peter. "Till watched his entire crew die, and then after a healthy beating from the crew..." Teach mimicked firing a pistol with his index finger and thumb, then turned the gesture into a wave. "Man overboard," he smiled.

Peter felt the bile in his stomach start to rise. He wanted to scream and cry and retch and a hundred other things that raced though his mind until suddenly they all went dim save for a single, clear thought: he was going to kill the pirate who had murdered his father.

"You know," Peter said, staring at his father's killer. "The plan was to keep you alive."

"Was?" Tinker Belle asked.

An eerie calm settled over him as he spoke. "But that's not the plan anymore. You're going to burn with the fleet, pirate," he spat.

"What?" Tinker Bell exclaimed. "Peter! The plan!"

"I don't care," Peter yelled, pointing at the man. "He dies!"

Teach drew a second sword and began to swing them around him. The silver blades blurred and hummed in the air. Teach walked slowly toward Peter, swaying slightly as the mers continued to pound the hull of his ship, his swords still weaving a basket of death around him.

"Doubtful," the pirate said.

"I'll let you in on a little secret," Peter said in a stage-whisper. "It'll be less painful if you surrender now."

"You first," came the pirate's reply, then he hurled both of his swords at him.

Peter flipped away from the spinning blades. They passed just under him and buried themselves in the mast. Peter landed deftly atop the swords protruding from the mast, glaring down contemptuously at the man.

Teach drew a third sword, this one somehow hidden in the folds of his coat, and continued to advance.

The pirate brought his sword across in a strike intended to cut the boy's legs out from under him. Peter leapt away from it, landed on the deck, then stepped in close, and aimed a strike at Teach's sword hand. The pirate immediately adjusted the angle of his sword and caught Peter's blow. At the same time, Tinker Belle struck, acting almost like a third limb for the boy.

But the pirate was quick. He saw her coming and flicked his wrist at the fairy, connecting hard and sending her spinning away.

Peter took his eyes off of Teach for a second, just long enough to see that Tinker Belle had recovered and was soaring back toward him. Then he felt something cold and solid press into his stomach.

He looked down to see Teach's pistol then heard the trigger click as the man fired it.

TWENTY EIGHT

Shiiklah's thick tail slammed against the side of the ship again, weakening the area next to the hole she and her warriors had made. The mers had selected an area of the hull just above the waterline. And with a combination of tail strikes and a little help from their coral blades, the mers were nearly finished with their new entrance.

Peter had given clear instructions that the *Dawnriser* was to be left fully intact as their plan was ultimately to allow Teach to escape to warn others away from the island. But Shiiklah thought about how boring all those months at sea must get. This modest breach would give Teach something to do on the voyage home.

She struck the hull one more time and was rewarded with the

sound of snapping wood. She imagined the vibrations from her tail thundering through the hull and up the spines of every pirate on board.

The mers around her pulled the splintered wood off of the ship, enlarging the hole enough so they could fit though.

Shiiklah hissed in delight as the party noiselessly slipped out of the water and into the *Dawnriser's* hold.

The mers slowly made their way through the bowels of the ship. The sound of fighting on deck was muffled by the layers of ship between them and their prey. The floor boards creaked as the creatures glided across the floor.

Suddenly, the sound of frantic footsteps grew louder.

At Shiiklah's gesture, the mers melted into the shadows.

Three pirates scurried past, oblivious to the death that currently inhabited the shadows around them.

"Lets get out of here," one of them cried.

"But what about the captain?" another responded. "He'll gut us alive if we jump ship."

"Yess, jump ship," Shiiklah thought. *"More fun, my mers."*

"We're dead anyways, do you see those things outside? Do you hear that pounding?"

"What's going on? I've never seen anything like this."

"I wager they're here for Teach, and he's on his own, I'm going to save my own hide."

The speaker turned to leave. Shiiklah clacked her tongue once and a scaly arm reached out and yanked the speaker into the shadows. A moment later, his lifeless body collapsed to the ground in front of the two remaining pirates.

The surprised pirates stumbled away from the man. Their surprise turned to horror as Shiiklah materialized from the shadows in front of them. In the same breath, two mers appeared behind the men and grabbed them, lifting them off the ground.

"Teach," Shiiklah demanded, approaching the men.

Neither man spoke. Instead, all the blood drained from their faces as they both went rigid with fear.

"Ssspeak," Shiiklah hissed.

"I...I don't know where he is," the first pirate stammered.

Another mer appeared from behind Shiiklah and killed the speaker with a single slash from his coral rapier.

"Please, the last time I saw him, he was in the captain's quarters," the last pirate said. "Please, believe me. That's all I know. I don't know what's going on. I just left the navy. I don't know what any of this is. Please don't kill me," he begged. "I have a family, I became a pirate to try to make a better life for them."

Shiiklah stared at the man, her blue eyes considering. Then she peered into the darkness, over the man's shoulder. And the man was abruptly deposited on the ground.

"Oh thank you, thank you," the man wept.

A few moments later, the man's sobbing died down and he looked up, but Shiiklah and her mers had slipped back into the shadow.

She watched him as he slowly rose to his feet. He looked around slowly, obviously expecting a strike to kill him at any second.

Suddenly, the door at the far end of the room kicked open and half a score of pirates came running out, brandishing all manor of swords and pistols.

"Jasper, what's with that face? Here, let's give these pixies a taste," one of the pirates said, throwing the man a cutlass.

The sword hit Jasper in the hand then clanked to the ground.

He stooped to pick it up, then seemed to think better of it and stood, leaving the weapon untouched on the ground.

Shiiklah stood in front of him again, her thin, white sword in hand. The men who had just rushed into the room lay on the floor, unmoving.

The man jerked in surprise when he saw her again.

"Return home, Jasper of Man," Shiiklah hissed, her eyes changing from blue to black as she once more blended into the darkness.

"W-what are you?" Jasper stammered.

"Death," came her reply from the shadows. "Death."

Mad Rogue knew the sounds of fighting, or rather the sounds of dying, well. His ears were telling him that pretty much everyone on deck was dead. And when those little devils were finished up top, they'd be coming below, which meant it was time to leave. The *Royal James* had lost two captains now. First, Captain London, slain by that flying boy, Peter Pan, and now Two.

At any rate, this was no longer the ship for Mad Rogue. There was trouble afoot – to say the least – and when things got bad, there was only one person who could make things worse to set everything right.

Teach.

It was odd reasoning, to be sure, but it made perfect sense to Mad Rogue.

He heard something scrape and rattle against the hull then felt the ship's anchor release its hold on the ship. The *Royal James*, now free of its tether, began to drift aimlessly.

"Well that settles it, then," Mad Rogue said and climbed out of a porthole onto the ship's exterior.

The night sky was ablaze with ships burning and countless fairies streaking across the sky.

The *Royal James* drifted aimlessly through the cove before sidling up next to another ship, the *Dawnriser*, if Rogue was correct.

"Capital!" Mad Rogue cheered, knowing that this was Teach's ship. He checked to make sure Little Kite was still securely clenched in his fist, then leapt to the *Dawnriser's* side and scrambled through an open porthole.

The cabin he fell into was dark. He waved his hands above his head, groping for a hanging lantern. Finding one, he produced a match from a pocket, ignited it on a tooth, then lit the lamp.

"Ah, the galley," Mad Rogue exclaimed. He stuck Little Kite into the brim of his hat and began rummaging through the ship's kitchen.

"Pixies are small, so very small," he muttered to himself. "Too small for sharps, too small for bullets. Ah," he said, shoving a barrel out of his way to see better. "Perfect!"

He rose, brandishing a huge cast iron skillet. It was black, greasy, and more than two feet in diameter. He swung it experimentally. It was heavy, and took some effort to get it moving. But it would certainly do significant damage if it struck a pixie.

Satisfied with himself, he turned just as one of the doors flew open and half a score of pirates ran through the galley to the door on the opposite side of the cabin. They plowed though Mad Rogue, sending him sprawling. His new-found weapon flew from his hands, and the feather in his hat leapt free and drifted slowly to the deck.

"No, no, no," Mad Rogue wailed, throwing pots and shoving barrels out of his way. "Little Kite, are you here?"

Finally, he found the feather.

"Stay close, Little Kite," he said, clutching the feather to his chest. "There be fools aboard."

He picked up his skillet and followed after the men. He left the galley, using the same door the men had exited through, and entered the main hold. In the middle of the large cabin were the men who had just run into him, but now they were laying on the floor, dead, save for one pitiful-looking man in the center of the room, shaking.

Mad Rogue pointed at the man with Little Kite – a warning – as if the other men had spontaneously died as a result of upsetting him. He left the shaking man in the cabin, skipped around the bodies, and ascended a ladder that lead to a trap door that would bring him to the upper deck.

Climbing the ladder while holding a large skillet and a feather proved to be difficult but not impossible. Rogue pushed the door open above him, then climbed out onto the deck.

The situation seemed unchanged. Ships were still burning all around him, the sky was still lit with pixies and explosions and the ship still shook from whatever kept pounding on the hull.

Movement caught his eye. He looked up as a pixie shot toward him. He swung his huge skillet and was rewarded with an almost musical ring as the pixie collided with the pan, erupting in a shower of golden brilliance.

Mad Rogue turned the skillet over, inspecting his handiwork. He brushed the golden dust off of his skillet with Little Kite, blew the feather clean, then skipped off in search of his new captain.

"Oops," Teach said as jammed his pistol into Peter's stomach and pulled the trigger.

Peter squeezed his eyes shut, waiting for his insides to fill with pain and fire, but nothing came. He opened them and saw a confused Teach looking down at his pistol. Peter looked down to see Tinker Belle on top of the gun, her tiny arms and legs quivering as she strained to keep the weapon's hammer from striking the charge.

Peter batted the gun away just as Tinker Belle released the hammer, the gun discharging harmlessly into the deck. Meanwhile, Teach was bringing his sword around again.

Peter caught the strike on his dagger, then wrapped his free arm around Teach's sword arm to trap it. The pirate merely head-butted him. Peter stumbled back, his vision filled with stars, then felt himself rocking backward as the man's boot sent him sprawling.

"You've got decent skill, Spirit," Teach said. "I'll give you that. But I'm decades your elder. I've slain more men than you've ever met."

Teach stooped to pick up a second sword from the deck. He twirled both experimentally as he spoke.

"Your friends took us unawares," he admitted, looking at the countless golden lights streaking through the sky. "I'll give you that. But your advance has slowed. It is you who need to take heed. This island will burn. Take flight, leave, and count it a blessing that you survived."

Peter shook his head.

"You'll die long before you touch this island," he said, rising to his feet, then lifting off the deck into the air.

"Tell me your name, Spirit," Teach asked. "So I can properly mark your grave."

"That's Peter Pan, captain," a crazed, sing-song voice responded.

The voice belonged to a man in a red jacket with matching pants and hat, climbing out of a trap door in the deck. He held a large cooking skillet in one hand, and a feather in the other.

Mad Rogue.

Peter stared at the man who had helped Captain London torture him.

The crazed pirate fluttered his fingers at Peter.

"Hello, Peter Pan," he said.

"Peter Pan," Teach said. "The boy who wouldn't die. What's a 'Pan,' Peter?" he asked.

"The last man who asked me that died," Peter replied. "It's fitting you would ask."

"Well?" Teach asked.

"It's nothing you would understand," was all Peter said. Then he charged.

He flew toward the man and struck. Teach blocked and parried, his sword humming as he swung it, while William Till's dagger sang in his son's hands. The pair stabbed, punched, and kicked at each other, all semblance of precision and technique was replaced with fast, powerful attacks.

Tinker Belle flew toward Mad Rogue. He raised his skillet and swung it at her. She immediately tried to stop and reverse direction and managed to land on the skillet rather than be obliterated by it.

He turned it over to inspect his handiwork, but was taken off guard when she flew right into his face, cutting deep into his cheek with both daggers. She continued to circle him, landing attacks on his arms, legs, and chest.

He howled in pain, spinning in erratic circles with his skillet. Twice he nearly connected, but Tinker Bell managed to stay just out of reach.

"Tinker Belle?" Peter called. He could feel himself beginning to tire. With her help, they could keep Teach off-balanced, but with only a single target to worry about, Teach's strength and experience was beginning to prove a greater advantage than Peter's own abilities.

Tinker Belle flew fast, dizzy circles around Mad Rogue, then landed on his hat. The pirate continued to look around, frantic now in his searching. She held on tight, closed her eyes and concentrated. Her glow grew brighter and brighter until her blinding white light forced Peter to look away and even caused Teach to slow his attack. Then dust poured from every part of her. It gushed from her fingertips, hair, eyes, and legs. It filled the rim of the Mad Rogue's hat, then spilled over, covering the pirate in a brilliant, golden glow.

"Dust!" he screamed in surprise as the swirling dust ran down his shoulders and chest. Then he gasped as the dust soaked into his arms and hands, then the rest of his body.

Tinker Belle leapt off of his hat, her normal glow restored, if dimmed slightly. Mad Rogue finally saw her and pivoted to swing his skillet at her, but found that he didn't have the footing.

He looked down and found himself rising off the ground, his feet no longer touching the deck.

"Capt'n! Dust!" he cried joyfully as he slowly began to turn in the air, but Teach kept his attention fixed on Peter's unrelenting assault.

Tinker Belle zipped in suddenly and plucked the red feather from the pirate's grasp.

"Little Kite!" Mad Rogue cried, lunging for the feather. But the movement shifted his momentum and he began to both rotate and flip as he drifted higher and higher away from the deck. "Little Kite, come back!"

Tinker Belle dropped the feather, and returned to join Peter. The feather drifted to the deck almost seeming to wave goodbye as it wafted back and forth as it fell.

"Little Kiiiiite!" Mad Rogue sobbed.

But his pleading was left unanswered and Peter distantly registered the faint sound of Mad Rogue both laughing in victory of finding dust, and sobbing over the loss of his only friend, Little Kite.

A kick to his shin brought his attention fully back to Teach. The blow drove Peter to one knee, but he used the momentum to his advantage and brought his dagger down with him as he fell, driving it into Teach's thigh. The man swore, and instinctively reached to touch the wound. But Peter flew into the man, driving his shoulder into Teach's stomach and sending him somersaulting backwards. He heard the breath leave the pirate in a gasp. Peter raced after him and brought his dagger back to strike.

"Hear my father's song," Peter said, panting. "May it carry you to Hell's gates."

Adelaide wiped a hand across her brow, then wiped the sparkling sweat on her tunic.

"Is that the last of them?" Tolan asked.

"We've got one more crows nest to search, then that will be it," she said.

While the main force was busy raining down on the pirates on the deck, Adelaide had led a smaller force whose job it was to neutralize any pirates on night watch. The last thing they wanted was to have to worry about attacks coming from above. At first, Adelaide had announced that she would be leading the main assault while Tolan led the secondary assault. But every fairy in White Falls had flat out refused to allow their leader to put herself in such harm. Rather than face an uprising, Adelaide had agreed to limit her involvement in the second assault.

The group of fairies, about a score, made their way to the last ship.

"What's that?" Tolan asked, pointing.

Adelaide followed his gaze and saw a pirate, thirty yards away, flying, but slowly flipping through the air. And crying.

"Should we get him?" Tolan asked.

"I think not," Adelaide replied, shaking her head. "He's no longer a threat."

The party continued to make their way to the central ship and the last crows nest.

"It looks empty," Tolan said, approaching the crows nest.

"Die!" a voice cried as a pirate leapt up from lying on the floor of the nest. He brandished what looked like a length of sail rolled up into a whip. He swung it at Tolan, catching him squarely. His glow flickered and went dim as he toppled off of the edge and fell.

The remaining fairies blitzed the pirate. They overwhelmed him in seconds, putting an end to any future threat he might present.

Adelaide turned her attention to Tolan. She could see him falling. She could still make out his glow; he was dim, not dark. Dim meant alive, but at the rate he was falling... She dived after him. Bullets from errant shots zipped near her. The smoke from burning sails stung her eyes as she flew through billows of smoke. She was gaining on him, but he was still too far away.

Dark, fast moving patches began darting across the deck below. She thought her eyes were playing tricks on her at first, then she realized what she was seeing: kites.

The birds swarmed the ships, tipping the balance back in their favor again. One of them adjusted their course and angled up, then deftly caught the fairy with its talons. The bird, Grath, for she could make out his features now, passed Tolan to a pair of fairies who carried him off to one of the now-empty crows nest.

Adelaide sighed in relief, both that Tolan was safe and that the kites had decided to come after all.

"You honor us with your presence," she said to him, dipping her head.

The bird clacked his beak in greeting, flexed his talons, then joined his brethren in battle. Kites and fairies began swarming individual pirates, working in unison to lift them up off the deck. The pirates would flail and scream, only to fall painfully back on to the deck or splash into the water where mers waited.

Adelaide watched with a mixture of astonishment and pride as her fairies fought side by side with kites for the first time in years.

Peter brought his dagger down toward Teach. The man was

clutching his leg with one hand and trying to pull himself out of range with the other.

"Peter, no!" Tinker Belle cried. "You can't do this!"

"You heard what he did to my father," Peter bellowed. "He needs to die!"

Tinker Belle had him by the back of his shirt, trying to pull him away as he tried to advance on the scrambling Teach. She let go of him, flying in between him and the pirate.

"I know what he's done, and he'll get what's his," she insisted. "But not like this, if you do this, you'll be no better than him."

The words hit him, and for an instant, he wasn't Peter Pan, on a ship fighting pirates to protect some lost island. Instead, he was just Peter, walking up the cobblestone path with his father.

"As soon as it becomes about killing, you're no better than a pirate," William Till was saying. "What kind of man do you want to become?"

And suddenly, Peter saw with new eyes.

This was it.

This moment would define the rest of his life.

Would he allow hate and anger to guide his hand, or would he be ruled by something better?

Hate or love?

Peter lowered his hand and looked at the dagger, his father's weapon, somehow, a weapon of love. Using it in anger would dishonor William Till's legacy. He smiled and looked up at Tinker Belle and saw his sister.

"Thanks, Tink," he said. "You're right." He looked from Tinker Belle to Teach. "It's over," he said to the man.

Fairies and kites flew all around Peter, carrying pirates into the air or slashing rigging and sails.

"You're leaving this island and you're never coming back," Peter said, tossing a loose strip of sail to Teach.

The pirate caught it, wrapped it around his wounded leg and tied it tight. He looked up and around, no doubt seeing his fleet in flames, his men scattering. He removed his hat and bowed his head to Peter. Then, replacing his hat, said, "I can see the dice when they're cast, Spirit. I accept your terms."

Peter extended his hand. The pirate stared at it for a long moment, then with a painful grunt, rose to his feet. His hand closed around Peter's but instead of shaking it, he yanked the boy towards him then kicked him hard. The kick send Peter flying backward. Teach ran after him, his wound obviously not as serious as he had let on.

"I am Edward Teach, Blackbeard the Pirate! Scourge of the seas, lord of all pirates, and no child, flying or otherwise, will take my surrender," he roared.

Peter rolled to his feet and feinted, faking a strike at Teach's wounded leg. But instead, he jumped up, then propelled himself down on the end of one of the deck boards. The opposite end of the deck board tore free of the floor, flew up, and caught Teach hard under the chin. The pirate staggered for a moment and Peter flew forward, slamming into the man, propelling him down the stairs back into the captain's cabin. The door flew open as the two of them crashed into it with Tinker Belle in tow.

Peter and Teach landed in a tangled heap in the middle of the room. Teach threw Peter off of him, and Peter, clumsily trying to fly, was sent spinning away instead. Teach drew one of his remaining two guns and fired. Peter threw himself flat on the ground, the bullet hissing above him. Then he launched himself to the ceiling as Teach drew his final gun and fired it.

Peter landed lightly on the deck, his dagger still in hand, and the trio of pirate, boy, and fairy began to circle slowly.

"Now what?" Teach asked, his sword in one hand, his pistol held like a club in the other. "We carry on until we cut each other to pieces?"

They continued to circle, the cabin blocking out most of the sound of fighting outside. Even the mer's tails on the hull seemed to have stopped.

"You can't win," Teach said. "You've already shown you don't have the gall to kill me, and I won't surrender."

"Oh, you'll surrender," Peter said. "But you're going to wish you had done it a whole lot sooner."

They continued to circle each other, until the cabin door was behind Peter. Then he sheathed his blade.

"Fool," Teach spat, "Now I'll..." but what sounded like rustling beads and bone gave him pause, and he turned around to see retribution silhouetted in the window behind him.

"Teeeeacch," a wet voice hissed.

Peter stepped into the doorway and back out onto the deck. Tinker Belle followed him as he pulled the door shut, leaving Teach alone in the cabin with Shiiklah.

Peter guessed that Teach was wishing he had surrendered sooner.

TWENTY NINE

A bright morning sun watched waves lap at the rocks and boulders that lined the small island's shore. The island seemed just large enough to hold what once must have been an ancient stone fortress. All that remained from the destroyed fortress was wreckage, broken pillars and debris – shadows of what once was.

"What were our casualties?" Peter asked, looking at the assembled group.

"We lost around a hundred," Adelaide said. "The kites lost maybe a score, more wounded."

Peter looked to Shiiklah.

"None," she replied. "But several injuries," she said.

Peter noticed that a fresh wound had been added to her collection.

The battle had quickly shifted from a free-for-all to smaller skirmishes that had quickly died out. Three of the seven ships had attempted to leave. One burned to ash before it could leave the cove, with sailors trying to swim to shore finding themselves being dragged to the depths by mers.

Two of the ships, however, did manage to get away: the *Dawnriser* and the *Royal James*. Shortly after Peter and Tinker Belle had left Teach alone with Shiiklah to face the demons from his past, the two ships had been cut free, and the surviving crew had managed to tie enough sail to the masts to catch the wind allowing them to limp out of the cove.

The ships that had escaped faced a difficult challenge at sea. With minimal crew and supplies, escaping the cove did not guarantee survival.

Two ships had taken on too much water and were now at the bottom of the cove. Members of their crew who hadn't managed to swim to the relative safety of a surviving ship ended up joining the ships on the ocean floor.

That left two ships remaining.

A score of mers had stayed behind to make sure no one successfully made it to shore. A few brave, or foolish, pirates had attempted to row ashore. Some of the boats were turned back toward the ship, but most of them were capsized, their crew drowned.

Eventually, the remaining pirates got the message and focused their efforts on repairing their ships.

"Why are we meeting here?" Shiiklah asked, clearly uncomfortable.

"Because it's important," Peter said. "This is where unity was destroyed, I think this is where it should be restored."

Adelaide nodded in understanding.

"You can not recreate the Grand Council," Shiiklah said. "It dishonors them to try."

"Forget the Accord," Peter said. "We'll start a new one. We have a common goal, we want this island protected."

"We?" Adelaide asked.

Peter looked out across bay to the island and nodded slowly.

"We," he said, looking back to the fairy queen. "It's what Mara would want. She died protecting this island. I'm not going anywhere."

"I agree," Tinker Belle said.

"The pirates will return," Adelaide said. "They have always been able to find this place somehow."

"All the more reason for us to stick together," Peter insisted.

"I don't know," Shiiklah said, shaking her head.

"Blood matters," Peter said. "And I think we've all sacrificed enough of it for each other to make us all family."

The group fell silent, each one reflecting on the losses borne to them as a result of the single act of betrayal that had taken place here.

Grath was the first to respond. He clacked his beak and nodded in agreement.

Adelaide landed on the ground and placed her palm on one of the blackened stones where most of her kin had been murdered. "I would be a fool to lead my people anywhere else," she said. "I know Tam would want his death to bring unity, not strife."

All eyes looked to Shiiklah. The mermaid, scarred and weary

from years of conflict, stared at the burned stone floor.

Peter knew better than most how much power the past held over the future. But it was time to allow the future to be shaped by today's actions, not yesterday's.

He just hoped Shiiklah had realized that too.

"We will have to change everything," Shiiklah replied, looking up. "It will take much work."

"Nah," Peter waved, a smile splitting across his face. "It'll be a great adventure."

EPILOGUE

The waves tugged gently, inviting him into their depths. It was said that drowning was the most horrifying way to die. The terror of needing to breathe, but knowing that a final breath would replace the panic with agony, not relief.

But that didn't seem to be the case now. Now, it seemed like a fitting end to a battle well-fought.

He was at peace.

There was nothing left to do but surrender. He closed his eyes, took one final breath, then exhaled as he allowed the waves to pull him under. Suddenly, he felt himself being hauled out of the water. Strong hands forced his head up above the water.

"¡Mantenga la cabeza en alto!" a voice cried.

Abruptly he was hauled out of the water and dragged onto shore. Wet sand filled his mouth and eyes, but he didn't care. He stared at the sand in disbelief, then looked up to see two men standing over him.

"¿Conoce su nombre?" one of the men asked him.

Nombre? It was Spanish – *name.*

"Uh, my name," he replied, his head filled with fog.

The two men exchanged glances. One of them shook his head at the other, pointing to the gunshot wound in his shoulder.

"William," he answered. "William Till."

* * *

The ship's rocking stirred Teach awake. He immediately wished he were still unconscious. He tried to sit up, but his entire body seized in pain. His beard, once full and ferocious, was now patchy and bloodied. His face burned where handfuls of beard had been torn out. He rolled over, slowly, on to his back, feeling new wounds as they made themselves known. He coughed, spitting blood throughout the cabin. He could feel bones now--broken and out of place. That accursed mermaid had brought him within a hairsbreadth of death, then had vanished.

He breathed in, but the effort pressed his lungs into broken ribs, sending fresh reminders of the price he had paid for antagonizing those creatures.

And that boy, that terrible, flying boy.

He stared vacantly out the window, watching the island, now a small dot on the horizon, fade away.

"Keep your island, Peter Pan," Teach whispered. "'Tis nothing compared to the riches the New World has to offer."

To his relief, he felt himself slipping back into unconsciousness. But before he blacked out, the whisper of a plan started to take form. A little rest, then perhaps he would see what the Carolinas had to offer him.

After all, his luck could only improve.

* * *

"Looks like we missed the party," the tall man said as he sat in his cabin, watching frantic pirates repair the two crippled ships in the cove.

"From what they've said, it was a massacre, Capt'n," a short bearded pirate replied. "Pixies, mermaids, birds, and a some boy who can fly – Peter Pan, they call him."

"They must have something valuable indeed if they came out in such force," the captain mused.

"Well, there are rumors that the pixies guard caves filled with gold and jewels," the pirate replied.

"Hmmm," the captain considered. "I'd like to go ashore."

"Th-that may not be the best idea," the short pirate stammered. "Apparently there is something in the water turning back or capsizing any boat that tries to land. The men are calling the island Neverland – no one can reach it."

"A challenge, then," the captain said, smiling.

He rose, walked over to the window and looked out over the cove. With one hand resting on his hip, and the other on the hilt of a jewel-crusted sword, he watched the ships undergoing repair. He watched the forest that lined the beach, the waters that patted lazily against his ship. His ice blue eyes took in everything.

After a long moment, his lips curled into a smile.

"Good form, Mr. Smee," the captain said, twisting his mustache with his fingers. "I think we'll stay for a while."